4

D0465263

WILD NIGHTS

Also by Kate Douglas:

Wolf Tales II

"Chanku Rising" in Sexy Beast

Wolf Tales

Sharon Page:

Sin

WILD NIGHTS

KATE DOUGLAS
SHARON PAGE
KATHLEEN DANTE

APHRODISIA

KENSINGTON BOOKS

http://www.kensingtonbooks.com

APHRODISIA BOOKS are published by

Kensington Publishing Corp.
850 Third Avenue
New York, NY 10022

Copyright © 2006 by Kensington Publishing Corp.
"Camille's Dawn" © copyright 2006 by Kate Douglas
"Midnight Man" © copyright 2006 by Sharon Page
"Night Pleasures" © copyright 2006 by Kathleen Dante

All rights reserved. No part of this book may be reproduced in any form or by any means without the prior written consent of the Publisher, excepting brief quotes used in reviews.

All Kensington Titles, Imprints and Distributed Lines are available at special quantity discounts for bulk purchases for sales promotion, premiums, fund-raising, and educational or institutional use.

Special book excerpts or customized printings can also be created to fit specific needs. For details, write or phone the office of the Kensington Special Sales Manager: Kensington Publishing Corp., 850 Third Avenue, New York, NY 10022, attn: Special Sales Department, Phone: 1-800-221-2647.

Aphrodisia and the A logo are trademarks of Kensington Publishing Corp.

ISBN 0-7582-1489-8

First Trade Paperback Printing: September 2006

10 9 8 7 6 5 4 3 2 1

Printed in the United States of America

Camille's Dawn

KATE DOUGLAS

1

Textures. Right now, at this point in time, it was all about the texture, the colors, the scents and sounds and amazing sensations. It just didn't get much better than this.

Lucien Stone threaded his fingers through the tangled mass of his lady love's hair and followed the slow up-and-down movement of Tia's head as her exquisite mouth slowly but surely brought him closer to climax.

He remembered when her hair had been crinkly and coarse, the curls so tightly woven that combing it out could be a nightmare. Now, with Tia's metamorphosis to Chanku complete, it had grown softer, smoother, more accepting of his fingers, an inviting tangle of silken ringlets. He felt her scalp beneath the thick mass, shoved his fingers slowly around the curve of her skull, and then gently touched the tip of her ear.

Luc ran his fingertip around the outer shell of her ear and tickled the sensitive canal. Tia's lips slowly released his swollen cock with a soft little *pop.* She raised her head and smiled at Luc, her full lips shining and moist. Morning sunlight streaming through the window behind her cast a golden glow over her high cheekbones and turned her wild blond hair into a shimmering halo.

Luc's fingers tangled more tightly in her curls. He tugged, drawing her back to the business at hand.

She dipped low once more. The strands of her hair drifted over his belly and then brushed lightly across Luc's groin. The tip of her tongue stroked the hard underside of his aching erection and then dipped into the sensitive slit at the top. She opened her thoughts to him, sharing the flavors she tasted, the things she felt.

Caught in the sensations of Tia's mental link, Luc tasted his own bead of pre-cum when she licked the drop with the tip of her tongue. He felt the large vein running the length of his cock as her tongue slowly traveled from base to crown.

Luc groaned, his lungs expanding and his fingers tightening in Tia's hair until he had to consciously force himself to relax his hold. The last thing he wanted was to interrupt what she was doing . . . and doing so well.

Her skin felt like satin—its dark, golden color, the gift of her African American mother and Scandinavian father, a perfect counterpoint to his lighter hue. Luc was concentrating on the shade and silkiness of Tia's skin, comparing it to the coarseness of his own, when her lips found his scrotum.

Once more, she shared the sensation. She suckled one tight nut into her mouth, rolling it with her tongue, slipping it back and forth between her lips. He felt the solid, round ball as it slipped over her tongue, the soft slide of scrotal skin between her lips, all from Tia's point of view. At the same time, he experienced her tender ministrations firsthand, doubling the powerful sensations.

Her fingernails raked his perineum and tickled the underside of his sac. Luc moaned and grasped the covers with his free hand. She was definitely trying to kill him!

Tia hummed against his balls. The vibrations crawled through his gut all the way up his spine. Her lips tightened around one testicle, taking Luc just to the edge of pain. She held him there, licking and rolling the round gland beneath her tongue before she finally released his nut. Her slim fingers wrapped around the heavy length of his cock. Luc groaned as she slowly worked the broad head between her lips, ran her tongue beneath the taut crown, and then sucked him deep down her throat.

Blowing as if he'd run a mile, fighting for whatever remnants of control he could find, Luc felt the undulations of Tia's hips and knew she must be nearing her own orgasm. Raising his head just a fraction, he watched as Tinker, their packmate, feasted on Tia's slick pussy.

Dark as ebony and built like a linebacker, Martin "Tinker" McClintock had admitted his love for Tia from the very beginning. Luc not only trusted the big man with his life, he trusted him with his mate.

More textures. The odd word rolled around in Luc's mind as he watched Tinker's big hands spread Tia's cheeks, watched him dip low to suckle gently at Tia's clit. Then Luc's attention snapped back to Tia, positioned on elbows and knees between his legs, her butt in the air for Tinker's busy tongue.

Damn, what a gorgeous picture they made.

Luc's breath lodged behind his heart as Tia's fingernails raked over his ass and her cheeks hollowed with the force of each slow, measured pull on his cock. He planted his feet flat on the bed and raised his hips to meet her mouth, joining Tia's rhythm.

He linked with his packmate, if only for a moment, so that Tia's sweet taste lingered on Luc's tongue as well as Tinker's.

Tinker reared up from between Tia's legs and grinned at Luc. His dark lips glistened with Tia's juices, his broad, muscular chest expanding with each deep breath. He winked.

Then he began to dissolve, to shimmer and fade.

In less than a heartbeat, a huge wolf sat at the foot of the bed, tongue lolling, amber eyes glinting.

Then he dipped his long snout and longer tongue and disappeared between Tia's parted thighs.

Tinker's slick, wolven tongue snaked into Tia's swollen sex and licked deep inside. She screamed and convulsed, her orgasm hitting so hard and fast, she almost bit the mouthful of Luc she was working on. His cock slipped out of her mouth just as her pussy clamped down on Tinker's marauding tongue. The hard tip licked high against her spasming walls and Tia screamed again. Gasping for air, shuddering against Tinker's continuing assault between her legs, Tia lifted off her elbows, swung her head around, and glared at her lupine packmate.

Dear God, Tinker! Warn me when you're going to do that!

Tinker's laughter rolled through her mind and his long, rough tongue found spots inside Tia that made her see stars. Lungs pounding, she tried to go back to Luc, but Tinker's mobile tongue wasn't about to turn her loose.

It's okay . . . I'm enjoying the show. Besides, I'm with Tinker, and you taste marvelous.

She flashed Luc a wan smile. He shoved himself against the headboard, and Tia rolled over and lay back against his groin, spreading her legs wide. Tinker scooted down on his furry belly and, with sharp teeth and a tongue that should have been licensed, took Tia to the top and beyond once more.

She arched her hips as he went deep, clutched the blankets in her fists when he slowly dragged the rough side of his tongue from her ass to her clit. Once, twice . . .

Knowing Luc shared each taste, each clenching spasm of her pussy, took Tia even higher.

She bucked her hips, raised up on trembling legs. It was too much, too intense, but Luc held her in a viselike grip, his elbows clamped against her shoulders, his hands massaging both of Tia's breasts. He kneaded them roughly, pinching her nipples, rolling the tips between thumb and forefinger. Her body tensed. His thighs pressed against her hips, holding her still for Tinker and his amazing Chanku tongue.

Eyes clenched tight, lungs burning as if she'd run too far, Tia crested and then raced headlong over the edge again, giving it all up in a long, low howl of pleasure.

The rough texture of Tinker's wolven coat gave way to smooth, hot male skin. She felt him slide forward along her body, felt the meaty head of his cock press against her spasming sex, his warm, wet lips dragging at her now tender nipple.

Luc's grip on her breasts released, his fingers ran along her hips, and then he rubbed something warm and slick—her own juices?—against Tia's ass. She sighed with pleasure as Luc's cock slipped between her cheeks and pressed gently at her puckered opening, each time with a little more force, before finding entrance beyond the tight ring of muscle. He filled her there just as Tinker claimed her pussy.

Stuffed full, surrounded by love and the warmth of two spectacular male bodies, Tia arched her neck, pressing her head against Luc's collarbone as he slowly pumped in and out, matching his rhythm to Tinker's powerful thrusts.

What more could a woman want?

She opened her thoughts, found Tinker and Luc, each man lost in his own as well as the other's pleasure, sharing the sensations with one another. Tia joined their mental feast, passing on the amazing feelings of two solid erections slipping in and out of her slick, sensitive channels. She took their sensations as her own, felt the slide of Luc's cock against Tinker's, and then the same thing from Tinker's point of view.

She was hot and tight and oh-so-slick inside both her passages, and the men loved it. Almost as much as Tia loved it. Her lungs pumped air as she flew higher and higher with Luc and Tinker's growing arousal. She stayed inside their minds, a sensual voyeur sharing her own rushing wave of desire, sharing theirs.

Tia knew the instant Luc and Tinker drew close to a simultaneous peak, each of them climbing higher, pressure building, the rush of blood in veins and air whistling in and out of lungs. Luc's arms came around Tia, and he held her tight, thrusting forward until she felt the crush of his rough pubic hair against her buttocks. At the same time, Tinker buried himself deep inside, pressing his tight balls against Luc's.

She knew how it felt, how Luc loved the feel of Tinker's pouch slammed up against his, loved the slide of his cock tight against his packmate's, separated by nothing more than a thin wall of tissue deep inside Tia's body.

Tia opened her mind, her body, her heart . . . gave it all to sensation, to the textures of rough and smooth, slick and wet . . . and heat . . . always the heat of man and beast and lover. To love itself. The love of her mate, the love of her friend . . . the love of the amazing breed that was Chanku.

Tinker left first, dragging himself off to his own apartment across the hall. Shaking his head, mumbling something to himself that sounded like, "Those two are trying to kill me," he quietly shut the door behind him.

Luc went in to shower. Tia joined him long enough to rinse off and then slipped out of the bath before Luc came up with any more ideas of how they should spend the rest of the morning.

When he strolled out a few minutes later, Tia was sitting in an old rocker by the window, her naked body wrapped in a multicolored quilt, her thoughts a million miles away . . . actually, a few city blocks from their room.

Luc leaned over and kissed her and then straightened up. She nuzzled against his groin and kissed the damp curls of hair at the base of his flaccid cock. "I love you."

Why, whenever she said those words, did her eyes sting and her throat feel full?

Luc leaned over and kissed her on the mouth. "I love you, too. But why do I get the feeling you're not very happy right now? You should be sated and satisfied and glowing. . . . Well, at least satisfied."

Tia wished the only thoughts filling her mind were of Luc and the way he made her feel, but other worries had taken this quiet moment to invade. She shook her head, unsure how to put her concerns into words. "I'm worried about Dad."

Luc jerked upright and frowned; then he shook his head, grinning. "What is it about unbelievable morning sex with two absolutely perfect men that makes you think of your father?"

Tia laughed. "Absolutely perfect, huh? Well, when you put it that way . . ."

Luc sat down on an old trunk under the window and took her smaller cold hands in his warm ones. "Why are you worried about Ulrich? The man's healthy as a horse, he's still doing a hell of a job running Pack Dynamics, and he's actively searching for more Chanku. What more could he want?"

Tia shrugged. "What we have. A companion. Someone to warm his bed. A mate."

"Honey, I hate to disabuse you, but your father has not lived the life of a monk since your mother died. He's rarely alone at night."

"It's not the same. Other than us, he doesn't love anyone . . . doesn't have anyone to love him. Don't you remember what it was like before? You could have sex five times a day, every day of the week, but you still felt empty."

"Five times a day, eh?" Luc leaned close and nuzzled the

sensitive juncture between her neck and shoulder. "If we're still on that schedule, you owe me two more times."

Tia giggled and scrunched her chin down. "Cut it out. I'm trying to be serious here. I sense that emptiness in Dad. It's like he's never really moved on since Mom died."

Luc sat back and put his palms on his thighs. "I do know what you're saying." He sighed. "What can we do? It's not like we can just go out and dig up another Chanku female." He reached up and touched the end of Tia's nose. "It took me twenty years to find you."

She nipped at his fingertip and then took his hand. "I'm so glad you did, Luc. So very glad."

The past few weeks still felt like a dream to her. She had come home to San Francisco to a new teaching job, hoping to learn the true story of her mother's death. She'd discovered that Camille Mason hadn't been the victim of a nameless mugger. No, she'd been shot by a young rookie cop who saw a wolf running wild in Golden Gate Park.

A rookie cop named Lucien Stone. Tia knew now that Luc had regretted his action every day, still couldn't forgive himself for killing a young woman who was of the same amazing species as he was—Chanku. Shape-shifters from an ancient bloodline, born on the rugged, wind-blown steppes of the Tibetan Himalayas.

But Luc hadn't known about the Chanku. Not then. Not until he faced Ulrich Mason after Camille's funeral and learned the truth about the woman he'd killed. Without any warning, Ulrich had shown Luc what it meant to shift from human to wolf. He'd scared the young cop just about half to death.

Then Ulrich Mason had explained the ancient race of shape-shifters. He'd told Luc that Camille Mason was Chanku. So was Ulrich . . . and so was Luc.

It hadn't been until Tia returned to the city of her birth that she finally learned the truth about her own heritage, finally received the mixture of nutrients that allowed her body to develop the way nature had intended.

Only then had Tia embraced her Chanku heritage.

She gazed into Luc's beautiful amber eyes and saw the self-recrimination that would never go away. Though it had been an innocent mistake, Tia knew Luc would always feel guilt for having killed Camille Mason.

He'd robbed a young girl of her mother, a wonderful man of his mate, and ended the life of a vibrant young woman much too soon. Tia leaned forward and kissed him, and Luc wrapped his arms around her shoulders as if Tia were his lifeline.

"We'll think of something," Tia said. "I'm not sure what, but we have to do something."

Luc nodded. "You're right. But, for now, you need to go teach a classroom full of rug rats, and I have to get to work as well. We both have a full day of the mundane before things get interesting again." Playfully, he kissed her nose. "Don't forget, my sweet Chanku. We're running with the guys on Mount Tam tonight. It's a full moon."

The moon cast an eerie glow across the western slopes of Mount Tamalpais and trailed a silver band over the broad expanse of ocean not far from its base. The lights of San Francisco glowed under clear skies to the south. Five wolves filled a small meadow on the southwestern flank of the mountain, their eyes glinting like stars in the moonlight.

Four of them, all males, sleek muscles rippling under dark coats and sharp teeth flashing, nipped and parried with one another. Their battle might be play right now, but the underlying power in each of the animals hinted at how easily their actions could tip into violence.

The lone female stood aside, smaller boned, features more delicate compared to the larger animals, yet self-assured and enjoying her level of command. Tia settled back on her haunches and watched as Luc, Tinker, AJ, and Mik went through their nightly ritual of essentially finding out who was top dog.

Luc, of course, always took the lead, with Tinker faithfully by his side. Mik and AJ, lovers for many years, generally yielded to Luc without question.

Luc, of course, would always defer to Tia. Love and the order of the pack was an amazing combination.

Tia yipped once, turned, and raced up the trail. The rough-and-tumble ended immediately as the four males fell into position behind her. This was the time she usually loved most, the freedom she felt when they raced through the forest as Chanku, the occasional hunt for deer or rabbit, the clean night air and the solidarity of their pack.

Most nights her human worries faded into the background, much like the hum of traffic on the nearby freeway. Tongue lolling, tail streaming behind her, Tia bit back the howl that might alert the locals there were wolves in the forest. She picked up the pace and raced into the darkness.

Tia truly loved the night, loved the freedom of Chanku, the freedom of running at the head of her pack.

Usually.

Tonight, though, Tia raced far out in front of the others, heart heavy, Chanku eyes alert for any danger, her human mind unwilling to release its hold. In spite of the call of the wolf, the woman worried about her father.

2

They ran for more than an hour, five wolves in the moon-light, when Tia suddenly pulled up, eyes wide and mouth gaping. *Luc! I need to get to Dad. Now!*

What's wrong? Luc skidded to a halt beside Tia, his sharp nails kicking up clods of dry turf. She looked frantic. Her ears lay back against her skull. Even her hackles were raised, as though something threatened her.

I don't know. Only that something is terribly wrong. I need to go to him.

Luc nodded at the others. *Go ahead, guys. I'm taking Tia home.*

Do you need our help?

Tinker, concerned as always, waited for Luc's answer. Luc shook his head. *No. Enjoy the night. I'm sure everything will be okay.*

Tinker nodded and then whirled and chased after Mik and AJ. Luc and Tia raced back to their car. Within minutes they'd shifted, dressed, and were heading back across the Golden Gate Bridge toward San Francisco.

Tia wrung her hands, obviously upset about something, but her mind was blocked to hide her thoughts, and she stared straight ahead, as if willing the heavy traffic to clear and the car to move faster.

When they reached Ulrich's home in the Marina District, Tia was out of the car and racing up the walk before Luc even had the vehicle parked. He followed Tia up the steps, feeling her fear, sensing her overwhelming concern for her father.

He felt nothing from Ulrich. Nothing at all from the man who was his closest friend.

It all made horrible sense when Luc stepped through the door. Tia kneeled at Ulrich's feet, a loaded revolver in her hand. She was carefully removing shells from the chamber.

"Why, Dad? Why would you even consider . . ."

Ulrich shook his head. From the slur in his voice it was obvious he'd been drinking. "I'd already decided not to, sweetheart. I'm sorry you had to find me like this."

"Oh, Daddy. . . ." Tia set the empty revolver on the table, leaned close, and wrapped her arms around her father. Luc stayed back, not wanting to intrude on such a private moment. Guilt ate at him. If Camille were still alive, Ulrich wouldn't be here alone, drinking, with a loaded gun.

Ulrich raised his head, his eyes suddenly clear, and stared at Luc. *That's not true, Luc. This isn't about you.* He swept his hand over his daughter's tangled hair and held her close. *Sweetheart, will you and Luc do something for me?*

Tia raised her head and stared at her father through tear-filled eyes. The misery on her face tore at Luc's heart. "Anything, Daddy. Whatever you want."

Ulrich sighed. "I had a long talk with Anton Cheval tonight, with regard to a letter that arrived from him this afternoon. Please don't think I've lost it, but I want you and Luc to go back to Montana with me. Anton thinks he can contact your mother's spirit. He said Keisha has felt Camille in her dreams, that she's near, that she needs to communicate. The thing is, Anton wants to try something that will bring your mother back, if only for a short time."

Tia sat on her heels, obviously stunned, and definitely unsure. Luc shifted his gaze from Tia to her father. What Ulrich said sounded impossible, but the Chanku alpha, Anton Cheval, had managed the impossible on more than one occasion. Luc wasn't going to be the one to say the man couldn't do anything he claimed.

Not only was Anton an alpha Chanku, he was a powerful wizard with abilities well beyond those of anyone Luc had ever seen. In fact, it was common knowledge among them that Anton already had been a powerful wizard when he discovered his Chanku heritage while researching ancient, arcane rituals.

If anyone could bring back the dead, it would be Anton. Tia obviously had come to the same conclusion. She nodded, agreeing. "Whatever you want, Dad. When?"

Ulrich pulled an envelope out of a drawer in the table beside his chair. He opened it slowly and showed it to Tia. "It has to be done this week, on Halloween night, if we're going to try it at all. On Samhain."

Tia frowned. "*Sow-in*? What's that?"

"Basically it's another name for Halloween. According to Anton, that night is the time when the veil between the living and the dead is open the widest. The period lasting from just before midnight to dawn. Anton thinks he can contact your mother during that period, but only if we're all there, all of us calling to her."

Ulrich looked directly at Luc when he spoke, though his words were obviously for Tia. Luc felt a shiver run along his spine at the intensity in the older man's voice.

"We are the people who meant the most to your mother. Me, as her husband." He brushed Tia's hair back from her face and planted a kiss on her forehead. "You, as her only child."

Then he turned to Luc once more. "And, you, Lucien, as the man who ended her life. No. Don't look at me that way. Camille brought it on herself. Her actions caused her death, not yours. It wasn't your fault. Still, all of us felt a loss with Camille's death. Sometimes I think you, Luc, lost more than either Tia or myself. You lost your innocence, your sense of purpose. . . . Though, I hope, by gaining your Chanku heritage, you made up for some of that loss."

Luc sat down on the couch, hard. "I don't know what to say." He wiped his hand over his eyes, as if he might sweep away the memory of the breathtakingly beautiful wolf staring at him across freshly mowed grass, the bright flower of red when his bullet pierced the animal's shoulder—the broken body of a beautiful woman lying on the ground.

Luc raised his head and looked into Tia's eyes, expecting condemnation and finding only love. She spoke to her father, but her gaze never left Luc. "When do we leave, Dad?"

Ulrich cleared his throat. "We go tomorrow. Anton will send his private jet. He needs a couple days to prepare and wants us close. He said he's never attempted this before." Ulrich's voice cracked. He coughed and then sighed deeply. "Thank you. Thank you both. Whether or not he is successful, we'll know that at least we tried."

Tinker didn't join them that night. Tia heard his door open and close across the hall, heard Mik and AJ's laughter, and realized the three men had elected to spend the night together. Tia lay alone in the big bed with Luc, glad that only her mate was with her tonight.

She'd felt her father's pain, if only for a moment, and then he'd shielded, hiding the worst of it from his only child. Tia'd been shocked by his anger, the fury he carried in his heart over his wife's death. He missed her terribly, he loved her still, but he'd not forgiven Camille for her foolhardy decision to run as Chanku during daylight, when risk of discovery was high.

Ulrich had never before allowed Tia to see so deeply into his true feelings. Always he spoke of Tia's mother with love and admiration. For the first time Tia sensed the anger that boiled just beneath her father's calm surface.

He'd carried that anger for twenty years. Let it seethe and fester, while all the time speaking of Camille with warmth and love. Tia lay awake, dissecting her own feelings. Yes, she missed her mother, missed the hugs she couldn't remember, the bedtime stories that had framed her childhood. Missed the warm smile and the unconditional love only a mother could give.

But did she really remember that love? So much of Tia's childhood remained a blank in her memories, a great void where the good thoughts should lie.

Her memories, the little vignettes she thought about, were mere fantasies Tia had created over the years, events and images of things she knew she must have done with her mother; but they lacked the conviction of reality. Mixed with those childhood fantasies were strong feelings of anger, of rejection. Feelings Tia had never before wanted to explore.

Tonight her father had shocked her enough that Tia forced herself to face the truth. Camille had risked all for the freedom of running as a wolf. Not satisfied to run only at night, she'd condemned her daughter to grow up without a mother, condemned her husband to a life without his mate, condemned an innocent young man to a life of guilt over a meaningless death.

The reality of her feelings washed over Tia like a cold shower. She wrapped her arms around herself and shivered.

Suddenly aware of a sense of distance between herself and Luc, Tia reached for him. He came to her willingly, eagerly, and she knew that he worried about the trip to Montana. Worried that Anton might actually be successful.

Now shame mingled with her repressed anger. Luc's memories would be horrible. How could she have missed what must be passing through his mind?

Luc feared facing the ghost of the woman he had killed.

Offering her own absolution, Tia turned to him with her arms wide and her mind free of barriers.

"I love you," she whispered. "Whatever happens, I love you."

A sense of peace swept over Luc, a feeling that no matter what they might face, he would always have Tia's love. Luc nuzzled the soft skin beneath her chin, trailed kisses along her throat, found her left breast with her heart beating steadily beneath the golden flesh.

For a moment he hesitated, remembering the sight of Camille lying in the wet grass, the red spatter of blood spreading across her chest, the sightless eyes a tragic parody of her daughter's, which were always so filled with life.

Just as Camille's must have been before that day so long ago.

Tia wrapped her arms around Luc's neck and drew him close. Her lips were warm, her tongue alive with passion, licking at the crease of his lips, entering the moment he parted for her.

Luc smiled against her mouth, sensing her arousal, her body's desire for his. There was no reason for extended foreplay, no need to tease or titillate. This time he reached down, found her wet and ready folds, and grabbed his cock in his fist. With one thrust Luc entered her, felt her muscles clasp him in greeting, knew she was ready.

His second thrust took him deeper, hard against the tight ring of her cervix, the solid mouth of her womb. Luc withdrew slowly, caught in the warm grasp of her sex. Once more he thrust deeply and then withdrew.

He felt Tia's fingers fluttering across his thighs, over his buttocks. One finger found the tight crease between his cheeks, traced the sensitive flesh from his ass to his balls.

He felt her fingers beside his cock, sweeping through the fluids that lubricated his slow thrusts. She trailed damply around his balls, across his perineum, back to the crease in his butt.

Luc groaned, his entire body sensitized to Tia's light strokes, when suddenly she found the tight ring of his sphincter, rimmed the sensitive muscle, and penetrated him as deeply as she was able with her cool, slick finger.

He hadn't resorted to doing his multiplication tables in years, but Tia's probing finger, sliding deeper with each thrust, finding a rhythm to match Luc's slow but steady penetrations, took him higher, further than he'd imagined.

Suddenly she pressed against something, some small part of his anatomy that seemed to contain every nerve ending in Luc's entire body.

An electric charge surged from butt to balls to cock. Luc's climax shot through his lower half like a screaming comet. He arched his back, shooting deep inside Tia, shouting out as she added a second finger, filling his ass, pressing down on whatever magic button controlled him.

Luc's climax went on and on. Tia joined him, crying, trembling, her fingers slipping free of his body.

They clung together, both of them shivering in the aftermath of orgasm, unsure what tomorrow would bring but totally certain of the power of their love, their commitment to one another.

They met Anton's private plane at San Francisco International Airport. The wizard's personal valet, Oliver, welcomed them aboard. Luc, Tia, and Ulrich settled into their comfortable seats for the flight to Montana.

Luc found a blanket for Tia so she could rest. He'd kept her awake most of the night, making love to take her mind off the trip. Now, sated and sleepy, she curled up in a comfortable seat with a blanket wrapped snugly around her.

Ulrich sat alone, his face set, his thoughts unreadable.

Once he got the others settled, Luc found Oliver in the forward cabin. He'd actually grown fond of the tiny man of indeterminate age and heritage who managed such a wide range of jobs for the powerful wizard.

One day, Luc thought, he'd learn Oliver's story.

The two of them played cribbage all the way to Montana while Tia slept and her father stared silently out the window. By the end of the trip, Luc and Oliver had evened their score.

3

Luc and the others had been to the home of the Montana pack more than a month ago when Ulrich had been kidnapped, but the changes in the surrounding landscape in that short time had been dramatic. Brilliant splashes of orange, gold, and red mixed now with the dark evergreen forest. The emerald meadows had gone to brown, and there was a hint of frost in the air.

A transformation had occurred in Ulrich as well, merely over the course of the flight. He walked into the sprawling house like the confident alpha Luc knew him to be. Tia, however, seemed quiet and withdrawn, her mental shields tightly closed.

She didn't brighten until her cousin, Keisha, appeared on the front deck, holding tightly to Anton Cheval's arm.

Luc paused, almost midstep, sensing something secretive about Cheval's mate. He studied the tall, slim African American woman long enough that Tia turned back and looked at him with a question in her eyes.

Keisha obviously was carrying something more than a secret. Though her slim waist appeared almost unchanged, there was something in the light in her eyes and the way she held her hand protectively over her abdomen that gave her away. When Luc cocked an eyebrow at Anton, the wizard couldn't control a wide grin.

"Keisha?" Tia suddenly picked up on the silent communication. "You're pregnant? Oh, my goodness!" Tia raced up the long steps; the women hugged, Tia cried, Anton glowed.

Luc followed Tia up the stairs at a slower pace and watched Tia hug her cousin. Without consciously willing it, he imagined Tia growing his child, her slim waist thickening, her breasts swelling.

Need slammed into Luc, a sense of wanting, of urgency so powerful it rocked him. He paused a step, caught his breath, and shook off the feeling; then he turned and, smiling broadly, shook Anton's hand.

"Congratulations."

"Thank you. We're very excited, but . . ." Anton glanced at Keisha, who was totally wrapped up in Tia, and walked Luc and Ulrich to one side. "I'm glad you've come. Both of you. I'm guessing Ulrich's filled you in somewhat, Luc, but there's a lot more to this than I've told either of you. The visitations, and that's all I can consider them, began shortly after Keisha conceived. At first she merely dreamed of her Aunt Camille. The dreams have become more intense; the strength of Camille's presence is very unsettling. I'm worried about my mate, Ulrich, concerned as to the reason your late wife has seemed to fixate on her."

Ulrich shook his head, obviously perplexed. Luc studied Keisha for a moment, comparing her to Tia.

Other than Keisha's much darker complexion, the resemblance was phenomenal. "Did Camille look like Keisha?"

Ulrich nodded. "Very much so. The resemblance is striking."

"Could Camille's spirit be fixating on Keisha's unborn child, remembering her own daughter? Maybe she sees Keisha and thinks of herself when she was pregnant with Tianna."

Anton turned to study his wife and then looked back at Luc. "I hadn't thought of that, but it makes perfect sense. It's definitely been unsettling. Her presence is strong enough that even I've seen her. I know she's unhappy. Something ties her to this plane, but she can't seem to tell us what or why. We need to find out what's holding her back, what's keeping her from moving on in the natural progression of all spirits after death."

Ulrich turned away from Luc and Anton and stared out over the meadow. His voice was measured, defensive. "My wife was an amazing woman. Vibrant. Brilliant, stubborn, and uncontrollable in many ways, but very loving. I can't imagine she would harm your wife or your child."

Anton stepped beside Ulrich and grasped his shoulder. "I don't believe she means harm, but she obviously is very troubled. I want to help her, not harm her. Plus, I want my wife and I to get a decent night's sleep without waking to Camille in our bedroom." Anton chuckled softly and shrugged his shoulders. "Your wife needs to find peace if we're going to get any. I've been studying the rituals, looking for solutions good for everyone involved, including your wife's spirit."

Anton glanced back at Luc and then spoke very softly to Ulrich. "However, what I ask may be very painful for you. I want to try something I've never attempted. I'd like to send you through the veil that separates life and death, the corporeal world from the ethereal. I'm asking you if you're willing to spend one night with Camille, to cross over to the spiritual plane and see if you can find out what holds her here, what we need to do to give her peace."

Silence stretched between them for a long moment. When Ulrich turned around, there were tears in his eyes. "If you could give me one night with the woman I've loved all these years, it would be a gift beyond treasure. If there is any way to give her peace..." His shoulders sagged, and Ulrich took a deep breath. "To give any of us peace, we need to do whatever it takes."

Anton nodded slowly, as if weighing Ulrich's words and his own reply very carefully. "The hardest thing, my friend, will not be going through the veil to your wife. The difficult part of the journey will be when you need to return. You must come back to us before dawn or stay forever on the other side."

Ulrich's shoulders slumped. "I understand. It'll be like losing her again, only forever this time."

Anton shook his head. "Not that long, really. Life on earth is short, by comparison. Eternity is..." Anton smiled at his own joke, "forever." He held out his right hand for Ulrich to grasp. "You must promise me you'll come back of your own free will, or I can't attempt to send you across. From what I've seen of you, I trust you're a man of your word."

Ulrich hesitated but a moment, nodded, and took Anton's hand in his. Luc realized he'd been holding his breath and let it out in a long, slow sigh. All this talk of death and veils and planes. None of it made sense. He watched Tia and Keisha, still talking, Tia with her hand on Keisha's almost flat stomach, their faces animated, filled with laughter.

Now *that* made sense.

A shiver raced over his shoulders.

Luc felt as if a hand caressed his cheek; then the presence moved toward the house. He turned and glanced at Anton, saw the other man's gaze follow something toward the front door. Anton turned back, his amber eyes locking on Luc's with mesmerizing intensity.

Yes. She was here. You didn't imagine it. Anton spun around and slapped Ulrich on the back. "Come inside," he said, as though the ghost of Ulrich's wife hadn't just wandered across the deck. "Alexandria and Stefan have set out a late lunch for us. We can discuss what comes next over a good meal."

Sitting at the foot of the long table, Ulrich felt the separation between himself and the others in the room more intensely than ever before. Each of them was paired with a lover, just as he'd once been paired with Camille.

Damn her! Why did she have to take so many risks? Ulrich wondered if he'd ever get past the anger, the sense of helplessness over the loss of the one woman he'd ever loved.

Hadn't her adventurous personality been part of her charm? Hadn't he been drawn to the cocky attitude, the strength, the absolute mastery of the woman?

Yes. Ulrich sighed.

Would he ever be able to think of Camille without blaming her for all the years he'd spent alone?

Camille had missed so much. Ulrich caught Tia smiling at him and flashed her an answering grin. Who would have thought he could have had a part in creating such an amazing young woman? Bright, beautiful, headstrong like her mother but with her stubbornness tempered by just enough of Ulrich's own common sense.

Damn her! Camille should have been there to help raise her daughter.

But if she had, would Tia have turned out as well? Would she have been something better? Ulrich couldn't imagine anything about Tia that could be improved.

Then there was Luc. Like the son he'd never had, the son Camille might have given him, had she lived. Luc had ended Camille's life and then done his best to atone for what he considered his most egregious sin. He'd more than atoned. He'd become indispensable, and, even more than that, loved.

Anton's laughter caught Ulrich's attention. The Montana

alpha didn't laugh all that much, but it was obvious that the child Keisha carried had softened the enigmatic wizard more than anything else could. Usually Stefan was the one laughing, making jokes, teasing his packmates.

The sense of love in the room was a palpable thing, alive and growing, excluding Ulrich by its obvious pairing. Anton and Keisha, Alexandria and Stefan, his own daughter Tia and the man by her side.

Ulrich sighed and closed his eyes against the sting of self-pity. He must be getting old, to feel so maudlin.

Not old, my love, merely lonely.

Camille?

It had to be her. Ulrich's head snapped around, but of course there was nothing behind him.

Soon. We'll be together soon.

He must be hearing things. The conversation ebbed and flowed around him, late afternoon sunlight streamed through the windows . . . and that couldn't possibly be the voice of his long-dead wife.

Ulrich glanced up and caught Anton watching him. The small nod and half smile the wizard flashed his way made Ulrich shiver.

Anton pushed his chair back from his position at the head of the table and stood; then he lightly tapped his fork against his wineglass. The crystal rang like a small bell. Chatter and laughter among the others in the room came to an immediate halt.

"First I want to formally welcome our guests." Anton nodded toward Tia and Luc, but his gaze rested on Ulrich. "I also want to explain exactly what I have in mind, as there's a certain amount of preparation all of us need to do before tomorrow night."

Keisha smiled up at her mate. Once more Ulrich was reminded of Camille. Was the similarity in appearance between the two women, the fact Keisha carried her first child, the reason for Camille's reappearance?

"Halloween, or Samhain, is traditionally the time we honor our dead. It's the one night of the year where the veil between the living and dead is at its most fragile, when the dead can more easily pass from the ethereal plane to our earthly one. Keisha and I have sensed Camille's presence on this side, the side of the living, where she shouldn't be, and it's grown stronger each night. Tomorrow night, if everything works, I want to do two things. Find out what is holding Camille here, and, hopefully, give Ulrich the opportunity to find closure with his wife. I suspect that lack of closure is what's holding her tied to the world of the living."

Ulrich stared at Anton for a long moment, considering the wizard's words. Anton had just accused him of hanging on to Camille's spirit, of holding her back. The purpose of this whole visit suddenly made all too much sense. "I hadn't thought of it like this, but, essentially, you're asking me to condemn Camille, once more, to death."

Anton shook his head. "No, my friend. She is already dead. I'm asking you to let her rest."

Put that way . . . "What do I need to do?" Ulrich reached for his wineglass, realized his hand was shaking, and placed his palm flat on the table beside his plate.

"We all have to prepare. I'll need the combined energy of everyone in this room to part the veil and hold it open long enough. My wife appears to be Camille's focal point. Ulrich suggested it was Keisha's appearance as much as the family relationship of aunt to niece; Luc thought it might be that plus the fact Keisha carries our child, reminding Camille of her own role as a mother."

Tia's head snapped up. She looked directly at Keisha, and her skin flushed a dark bronze. "I never thought of that. I've been feeling so jealous, wondering why my mother would come to you and not her own daughter. That makes so much sense. Keisha, I'm sorry."

"For what?" Keisha reached across the table and grasped Tia's outstretched hand in hers. "You have every right to be resentful. I hardly remember your mom. . . . Believe me, I've been feeling just as resentful, wishing it was my own mother popping into my head, not yours!"

"This is one of the things we need to clear from the room. Any suspicion, any sense of ill will." Anton smiled at his wife. "Tomorrow night when we call Camille, we will all have purified ourselves as much as possible. I want you to consider at least an hour of quiet meditation, preferably somewhere alone, before we meet here tomorrow night at dusk. Clear your thoughts of all distractions, all anger, jealousy, all fear . . . and, while I know it's asking a lot of this particular group, no sex from now until after we're done."

Stefan's dramatic groan made even Ulrich chuckle.

Anton grinned. "Think of the energy you'll add to this project, all that bottled testosterone struggling to escape. We need you, Stefan."

Laughing, Stefan tossed a napkin at Anton, who caught it neatly in one hand as he continued. "We'll all need to rest well tonight and tomorrow. We'll eat well at midday and then fast until dusk, when I want you to meet me in the meadow behind the house. Once we establish a circle and make contact, we need to hold the link until Ulrich returns before dawn. If we lose it, we could lose Ulrich."

He said it so matter-of-factly, Tia's head spun in an arc as her gaze shot from Anton's to Ulrich. Her father looked directly at her, shrugged his shoulders, and smiled. *Don't worry. It will all be fine. I'll be okay.*

Are you sure?

Ulrich nodded, keeping the connection between the two of them completely private.

His daughter blinked rapidly, her eyes sparkling with what could only be tears. Her hand came up and she brushed them away, the quick and angry motion of her fingers so much like Camille, Ulrich's heart actually hurt. As he watched, Tia's shoulders straightened, and she glared at him.

Well, you'd damned well better be careful, because if anything happens, I'm coming after you, and you'll be sorry.

Ulrich's burst of laughter caught everyone by surprise. Tia had just repeated the very threat he'd used on her when she was a child. He held up his hands in mock surrender.

"My daughter has just made a point of reminding me who the lead alpha in our pack is. She's more like her mother than she realizes. You may all rest assured, should Anton be successful in sending me to the other side, I will be back on time."

4

Freshly showered and shaved, wearing only the simple white robe Oliver had left in his room, Ulrich took one last look in the large mirrored closet door at the man who would attempt the impossible in a few short hours.

A candle flickered from a nearby table, the small flame barely visible in the late afternoon light. He'd thrown open the window shades to the perfect fall day, and sunlight spilled across the polished wood floors.

Was he ready? As Anton instructed, Ulrich planned to meditate for the next hour, find his center, and calm his racing heart before meeting with the others, but, now, looking at his reflection, Ulrich's body shivered with surging emotions and the rush of adrenaline.

What would Camille think of him when he appeared to her?

He turned to one side, examining his reflection. Except for the white hair, he didn't look or feel his age. No extra weight, his skin smooth and unlined, his eyes clear, their amber lights positively glowing tonight. Ulrich took a deep breath, sucked in his nonexistent belly, and then let it out with a sigh of self-disgust.

"Who the hell are you kidding, you old fart? You're a fucking sixty-three-year-old hoping to spend the night with a woman who will forever be thirty-eight years of age."

Ulrich sat heavily on the edge of the bed as the enormity of what they planned to attempt slammed into him. The years of anger, of need, of pure, unmitigated wanting, immobilized him and settled into an ache under his heart.

Dear God, how he missed her.

Anton had asked that each of them come to him with a clear mind and an open heart. *Impossible.* Nothing seemed clear . . . nothing at all. Not like this.

Ulrich slowly stood up, removed the white robe. He folded it neatly, set it on the bed, and shifted.

Only when he was the wolf could his body find peace.

Shaking off his human cares, the huge wolf that was the better part of Ulrich Mason paced the small area between the end of the bed and the wall and then settled down on his haunches to stare at the tiny flame. His thoughts might be that of the man, but the heart beating in his chest was that of the alpha wolf.

Tonight he would once again be reunited with his mate. He would think only of this night, not of the days beyond. Freeing his mind from worry, the wolf let peace steal his soul.

Tia sat cross-legged in the middle of the bed. She held in one hand a photo taken years ago of her mother and herself. It was an old color image from shortly before Camille's death. Both of them were laughing, their eyes bright, their smiles carefree. Tia stared at the picture and tried to remember her mother's scent, the way Camille's arms felt wrapped around her waist, the feel of her mother's lips against her cheek.

Tia knew all these things had happened, but the memories were lost. Staring at the photo, Tia realized all she really wanted were fresh memories, something to hold her mother close to her in all the years ahead.

Something to chase away the lingering resentment she'd never been able to shed, the feeling of abandonment when Camille had suddenly disappeared from six-year-old Tia's life.

Could Anton give her that much? It seemed so little to ask, yet it would require much of the wizard's skill.

Tia held the photo close to her heart. She opened her mind to possibilities, her heart to love.

Luc filled the space. Completely.

Smiling, Tia pushed thoughts of her mate aside and concentrated on the night ahead.

Keisha ran the brush through her hair, staring at the face of the woman in the mirror. She could be her Aunt Camille, so closely did they resemble one another. Was that the reason Camille had returned here, to Keisha's home in Montana, rather than to Camille's home in San Francisco?

Why now? Was it the baby she carried? Her hand protectively covered her flat stomach. Fearing for her child's safety, Keisha almost had considered not joining the group tonight, but it was obvious Anton counted on her.

Keisha smiled. She would do anything for Anton Cheval. Anything at all. Even face the ghost of a woman who had been dead for more than twenty years.

Shaking her head at the absurdity of calling up the dead, Keisha set the hairbrush on her vanity table and moved to the comfortable old rocking chair Anton had found in the basement.

Freshly painted now, filled with soft pillows and an even softer lap blanket, it would be perfect for rocking their child.

What better place to meditate, to find peace, to clear her mind of any fears and misgivings she might feel?

Keisha knew she had already survived the worst life could throw at her. A meeting with the ghost of her dead aunt was nothing. So long as she had Anton beside her, Keisha could handle anything.

Bring it on. I'm ready.

Smiling, she tapped the floor with her toe and set the rocker into motion. Opening her heart, Keisha felt the peace of the day settle over her mind.

Stefan heard the shower go on in the guest room next to his and knew Xandi readied herself for this evening. He'd already showered and shaved earlier, donning the soft white robe Anton had given him.

He knew this evening was important, but, damn, he missed Xandi. Why in the hell they always ended up without sex when the San Francisco pack showed up, he wasn't sure, but for some reason it seemed to happen that way.

It's been only twice, you idiot.

Okay, so he could go a couple nights without Xandi's sweet, responsive, and loving body in his arms, but, dammit, didn't these people realize he had a lot of years of celibacy to make up for? Chanku were sensual creatures. His five years caught halfway between human and wolf hadn't been conducive to picking up chicks in bars, much less finding a willing female to bed.

Five long years without sex. He'd managed fine without the chicks. He couldn't imagine life without Xandi.

When he'd rescued Xandi, her body had been half frozen, her hair a solid sheet of ice he'd had to pry from the frozen ground.

He'd gotten her into his warm bed just in time to save her life. Stefan shuddered, remembering the fear coursing through him when he'd realized she'd almost died.

Thank goodness she'd survived, because she'd certainly turned the tables and saved his pathetic life. He tried to imagine Ulrich Mason's lonely existence. . . . Twenty years without the woman he loved.

That poor bastard. Stefan shivered, feeling small-minded and selfish. He had the love of his life; the least he could do was help reunite Ulrich with his, if only for a night.

His thoughts searched for Xandi. He sensed the steady spray of the shower and steam rising around her perfect body. Content in the knowledge that she was close by and safe, Stefan sat in the middle of their bed—the bed he'd slept in alone last night—with his legs crossed and his hands resting on his knees, palms up. He breathed deeply, finding a rhythm that took him almost immediately into a meditative trance.

Stefan opened his heart, opened his mind, felt the first wisps of a gentle peace settle over him. He let his thoughts rest on Ulrich, wondering about all the years the man had spent without his mate, and for a moment Stefan's concentration faltered.

No, he wouldn't even try to imagine life without Xandi. He'd been there, and it was hell. Instead he thought of Camille Mason, the ethereal spirit all of them had felt over the past couple weeks, and he pictured Ulrich's joy should they be successful tonight.

Smiling, Stefan finally found his center, found the peace that had eluded him, and prepared for the coming night. He took one last glance out the window, saw the perfect sky, and sighed. Damn, but he wanted to run.

Now, to find that elusive center once again. . . .

Xandi slipped the white robe over her damp body and combed her fingers through her hair. She knew Stefan had already begun to meditate. She could sense him, so close had they become, two halves of the whole. She imagined his reaction when she finally told him her secret.

Keisha wasn't the only one who had conceived. Xandi's palm flattened over her belly, and she smiled. This child would be a creature borne by the most wild mating his mother had ever experienced.

She'd known from the beginning she would have a boy, had felt his strength in the first tiny cells created immediately after conception. That night she and Stefan had hunted alone. They'd brought down a deer, running the beast to the ground, feeding until they were sated, and then crawling off into the brush to clean themselves and sleep.

Later, when Stefan took her while still in their wolven forms, she'd known it was time. Xandi almost shivered with the power she'd felt when she consciously released an egg for fertilization, knowing this was her choice, approved by her mate yet still entirely up to her.

He'd been big and rough, clamping his jaws around her throat to hold her still, his claws raking her shoulders, his cock penetrating deep and hard. When he tied with her, when the knot formed inside her sex, she'd felt the steady throbbing pulse for what seemed like hours as he pumped his seed into her womb.

Xandi clasped her hands and bit back a whimper. Her body was a seething stew of hormones in the early weeks of her pregnancy. She needed Stefan with an ache that was almost painful.

Well, Anton said he wanted sexual energy tonight. If the pulsing dampness between her legs was any indication, Xandi figured she could call up just about any ghost Anton might think of!

Grinning like an idiot, knowing she would have to tell Stefan as soon as this night ended, Xandi settled herself on the small rug in front of the French doors to the patio. Clearing her mind, opening her heart, she placed both palms over her belly and let peace flow over her soul.

*   *   *

Luc paced the width of the bedroom and back again, the white robe swirling around his legs, his libido raging and his blood singing with the overload of adrenaline coursing through his system.

Why the hell Anton wanted them celibate for this damned ritual of his, Luc didn't know, but he sure as hell couldn't sit and meditate with his cock big as a baseball bat and twice as hard.

He needed Tia, wanted the softness of her warm and welcoming body, the calming influence of her gentle hands. Damn it all, he'd wanted to apologize to Camille Mason for twenty years, explain to her why he'd pulled the trigger, how he wished he could undo that terrible act, but if he couldn't relax, he might screw up whatever Cheval had planned.

He couldn't do that to Tia, couldn't do it to Ulrich. Both of them had more need of closure than he did. Hell, all Luc wanted was a way to rid himself of the guilt he'd hauled around for twenty years.

The weight of it was killing him.

The robe snagged on a corner of the bed and stopped him in his tracks. Luc leaned over to free the fabric from the metal frame and saw something shiny lying under the bed.

He reached for it, picked it up, and felt his heart stand still. It was the same framed photo he'd looked at the night of Camille's funeral. It must have fallen out of Tia's suitcase when she'd moved into the room next to his.

Luc stared at the photo, the mother and daughter so much alike it brought tears to his eyes. He might as well have been that same rookie cop twenty years ago, standing in Ulrich's house waiting for Ulrich to come down the stairs after tucking his tiny daughter into bed.

"Ah, Camille. You've missed so damned much because of me, yet your death is what brought Ulrich and me together; it gave me the world of the Chanku, it's what brought Tia into my life. Even more than I want to apologize, I need to thank you."

Luc set the photo on the low vanity dresser and sat down on the small bench in front of it. Staring at the picture of Camille and a five- or six-year-old Tia, Luc felt his heart rate slow and the tension ebb away.

He touched the woman's picture with the tip of his finger, honoring her in the only way he could. Calming his racing thoughts, relaxing his body and mind, he let the peace of the afternoon slowly seep into his heart.

Anton Cheval stood beneath the stinging spray of the shower and let the hot water melt the tension flowing through his body. Aware on an almost visceral level of all the other inhabitants of his household, he sensed the moment when Luc, the last of them to settle down, finally discovered the peace that had escaped him all afternoon.

Anton bowed his head, feeling the power flowing into him from the other inhabitants of his house. The water ran hot, turning his olive skin a dark brick red, joining the heat on his skin to the cauldron of energy building inside his body. His cock rose, rampant against his belly as the power and life raced through his veins.

He missed Keisha's warm body, her loving, gentle spirit. Come the dawn, he had hours of celibacy to make up for, but, like the others, he would wait.

What Anton hoped to accomplish tonight would take every bit of strength he possessed, all his arcane knowledge . . . and more than a little bit of luck.

He'd once accused Stefan of the sin of hubris. Was he suffering from the same self-delusion, that he could bring the dead to life?

He thought of the shroud of loneliness that followed his friend Ulrich, the *little-girl-lost* look clinging to Tia, the lifetime of self-recrimination haunting Lucien Stone, Keisha's fear for their unborn daughter . . . and the sadness of the wraith who had taken up residence in their home.

He couldn't ignore Camille Mason's plea for help. If there was a way to help her move on, to aid the others linked to her, Anton would find it. He was ready to do whatever he could.

He bowed his head as the hot water sluiced over his shoulders, and he gave thanks to the powers that ruled the universe, the spirit beings that so graciously accepted his amateur attempts to understand the ethereal plane.

Would they help him tonight? He had to believe. The peace of many lives depended on his success.

Anton willed his rock-hard erection to relax. His cock slowly returned to its flaccid state. The water cooled, chilling him beneath the spray.

He took a deep breath and reached for the center that would hold him steady this night. He felt his heart rate slow, his body calm. He stepped from the shower and slowly dried himself, soaking up the peace that had eluded him until now. He took his time shaving, ran his hand over the smooth skin along his jaw, and knew Keisha would approve.

Smiling, he pulled the white robe over his damp body, combed his hair into a tight queue, and tied it out of the way; then he went outside to prepare.

5

Luc watched carefully as Anton lit a small fire in a stone-lined pit in the meadow behind the house and then loosely arranged six chairs nearby in a circle. He placed a single chair off to one side. The sun had already disappeared behind the tall trees, and dark shadows grew darker, even as the flames rose.

Next to the fire was an intricately carved wooden table covered with a dark gold, silken cloth that shimmered like precious metal. Anton pushed the loose sleeves of his white robe back to his elbows, lit a candle, and set it in a holder on the cloth; then he held an incense stick in the flame until it began to smoke. He set that in an iridescent abalone shell. Luc noticed that the candle flame burned straight, without wavering, in spite of the light breeze stirring the treetops, yet the smoke from the incense wafted out over the chairs and hung there in a richly scented gray cloud.

Other objects Anton placed on the surface of what must be his altar included a beautifully carved knife with a bone handle, a shiny black stone that appeared to be obsidian, and a statue of a wolf, perfectly carved out of a redwood burl.

Next, Anton put a small amount of salt in a seashell and set it to one side and then poured water from a cloth-covered pitcher into a crystal goblet he set next to the candle. The last thing he did was place a small tray in the center of the table. On it sat a ripe pomegranate that had been cut crosswise in half. The brilliant red fruit held the perfect shape of a pentagram.

Luc sensed Tia's presence. He glanced up and saw her walking toward him with Keisha and Alexandria. The women held hands with Tia in the middle. Their white robes gave them a mystical, dreamy appearance. All three wore their hair long and flowing and walked barefoot across the short grass.

Tia glanced up and smiled at Luc. He fought every Chanku instinct to grab his mate, shift into the wolf, and run away with her. His hands felt cold; his muscles practically quivered with the need to be far from whatever Anton was setting into motion.

Stefan approached from the woods, brushing his hair from his face with one hand, wiping grass and twigs off his mud-stained robe with the other. Luc grinned at the sheepish look on Stefan's face. No doubt he'd just come in from a run. Obviously, the lure of the woods had been stronger than Anton's instructions.

Luc felt jealous as hell. He quickly tempered the emotion, set it aside.

Ulrich was the last to arrive, looking uncomfortable in his bare feet and white robe. He stared at the altar for a moment and then glared directly at Luc.

All we need are pointy hats and masks, and we'd look like a bunch of fucking Ku Klux Klanners.

Luc bit back a snort. He cast a quick glance at Anton and saw the man's lip curl into a smile. Nothing escaped him. Ever.

Anton finally looked up from his preparations. "I want each of you to stand beside a chair." He grinned. "Choose wisely. You're going to be in it for a while. Ulrich, please carry that one into the center." Anton pointed at the one chair he'd set off to the side. "I've cut a pentagram into the grass. It's hard to see in this light, but it's there. Put your chair in the center of the star, facing the altar."

Ulrich did as he was told, placing his chair legs directly over the five-pointed star's center.

Anton picked up the knife and carefully touched it to the obsidian, sprinkled salt over the blade, dipped it in the water, ran the blade through the flame and then through the smoke from the incense. He lifted it high, as if offering the silver knife as a gift.

Luc held tightly to the back of his chair as Anton knelt down and used the knife to cut a circle in the grass around them. He carefully enclosed the chairs, the people, and the pentagram within its boundary.

"Stay within the circle and sit down now, if you will." Anton took the goblet of water, sprinkled a few drops over the circle, tossed a few grains of salt, and then held both the candle and the incense inside its boundary.

Luc felt an odd pressure about him, as if the air had developed a charge. He realized he was hearing a soft chorus of some kind and glanced to his left where Tia sat with her head bowed. She and the other women were chanting, the words low and incomprehensible to Luc. He looked up at Anton, curious yet loath to interrupt.

Anton placed a picture on the altar. Luc recognized another of the photos of Camille that Tia had brought with her. The chanting grew louder. Anton picked up the tray with the pomegranate, stepped within the circle, and sat down. The chanting abruptly stopped.

Anton's voice took on the low, mesmerizing quality Luc remembered so well from their last visit. "I want you to relax, to feel the warmth within the circle. The night will grow cold, but you will remain comfortable within its protective shield." He passed the plate to each of them. Everyone took a few of the pomegranate seeds. Anton set the tray at Ulrich's feet.

Luc stared at the seeds in his hand. Blood red in the dying light, they seemed totally innocuous yet strangely powerful.

"Taste one of the seeds. Close your eyes, experience the sharp tang, the sweet flavor, the hard seed within the soft pulp. Roll it on your tongue. Realize you can taste the flavors, feel the textures, because you are alive, you are a part of this earthly plane."

Luc tasted the sweet tart flavor, found the hard seed with his tongue, and thought how simple an act, yet meaningful, to taste something. To experience the flavors.

"Concentrate on the spirit of Camille Mason. Draw her close with your thoughts. Those of you who know her: my wife, Keisha, who is her niece; Tia Mason, her only child; Ulrich Mason, her husband; Lucien Stone, the man who killed her."

Luc flinched at Anton's bald statement. Tia reached out and tightly grasped his hand. Ulrich turned his head and looked directly at Luc, but there was no condemnation in his gaze.

"Finish the remainder of the seeds you hold. Taste them, concentrate on the flavor, the texture, the sweet and the tart. The purpose of the seed, which is to bring life."

Luc tried to follow Anton's instructions and concentrate wholly on the few pomegranate seeds in his mouth, but he'd grown more aware of Tia, of the tension within the circle, of the sense of something building in the air around them.

Anton's soft voice brought Luc back. "Think of life. There is sweet; there is tart. There are bumps and valleys along the journey, good times and bad. Life is what it is, what we make of it. No more, no less."

Anton looked skyward and took a deep, slow breath. Then he exhaled and took Tia's hand on his right, Keisha's on his left. "I know you're close, Camille. Come into our circle. We offer you safety. Hopefully, we offer you a way home. Come to those who love you, those who hold you fast to this earthly plane."

The women began their chant again. Out of the corner of his eye, Luc saw the candle flame flicker. Tia's hand tightened in his left, but her voice was steady. Xandi held on to his right. There was only a small space between Luc's knees and Ulrich's chair, but something brushed his legs. The air felt heavy, ripe, as though something grew within the circle.

Xandi gasped, a sharp intake of breath as she stared at a spot between herself and Ulrich. She squeezed Luc's hand. Tia's fingers tightened around Luc's with bruising strength as a figure wavered, insubstantial at first, and then slowly seemed to draw on the energy within the circle, finding shape and substance.

Luc felt his heart literally skip a beat. Camille Mason stood just behind her husband, her black hair free and flowing about her shoulders, her eyes bright and alive. The white gown she wore matched the others in the circle.

Camille looked first at Anton, who smiled at her with a look of utter relief.

She gestured toward her husband. "Thank you. I promise to give him back."

Ulrich jerked around in his chair and stared at his wife. Camille smiled at him but held up one hand to forestall him. She leaned close to Keisha and placed her hand on Keisha's smooth belly.

"It was your babe who drew me back. You carry a daughter, just as I once did."

Camille's voice was strong and steady. There was absolutely nothing ghostlike about her. "For so long now, I've floated, neither here nor there. No color, no sound, no sense of anything living or dead, merely the frustration that I could not come back to life, nor could I move forward to the peaceful death I should have had. Then I sensed your baby, a little girl so much like my Tia. She drew me here."

Camille closed her eyes and took a deep breath, as though savoring the air, the expansion of her lungs. Her fingers trembled against Keisha's flat stomach. "Blessings to you, my niece. Your child will be just like you, strong and beautiful. She will be Chanku, and one with the forest. As we all are. Keep her safe."

Next Camille walked around the small circle, brushing by Ulrich as if he weren't even there. She paused in front of Luc and studied him thoughtfully. Finally she reached down and took his right hand, freeing him from Xandi's strong grasp.

"I did not want to die so young, but my death was not your fault. You were doing your job. No more, no less. What happened was fated, not only by my own willful actions but by the mysterious wheel of life none of us has the power to comprehend, much less control. For you to find Tia, to learn of your own Chanku heritage, for Pack Dynamics to come about . . . for so many other bits and pieces of the past twenty years, I had to die. The past happened as it had to. The future is yet to be determined. Don't let guilt undermine the wonderful life you have. Live without the weight you've carried for so long."

Camille squeezed Luc's hand, released it, and swept her palm across his cheek in benediction. There were tears in his eyes. Luc knew he was crying only because the vision in front of him wavered, disappeared for a brief moment.

As did the weight that had bowed his shoulders for the past twenty years.

Tia tried to swallow and couldn't. She felt Luc's strong fingers grasping hers, but when Camille turned to look at her, the rest of the world faded away.

"Mom?" Tia pulled her fingers free of Luc's hand and reached for her mother with both arms.

Camille gave a choked sob and out her hands. Tia practically leaped into her embrace, felt the slim arms around her back, smelled the suddenly familiar scent of her mother's favorite perfume.

Magically, all the memories Tia had held long buried rushed back. She remembered favorite meals and walks along Ocean Beach. Playing in the park and trips to the zoo and shopping in Union Square. Trolley rides on sunny days and walking with her mother across Golden Gate Bridge with the wind lifting her hair.

An entire childhood's worth of memories, all lost to the trauma of abandonment, all gone for so long, bursting now, like flowers coming into bloom, bright and colorful and filled with texture, scent, and sound. Sobbing, Tia hugged Camille tight for what felt like hours . . . but must really have lasted only a moment.

Much, much too brief a time in the life of a child.

Finally Tia felt her mother's arms relax. She dropped her own and stepped back. It was only then that Tia realized she towered over the much tinier woman. Sniffing, wiping the tears from her eyes, she grinned at her mother. Her voice cracked on a sob. "You're little. I'm taller than you!"

Tears streamed from Camille's eyes. "You're so beautiful, so much like your father." She reached up and brushed at the tears on Tia's cheeks. Tia leaned against her mother's soft palm. "Live well. You've found a fine man, but you need a wedding! I want to know my baby girl is married to the man she loves, and I want your father to walk you down the aisle. That's the way it's supposed to happen. I want my grandbabies to know their father loved their mother enough to marry her. I want to see you in that pretty dress with a big bouquet of flowers, looking just the way I did when I married your father. I'll be there, somehow. I promise."

Camille reached up and pulled Tia's face down to hers and

kissed her gently on the lips. Tia felt the life in her mother, felt the regret, and just as clearly, felt the years of her own resentment fade away.

When Camille stepped back and reached for Ulrich, Tia's shaking knees gave way and she sat back down in her chair. Luc's arms came around her, holding her close. She leaned into his shoulder and sobbed, but her heart was full of love, and her mind hummed with the childhood she'd completely forgotten until tonight.

Ulrich hoped like hell his heart could take the strain. Camille stood between his knees, and the look she gave him was so familiar, so full of mischief and her typical sass and bravado, he didn't know whether he wanted to shake her or make love to her.

Tears still streamed down her dark cheeks, but Ulrich wasn't sure if they were for Tia or for him. He reached for her, and Camille linked her fingers in his, tugging Ulrich to his feet.

He'd forgotten how tiny she was, how finely boned yet strong and determined. How utterly sensual and how much she turned him on just by being close. Now he stood over her, wanting to kiss her so badly he ached, yet afraid to do anything that might make her disappear.

Neither of them spoke. They stared at one another, so hungry, needing so much more than one night could give. Still, Ulrich felt Camille's familiar touch, felt her love in his mind and in his heart.

Ulrich glanced at Anton. The wizard sat very still, his face ashen in the low light. Ulrich suddenly realized what a strain this must be, holding Camille on this plane in such solid form.

He wrapped his arms around her and sighed when she pressed her cheek against his heart. She felt warm and solid and very much alive. Her voice came into his mind, so familiar, so very like his Camille.

C'mon, Ric. Get a move on, big guy. We've only got tonight and I want to make it last. I want you inside me, and we can't fuck here, not with this audience.

Ulrich threw back his head and laughed. He saw Tia's head come up with a look of surprise on her tear-stained face, saw Anton's wan smile as he waved them off with a weak flip of his long fingers.

The circle around them wavered. The light grew very bright and then dimmed. Ulrich felt a wrenching, tugging sensation, as if he'd pulled every muscle in his body.

He shook his head and blinked and tried to get his bearings. The circle was gone. The chairs, his daughter, the rest of the Chanku. All gone. He and Camille were totally alone in a beautiful meadow flanked by thick forest on all sides.

Alone, both of them naked, and Ulrich had never been so aroused in his life. He reached for Camille, and she slipped into his arms as if he'd never been separated from her, as if he weren't twenty years older with snow-white hair and a lifetime of experience his young wife had missed.

She whispered his name, came to him filled with need, her laughter dying on a soft sigh beneath his mouth, her body ripe and ready for whatever pleasure they could find, whatever old resentments they could ease.

Spirit she might be, but for this one night Camille was everything she'd ever been, the woman who had loved him, fought with him, given him more laughter and more grief than any one person had a right to.

It wasn't grief filling Ulrich's mind when he bowed down to kiss her. No, it wasn't grief. Not by a long shot.

6

A bright light flashed, flowing upward from the pentagram carved in the earth. Tia covered her eyes, and Luc dragged her body against his chest to protect her. There was no heat, just blinding brilliance. Luc shaded his face with his free hand and opened his eyes in time to see Anton slowly fall forward to the ground.

Keisha screamed. Luc steadied Tia in her chair and then reached for Anton. He lifted the wizard's surprisingly light frame and placed him back in his chair. Keisha hovered beside him, holding him steady. Luc checked to see that he was breathing, but when he placed his hand over Anton's chest, Luc felt the man's heart racing unsteadily.

"His color doesn't look good." Stefan brushed Anton's hair from his eyes. "Should we call for help?"

"We can't break the circle." Xandi's voice quavered. "No matter what."

Keisha held Anton against her shoulder, quietly sobbing. Stefan knelt beside the two of them. Luc turned to check on Tia. She knelt on the ground beside her father's body. Ulrich lay where he'd fallen, his eyes open and staring, his chest barely moving. Tia carefully closed his eyes with shaking hands.

Xandi watched the circle.

"Whatever you do," she cautioned again, "don't step outside the circle. Anton's orders. How is he?"

Stefan nodded. "I think he'll be okay. Whatever spell he just performed took everything out of him. Once he rests..." Stefan pulled Tia's chair closer to Anton. He could help support his packmate's limp body and comfort Keisha at the same time.

Her crying eased. Luc heard her sniff loudly. She reached for Stefan's hand, grasping his fingers with hers over Anton's chest, protecting her mate between the two of them.

Luc turned to help Tia. She held her father's body. Ulrich's head rested in her lap, and she sobbed uncontrollably, as though the emotions of the evening had been too much.

"Is he still breathing?" When Tia nodded, Luc knelt beside her and lifted one of Ulrich's eyelids. Only white stared back at him. He felt the soft rise and fall of the man's chest, but there was no rousing him.

"His body is here. His spirit has gone with Camille. We need to hold within the circle until he returns at dawn. We are the life force that will call Ulrich back. Do not leave the circle." Anton's voice sounded weak, but the command was still evident in every word.

The air within the circle remained surprisingly warm and comfortable. It carried the faint scent of the herbs, of rosemary, sage, and mint from Anton's incense. The small candle on the altar continued to burn steadily without flickering.

Tia stayed on the ground with her father. Luc sat in his chair, and she braced her back against his legs with Ulrich's head resting in her lap. Keisha stayed close to Anton, stroking his arm while his normal color slowly returned. Stefan moved back to his own chair beside Xandi. They huddled together on the opposite side of the circle, hugging one another, watching Ulrich.

Luc checked his watch. It was barely nine o'clock. Anton was right; it was going to be a very long night.

"So long, so damned long. Ah, Camille, I never thought to see you again. Where have you been? Have you felt pain? Loneliness?"

Camille gazed up at him, her eyes shimmering in the odd light. "I felt nothing, not the passing of time, not a sense of place or being. Only a wish to move forward, but I couldn't go. Something ties me here. I wanted to touch you, to see Tianna, but I couldn't. I merely waited . . . waited until Keisha conceived. I felt the babe's life. Felt the connection. Remembered life."

Ulrich thought of the long, lonely nights when he'd lain awake, imagining Camille in his bed once again. It saddened him to think she'd been somewhere, nowhere . . . caught in a strange and lonely place. Now that her body lay beneath his, their bed the thick grass of some ethereal meadow in a place far from the real world, he didn't know whether to weep or plunge his aching cock deep inside her waiting body.

Wasn't sure if what he wanted was love—or revenge for all those nights without her. He kissed her again, and she moaned against his mouth; her tongue found the seam between his lips and slipped inside.

Dear God, how he'd missed her! His big hand found her breast. He palmed the soft flesh, dark like fine chocolate, the underside as soft as silk, her nipple hard and proud and so tempting he had to pinch it between his fingers, had to tear his mouth from Camille's and take her insolent nipple between his lips.

He tasted her, and the lonely years fell away.

She cried out when he suckled the taut flesh; her hips bucked hard against his groin and trapped his cock between their straining bodies. Still working her nipple with his tongue,

Ulrich slipped his fingers over the smooth skin of her belly, found the tuft of dark, springy curls between her legs, the soft and swollen cleft of her sex.

So painfully familiar! He'd done this thousands of times in real life, in his dreams, touched her responsive body, made her sing beneath his fingers.

Camille thrashed against him, her movements desperate as she moaned and whimpered, begging him to take her. Instead, Ulrich used the tip of one finger to tease the soft, wet folds. He found her clit and rubbed it so lightly he knew it must be driving her insane.

She'd always loved the teasing, the long, slow foreplay when he built the tension and made her body tremble. This much he could give her again.

He dipped into her wet pussy and dragged her juices over her swollen labia, spread them down the cleft in her cheeks and teased the tight, puckered opening of her anus.

Each time he took her almost to the edge, each time he backed away, taking his fingers to another spot, another erogenous zone he remembered from all those long, sweet hours of foreplay so many years ago.

Ulrich moved to Camille's other breast and sucked and nipped his way to the top. He used his tongue to tease the hard tip, rubbed his chin against the sensitive underside, and then settled down to suckle her as if he were a newborn, his tongue holding her nipple tight to the roof of his mouth, drawing steadily with his cheeks and lips.

Sobbing now, Camille writhed as if her body would twist into a knot. He knew she'd loved their sex this way, the long, slow buildup, the teasing that went on and on until she was covered in sweat, her heart pounding, her mouth opened in a silent cry of need.

Ulrich brought her to that place, his fingers slipping in and out of her warmth, his cock riding against her thigh, his mouth pulling so hard on her breast he knew it must hurt, knew she wouldn't want it any other way.

He felt Camille shudder, sensed her orgasm was only seconds away. Ulrich raised up on his knees and turned her over. Crying, begging him to come inside her, Camille grabbed at the thick tufts of grass when he knelt behind her. She spread her legs, her breath bursting in great gasps like a bellows.

Ulrich grabbed his cock in his fist, pressed against her wet and waiting sex, and thrust inside, hard and deep. Camille screamed, the sound filled as much with pain as with pleasure.

"Ah, Ric . . . Ric . . . *Ric!*"

Her tight pussy clamped down on his cock, and her body shuddered as tremor after tremor rocked her. Ulrich never slowed, plowing in hard and fast, taking her even higher, waiting for the laughter, the love they'd always shared during rough and rowdy sex.

Now there was nothing. Her cries of pleasure ended, and he heard only Camille's grunts when he filled her, the harsh cadence of her voice begging for more, the rough whisper of the nickname she'd given him so many years ago . . . *Ric, Ric, Ric* . . . the sense of something missing holding more power than what they had.

Something in her voice, in the tone of her sobs, in the dark void where her mind should have been filled with encouragement and laughter, finally tipped Ulrich over the edge.

Snarling, growling with a combination of anger and love and need, Ulrich shifted. Sharp claws raked tender human shoulders, his huge cock thrust in and out of Camille's swollen sex as she shoved her hips back against his and, following Ulrich's lead, became the wolf.

Their mating turned into a battle, a power play between two alphas, fueled by hunger, seasoned by guilt and anger. The bitch might be smaller, but her will was great. She turned and nipped at the huge wolf riding her, grabbed his left front leg between her sharp teeth and bit down, drawing blood.

He snarled and thrust ruthlessly, felt the hard knot in his cock slip inside her molten sex, knew he swelled large enough to lock her tight against him, no matter how she twisted and fought.

There was no pleasure in this mating. Tied now, both of them exhausted, they collapsed into the beaten and torn grass. Ulrich thought of shifting back to human, but he'd missed her so much, both as wolf and as woman, he wanted to hold her locked to him just a little bit longer.

Even in anger he loved her. With all the resentment bubbling in his veins, he still wanted her more than life.

She turned her head, leaned over, and licked the small wound on his leg. Camille's vaginal muscles pulsed in rhythm around his solid cock, and she panted hard, but her eyes now were bright, and the darkness seemed to have fallen away from her.

I remember when we used to do this every night, when we fucked so hard I'd see stars.

It wasn't fucking, Camille. It was making love. I loved you.

She dipped her head, acknowledging the pain in his voice. *Will you ever forgive me?*

Ulrich growled. *You left me alone with a six-year-old daughter. I begged you not to run in the daylight, but you didn't care. You risked your life. By doing exactly what you wanted, you destroyed the lives of three innocent people.*

She tilted her head and looked steadily at him, long enough to make Ulrich feel uncomfortable. *Our daughter is a beautiful, brilliant young woman. Luc is a wonderful young man, the perfect mate for Tia, and you've found success with your business. I didn't destroy you, Ric. You've done all this because I died.*

It didn't have to happen, Camille. The anger rose in Ulrich once again, when all he really wanted to do was hold her, make love to her, find the warmth in her once more. He stared at the she-wolf, his mate, and Camille dipped her nose almost to the ground and then raised her head and gazed back at him.

But it did happen, my love. I was wrong and I paid a heavy price. I never thought beyond myself. I was selfish and believed I could live forever. She looked away at the perfect forest around them and sighed. *In a way, I've condemned myself to do exactly that—live forever. I'm caught here in a world halfway between life and death.*

Why can't you move on? What holds you?

Camille looked at him and shook her head, as though laughing at his stubbornness. Then she shifted, making the change so suddenly the wolf was tied with a woman.

Ulrich shifted as well and lay beside Camille, their bodies touching but no longer connected. He brushed her thick hair away from her amber eyes. "Will you tell me what holds you?"

Camille leaned close and kissed his nose. "You do, you idiot. Your anger, your resentment, your inability to forgive. You always were a stubborn bastard, but I used to think that was part of your charm. It's not so charming anymore."

She stood up and left Ulrich lying there with his mouth open, feeling like a damned fool.

Camille waved her hand, and a wisp of silk appeared out of thin air. She wrapped herself in the pale blue sarong and took off walking toward the forest; then she looked over her shoulder and paused for just a step. "While I used to find your stubborn-as-a-mule nature sort of cute, it's damned inconvenient when you're holding me hostage in a place that doesn't really exist."

Then she turned and disappeared into the woods.

Ulrich scrambled to his feet. He looked for his robe, but it was nowhere to be found. Remembering Camille's motion, he waved his hand in the air and thought of pants.

A pair of soft cotton jogging shorts fell on the grass at his feet. Feeling much like Alice after she tumbled down the rabbit hole, Ulrich slipped on the shorts and took off after Camille, jogging barefoot along the forest path.

"Do you think he'll be okay?" Tia twisted around and looked up at Luc. She'd been leaning against his legs for what seemed like hours, holding her father's still body, wondering what was happening in whatever place his spirit had gone.

Most of all, she'd been wondering about the amazing encounter she'd had tonight. Her mother's arms hugging her, the memories of a forgotten childhood spilling into her mind.

Unbelievable, but impossibly true.

Luc's hand swept over Tia's hair and tangled in her curls. His deep whisper sent a shiver along her spine. She wished they were back in their room, wished they were making love in the big bed where Luc had slept alone the previous night.

"He'll be fine. It's barely after midnight. They've been gone for only three hours. I expect your dad to be back by around six, just before dawn."

"What if he doesn't come back? What if he decides to stay with Mom?"

"He'll come back. Trust your father. Why don't you try to sleep? Everyone else is."

It was true. Tia hadn't realized they were the only ones awake. Anton had practically collapsed, once Keisha convinced him the integrity of the circle would hold while he slept. Xandi and Stefan had shifted, figuring they'd be more comfortable as wolves. They slept now, curled up nose to tail in front of their chairs, still well inside the circle.

Tia settled once more against Luc's shins, trusting him to keep watch. Her father's body hadn't moved. Breathing softly, Ulrich slept on with his head still resting in Tia's lap. She leaned back, looked up at Luc, and felt the warmth of his love surround her. "I love you. More than anything."

"I love you." He reached down and clasped her hand. "I like your mother's idea, by the way. I want you to be my wife. Will you marry me?"

Tia kissed his hand. Her throat filled with tears, and she couldn't talk, couldn't speak the answer Luc wanted.

Yes, she said, finally remembering there were other ways to communicate. *Yes, I'll marry you.*

Luc nodded. *Good. That's settled. Now sleep. We'll make plans tomorrow . . . after we spend a few hours in bed.*

Tia bit back a giggle. Not the most romantic of proposals, but she loved him. She'd take it.

Ulrich finally caught up to Camille near a small dark woodland pool. She sat on a log at the water's edge, one foot dangling in the clear water, looking the part of a sorrowful dark nymph gowned in gossamer.

Tears ran down Camille's cheeks. Ulrich sat beside her, felt the warmth from her body, smelled the familiar perfume she'd always worn, and ached with needing her. He leaned close, pushed aside the heavy mass of her hair, and kissed the back of her neck. Then he gently grabbed her by the shoulders and turned her so that she faced him.

Ulrich's voice sounded harsh, as if a stranger spoke his words. "I don't want to forgive you. If forgiving you means I lose you forever, how can you ask me to say the words? My anger has kept you alive to me, it's given me purpose, kept me from losing my mind for wanting you so much." He shook her gently, enough to show her how intensely he felt. "I love you, Camille. More than anything, I love you. I want those lost years back, want to fall asleep with you beside me, wake up to the sound of your singing, your silly jokes, the laughter we used to share. Hell, I even miss the fighting." He released his grip on her shoulders and raked his fingers through his hair, practically shaking with frustration. "Is there any way?"

She shook her head. "No. My time on Earth is over. You can leave me here, wandering in this half life for eternity, or let me move on." She grabbed his wrists with both hands. "I love you. I will always love you, but you still have a life to finish, a daughter who adores you, grandchildren who will need their grandfather to show them the way of Chanku. You can't come with me. Not now. You still have too much life to live."

Ulrich felt some of the resentment begin to melt away, replaced by the sadness and grief he'd kept at bay for so many years. He pulled her close. "Dear God, Camille. It's so hard. I didn't have a warning before, not a chance to think of any alternatives other than life without you . . . and I was so damned angry. Will we still have tonight?"

Camille's sob tore at his heart. Her tears scalded his chest. "One night . . . only a few more hours. Let's not spend them angry. Forgive me, please. Let go of the resentment and the anger and, yes, even the hate you've felt toward me. I was wrong. I was selfish and self-centered and foolish, but I've paid. We both have. Love me, Ric. Give me memories enough to last until we're together again. We will be together. I promise."

His heart thudded against his chest as blood rushed through his veins, his cock swelled, and Ulrich held Camille close against him for the briefest of hugs. Then he stood with her slight body in his arms and walked toward the center of the small meadow bordering the pond.

With the confidence of one who has witnessed the impossible, Ulrich imagined a large bed in the midst of the forest. Without breaking stride, he lay Camille on the sweet-smelling sheets.

7

Camille lay sprawled in the center of the big bed, her legs spread wide while Ulrich lapped and nibbled at her tender nether lips. He'd taken her so many times, in so many ways, yet still hadn't tasted her flavors enough.

They'd bathed in the pond, made love in the warm, shallow waters, run through the forest as wolves, playing like children yet always aware that none of this was real. There was no birdsong, no life other than the green forest, the thick grasses, and flowers along their path.

It was neither day nor night; there was no sun or moon, yet Ulrich constantly was aware of the passage of time. Of the hands of some unseen clock steadily ticking away his hours with Camille.

He drew her soft labia between his lips and then lightly suckled her clit. She moaned, arched her hips, and lifted her head. "More, my love. Please, Ric. I want more."

"Greedy little thing, aren't you?" Ulrich shifted, gave up his human form, and raised his wolven head. He stared at Camille with the perceptions of the wolf.

Her scent was richer, the savory, earthy smell of the woman he loved so much. Stretched out between her legs, he dipped his head and lapped at her lush folds, snaking his long tongue from her ass to her navel and back again.

Camille laughed when she cried out, arching her hips, begging for him to lick harder, deeper, begging for a lifetime of sensation in the few remaining minutes left to them.

Ulrich went deep, licking the streaming walls of her pussy, nipping at her sensitive clit with sharp teeth, and then soothing with his tongue.

Camille whimpered, leaned forward, and grabbed the thick fur at his neck, curling herself around him and holding on as he continued gently licking her sensitive folds and valleys. When her body shuddered and bucked, and he knew she could take no more, Ulrich finally stopped.

He didn't shift, though. Camille doubled forward, buried her face in the thick ruff of fur at his neck, and cried. The wolf whimpered softly, but there was nothing he could say, nothing he could do to change what had to come.

The only choice was no choice at all. He could choose death, but he would leave behind the ones who loved him, the ones who needed him the most.

Who would walk Tia down the aisle when she married Luc?

He raised his head and looked into Camille's tear-filled eyes and knew she understood. She smiled sadly at him and nodded in agreement.

"I was so selfish, Ric. So unbelievably selfish. Will you ever truly forgive me?"

He shifted and drew his wife into his arms. "I've forgiven you, my love. I have no choice. The anger was the only way I could cope with losing you. I love you. I'll come back to you one day, when my time in the world of the living is over."

Ulrich looked to the colorless sky and sensed the coming

dawn. Camille's final dawn, yet no sun would rise to greet her. Could he do this? Did he really have the strength?

Did he have the strength not to? His daughter needed him. Luc. The other men of Pack Dynamics.

He felt a tug, a very gentle pull, reminding him of time growing short. "My love . . . my one and only love." Ulrich sighed and held her close. "I feel the power of my life drawing me away. It's like a very fine line growing tighter, pulling me back."

Camille nodded. "I feel it, too, only mine is pulling me to the other side, away from life. Away from you and Tia." She threw her arms around him, holding on as if she could keep him close forever. "Oh!"

"What?"

Camille laughed. "I just realized I'm sending you back to another woman—two of them, in fact, who you'll love more than me, more than anyone you've ever known . . . and I'm not even jealous."

Outraged, Ulrich leaned back and glared at her. "There will never be another woman . . . definitely not two."

"Yes, there will, and they're the ones who'll hold you in your world until the very last second. Tia's going to give you granddaughters, two of them, with a lot of their grandmother's sass running through their veins."

Ulrich groaned. He tried to imagine two little Camilles in his life and gave up. That was a challenge he'd definitely have to grow in to.

Camille tilted up her head for his kiss.

Ulrich bowed and touched his lips to hers. He thought of the continuation of their race, of Camille's Chanku bloodline running through Tia, mingling with his, with Luc's, creating new life. Stronger life. A future.

He tasted Camille's tears, his own tears, felt the softness of her breasts against his chest, the steady beat of her heart, beating in counterpoint to his.

Finding the same rhythm, beating strong and steady, two hearts beating as one.

Felt the power that was life pulling him home.

Welcomed life. Accepted his future.

And then there was one heart. Beating. Beating.

Alone.

Luc must have slept. The sky to the east seemed lighter; the air within the circle remained warm, but he could see frost on the grass around them.

Stefan and Xandi were beginning to stir, but Tia slept soundly, still leaning against his legs. Luc tried to wiggle his toes, but they'd gone numb. He arched his back and stretched and then glanced at Ulrich.

Tears coursed across the man's cheeks, and his chest rose and fell with each ragged breath.

Luc touched Tia's shoulder lightly, but it was enough to wake her. She jerked upright and then settled as awareness returned. She turned her head and smiled at Luc first.

He whispered, "Look at your dad."

Tia frowned and immediately turned to her father. Ulrich opened his eyes and smiled; then he raised his hand to wipe his streaming eyes.

"Daddy! You're back! You came back!" Tia bent over her father, hugging him tightly. He reached up and patted her on the back and then slowly extricated himself from Tia's embrace.

"I'm back. I'm okay." He sighed and smiled sadly. "Ah, sweetheart, it was truly magical."

"Of course it was." Anton sat up, his arm wrapped tightly around Keisha. "I told you, I'm a very powerful wizard."

Ulrich scrambled into a sitting position and laughed. "No problem with ego either, I see."

Anton chuckled and squeezed his arm around Keisha.

"Daddy, are you okay? Is Mom . . . ?

Ulrich took a deep breath. "I'm fine. Your mother is free. She's moved on, but she'll be waiting for us." He patted Tia on the knee. "I'm exhausted. I imagine you are, too. Anton, is there something we can do to help you open the circle? I need about a week's worth of sleep."

"I'll handle it." Anton rose stiffly to his feet and tugged Keisha with him. He set his chair to one side, making a doorway to the altar, and then stepped outside the circle. He blew out the tiny stub of a candle, doused the incense in the goblet of water, and poured the salt into the goblet. He swirled it around a few times and then carefully poured the saltwater onto the dying coals in the fire pit.

Then he turned back to the circle and smiled at all of them. "Get some sleep, all of you. I'll put these things away and be in shortly. It's been a long night. Let's meet for a late lunch. We can talk then about what's happened."

Muttering to himself, obviously still half asleep, Stefan grabbed Alexandria's hand and, still naked following their shift, they stumbled back to the house. Grinning at the two as they wobbled sleepily up the steps, Luc helped Ulrich to his feet and held out his hand to Tia.

Anton watched the three of them walk back to the house—Luc, Tia, and Ulrich. Though not of his pack, he felt a true kindred with each of them.

He'd done well tonight. Ulrich, exhausted though he may be, walked tall and straight. Tia smiled, and the shadows that had been so much a part of her aura were gone. Luc, as well, seemed younger, lighter.

Anton wrapped each item from his altar in a silk cloth and packed them away inside a drawer at the front of the table.

Later, Oliver would make sure all was carefully put away. Only Keisha waited for Anton. Smiling, feeling much older than his fifty years, he took her hand and walked slowly back to the house.

Instead of their own private quarters, Keisha led Anton to the room they shared with Stefan and Alexandria when the four of them needed to be together. "Are you sure?" he asked. "I thought you might be really tired this morning after such a long night."

Keisha smiled, her look a mysterious blend of vixen, temptress, and virginal postulant. How could any Chanku look so innocent? Anton kissed her and then followed his mate down the hall to the larger room.

Stefan and Alexandria were just crawling into the big bed. They looked as exhausted as Anton felt. After a quick side trip to the bathroom to wash the smell of incense from his skin, Anton joined the others under the thick down comforter.

Like puppies tumbled into a warm basket, they curled around one another, kissing, hugging, touching, but slowly Keisha and Xandi nodded off to sleep.

Anton grinned quietly to himself. So much for Keisha's come-hither look. Quietly relieved, physically and emotionally stretched to the limit, Anton rolled over to sleep.

Stefan reached across the girls' huddled bodies and rubbed Anton's shoulder. "Hey, bro. You scared me out there. Are you okay?"

Anton rolled back over and smiled sleepily at his packmate. Stefan had raised himself on one elbow. His long, dark hair, shot with silver, brushed the pillow; his deep-set amber eyes glittered with concern in the morning light.

Love raced through Anton, a physical rush of affection that left him breathless. Love for Stefan so deep, so enduring it almost made him weep. He nodded, found control of his suddenly surging emotions, and then whispered quietly, "Yeah. I'm okay. Just worn out. I didn't sleep well night before last, worrying about what might happen."

"Everything went really well."

Anton nodded, swallowed back a lump in his throat. "It did."

Stefan lay back against the pillows and grinned, but he didn't say anything. After a moment, Anton raised on one elbow. "Okay. Obviously, there's more. What?"

"Keisha didn't tell you?"

"Tell me what?"

He flashed a broad smile at Anton. "Xandi's pregnant. We're going to have a little boy."

Keisha stirred, rolled to her side, and fell back to sleep. Alexandria snuggled close to Keisha and sighed quietly. Sleeping. As though Stefan hadn't just rocked the world.

Anton finally caught his breath and nodded his head toward the door. *Come with me.*

Grinning like an idiot, Stefan followed Anton out the door and trailed behind him down the long hall to the study.

Anton reached the study first and grabbed the cognac and glasses out of the bar. He watched the amber liquid flow from the decanter into the crystal glasses and saw instead the joy in Stefan's eyes. His heart ached, but it was a good feeling, a sense that he was filled with so much happiness there wasn't room for the damned thing to beat.

Anton glanced up as Stefan entered the room. The beauty of the man who was both lover and friend, as close as any brother could be, once again took Anton's breath.

Tall, dark, and gloriously naked, Stefan walked across the wide room without any self-consciousness at all, his lean yet muscular body moving with the grace of a dancer, his long, dark hair framing a face of both mischief and intelligence.

Now Stefan's brilliant amber eyes shimmered with emotion,

and he looked ready to burst. Anton held out his arms, and the two men embraced.

There was no awkwardness between them as they hugged, their bodies meeting, hearts pounding in sync as they held one another tightly. Anton almost wept when he thought of the changes Stefan and Alexandria had brought into his life, the family they'd given him, the sense of place and peace. As he slowly moved out of Stefan's arms, Anton gave thanks for the deep, abiding love he'd found with this amazing man.

Now both he and Stefan faced their greatest challenge yet.

Fatherhood.

It boggled the mind.

They took their glasses and stood in front of the large picture window overlooking the broad meadow behind the house. Morning sun streamed through the glass, and frost sparkled in the shaded areas along the edge of the forest.

Oliver must have already gathered up the chairs and altar. Smoke still rose from the fire pit, but only a dark scar marked the place where the pentacle had been.

Where Anton had parted the veil between life and death, if only for one night.

He held up his glass to Stefan's. His throat felt full, and his eyes burned, but he couldn't recall ever experiencing such joy. That he and Stefan should be able to share the miracle of fatherhood . . . It was more than Anton ever could have dreamed.

"Congratulations, my friend. That is the most amazing news."

Stefan tapped his goblet against the edge of Anton's. So often his response was a silly joke or gesture, but now his eyes shimmered with the same emotion as Anton's. "Xandi just told me this morning, right after Ulrich returned. She's a couple weeks behind Keisha, but not that far. You and I, my friend, will be raising our kids together."

Anton took a sip of his cognac. The clock chimed. . . . He

silently counted to seven and burst into laughter. "I wonder if, after the babies come, we'll spend a lot of time in the study drinking cognac at seven in the morning?"

Stefan sipped at his drink, glanced over at Anton, and chuckled. "Probably not naked. Things will have to change when we have children."

Anton nodded. "I know. It's been a magical time, the freedom, the loving."

"The loving will have to be a bit more discreet, but I don't want it to end."

Anton tipped his glass against Stefan's and then threw his arm around his friend's shoulders and kissed him on the mouth. "To discretion."

Stefan kissed Anton back. "To fatherhood."

Both men drank deeply, their arms draped loosely around one another's shoulders. Anton stared out the window. He felt Stefan laughing quietly beside him.

"Holy crap. I'm gonna be a daddy."

Anton grinned and rubbed Stefan's shoulder. *I know exactly how you feel.* Scared, elated, excited . . . any word would do. Anton took another sip of his drink and tried to imagine life in his huge home filled with the laughter of children.

Keisha had come into his life in his fiftieth year, blessing him with love and laughter, and, now, a child. He still felt like a young man. None of them really knew if the Chanku lived longer than mere humans, but if Ulrich was any example . . .

Anton wondered how the man had fared last night. If he'd resolved all the issues with his late wife. If he was ready to once again embrace life.

Just as Anton needed to embrace Keisha. He leaned close to Stefan and rubbed his head against his friend's, much as two dogs might nuzzle one another.

Or two wolves. "I love you, my friend, but I've got a beautiful woman sleeping in the other room."

Stefan set his glass on the sideboard. "I understand completely. C'mon."

Anton followed Stefan down the hall and crawled into bed just as Stefan reclaimed his spot on the far side. He felt himself slipping into sleep almost immediately, caught for just a moment on soft words echoing in his mind.

Stefan's words, an echo of his own sleepy thoughts. *It's all good, isn't it? All of it. So damned good.*

Anton pulled up the blankets. *Good night, Stefan.*

8

Luc pulled the shades tight and left Tia alone in their room while he helped her dad across the hall to his bed. Ulrich had seemed a bit disoriented from his journey through the veil, though not harmed in any way. Still, Luc hadn't wanted to leave her father alone.

Another reason for Tia to love him.

Sleep couldn't come soon enough. Now, lying in their big bed, waiting for Luc to return, Tia still wasn't sure if she'd dreamed the past night, or if it was really true.

She hugged herself, remembering her mother's arms around her waist, Camille's scent, her soft laughter. Memories of her childhood crowded her thoughts, making Tia feel whole for the first time since her mother's death.

To think her child's mind had blocked out the good in order to forget the bad! It seemed so unfair now, in hindsight, but it had probably been the healthiest thing, the only way the child could survive.

Tia was still going over memories long forgotten when Luc

slipped back into their room. She raised the covers and moved aside, giving him room to crawl into bed with her. "Is Dad okay?"

Luc leaned close and kissed her. "He'll be fine. He's exhausted." Luc chuckled and pulled Tia close against his body. "I think he and your mom did a lot more than talk last night."

Tia giggled and elbowed him in the stomach. "Too much information. There are some things I'd rather not know."

"He did say we're going to have daughters someday. Camille warned him they'd be a handful. I think impending grandfatherhood was part of the reason he chose to come back and not to stay with your mom. He figured we'd need his help."

Luc's hand settled protectively over her belly, as though he were imagining those same daughters growing there. The sweet gesture left Tia feeling warm, loved. "I'm not ready for babies yet. Someday." She tilted her head and kissed Luc's chin. "I worried he might not come back. He loved her so much."

"It was his anger that held her, his resentment that wouldn't set her free." Luc nuzzled the back of Tia's neck, nipped at the tender skin at the juncture near her shoulder. "I don't know if I could forgive you, either, if you were to leave me."

Tia rolled over within his embrace and kissed Luc full on the mouth. "Not a worry. We've got way too much to live for. If Dad's right, we're going to have the next generation of Chanku to raise."

She felt Luc growing hard against her belly, felt the tension building in her own body. No matter how tired she felt, nor how much they loved, Tia's body was never fully sated, her heart and mind always eager for Luc's sensual touch.

His hands stroked her gently; his lips made a velvety, warm foray across her body. Tia arched her back, mewling softly with each new sensation. She felt the slow bloom of desire growing, unfolding as Luc built her arousal with each touch, each caress.

His body was hot and hard, his lean muscles tense with his own arousal, but Tia's turned pliant and welcoming with each touch, each whispered word of love.

He trailed warm kisses along her throat, around her tightly contracted nipple, finally taking it between his lips and sucking until she whimpered.

Moving lower, he tongued her navel, nipped the soft skin on her belly, licked once across her greedy clit. Tia clutched his shoulders, tangled her fingers in his hair, and lifted her hips to meet his mouth.

Luc slipped his hands beneath her buttocks, lifted her to his mouth, and feasted on her needy sex. She felt the scrape of teeth over her labia, the kneading pressure of his long fingers as he massaged her buttocks.

Wet, greedy sounds of Luc's tongue and lips, soft whimpering moans rising from Tia without form or conscious thought, the quiet rustle of sheets and blankets—all leant punctuation to the silence in the room.

His tongue found the slick valley between her labia, lapped at her juices flowing fresh and hot. His finger brushed the taut muscle between her cheeks and pressed hard, matching the rhythm he set with his mouth.

Tia clutched at the sheets, arched her hips, cried out when his lips settled around her throbbing clit. He suckled hard, pressing his tongue against the tiny bundle of nerves just as his finger breached her anus.

She screamed, a hoarse cry of pleasure and release, her muscles clenching almost painfully, pussy contracting, muscles straining against Luc's thick finger, his hot, wet tongue.

On and on, the tender assault never ending, her climax building once more as Luc quickly backed away, knelt between her legs, and thrust his cock hard and deep inside her spasming pussy.

No matter how often or in how many ways he loved her, Tia still needed time to adjust to his size. Luc filled her, the broad head of his cock and thick girth barely fitting inside her tight passage, touching every nerve and fiber with muscle and heat.

Tia cried out again, a long, low howl of completion. Suddenly Luc was in her thoughts, in her mind, sharing her orgasm, sharing his own as it built and grew, as his balls contracted and pulled close against his body.

She felt the pressure, the almost painful pleasure he experienced with each driving thrust. Harder, faster, touching the hard mouth of her womb as his hips drove forward, feeling the tight walls of her pussy grab his cock like a velvet fist each time he withdrew.

Tia's climax faded. Luc's built, bringing her back to join him at the peak. She was there in his mind, in his heart. When Luc finally gasped her name, when his cock spasmed and his hot seed bathed her womb, Tia *was* Luc.

As if they'd planned for this, both Tia and Luc shifted at the same time, their bodies morphing, the call of Chanku overwhelming their human minds and bodies.

Two wolves, locked together between one heartbeat and the next, their four-legged bodies tangled together, mouths open and panting, tongues lolling.

Tia breathed in deeply of Luc's scent and felt the events of the night begin to take over. Thoroughly exhausted, her tight muscles still clinging to Luc's swollen cock, Tia lay her muzzle across his furred shoulder and groaned. Sighing, Luc rested his broad head on Tia's back.

Later, the visit from her mother, her father's journey ... later, it might all make sense. When they'd slept, when they'd eaten ... and, just maybe, after they'd made love again. For now, she drifted off to sleep, still firmly tied to the one who commanded her dreams.

Ulrich lay awake, too exhausted to sleep, too wound up to relax. Camille's scent still clung to him, something that made no sense as this corporeal body had stayed behind, but he would swear he still smelled her seductive perfume, still tasted her feminine flavors on his tongue.

He'd heard Anton and Stefan return to bed, the muffled cries of Tia and Luc. Ulrich tried to remember if he'd thanked Camille for suggesting that the two marry. It was so easy to forget the legalities after bonding with your mate. The paperwork, the formal steps seemed unnecessary after such a powerful experience, but Camille was right. It was important.

They'd married. A civil ceremony performed on the beach at dawn, but Ulrich would never forget how beautiful Camille had looked in her wedding gown, her arms filled with flowers, the morning sun sparkling off her raven-black hair.

She'd looked at him with such love in her eyes.

Such promise.

His eyes filled with tears. He'd promised himself he wouldn't cry. She'd been gone for twenty years, after all, dammit.

But you never grieved.

No, he'd been too busy raising Tia. Forming Pack Dynamics. Too busy being angry and resentful.

Now, with her soft skin still a fresh memory, the warmth of her lithe body pressing against his, the knowledge Camille was truly gone . . . now he grieved. Now he experienced the true despair he'd denied himself for so many years.

Not here. Not inside four walls where he might be heard. These people had all gone through so much for him.

Quietly Ulrich let himself out of the bedroom door that led to the deck. He shifted as he ran. Two bare feet slapping on the wooden deck shimmered, shifted, and became four paws. Extending his front legs, he leapt off the deck and raced for the woods, running, running as if the hounds of hell pursued him.

Grass flew in great clumps, torn from the ground by his sharp nails. Small woodland creatures ran into the brush, and birds stopped their song.

Ulrich stopped on a low rise and howled, long and low, the sound echoing off the hillsides, tearing at his throat as he forced the sound longer, louder, a Chanku benediction for his lost mate.

Then he ran again. Gasping, lungs screaming for air, Ulrich ran on. Frost still coated the shaded spots, wisps of fog hung in the lower areas along the track. He ran until his legs gave out, until he lay on his side in the cold grass, shifted back to his human self, and wept.

His body shook with the force of his grief. His lungs burned, his throat ached.

She was gone. He'd set her free and condemned himself. Had he taken the coward's way out? Should he have abandoned life, abandoned all who loved him on this plane to join Camille on hers?

Could Anton send him back? Would Ulrich find her there?

No. I am gone from that place. Thank you, my love. Thank you for setting me free. It was time to move forward. Time for both of us.

"Camille?" Rubbing his face with both hands, Ulrich sat up.

He heard it then, a soft whisper. Camille's voice.

Good-bye. For now, Ric, good-bye.

The silence then was absolute, but only for a moment. Birds came out, one by one, their voices mingling in song. Sunlight streamed through the treetops. A rabbit hopped past, obviously unaware of the threat.

Ulrich rolled to his knees, thought about standing, and shifted instead. He drank from a small pond and then slowly retraced his steps to Anton's home. Head hanging low, blood running from a long scratch on his shoulder, he looked beaten and bowed.

He felt anything but. His tears had washed away the last remnants of an old and dying grief. Camille was gone, but she'd freed him of the weight he'd carried for all the years since her death.

Ulrich sensed the house just ahead, saw the roofline as he topped a low rise. He sat there for a moment, one large wolf staring down at the sprawling ranch house.

Then, with a sweep of his tail, his head held high, he trotted slowly down the hill, thinking of Camille's warning.

Two little granddaughters, filled with Camille's sass and sense of mischief and adventure. He was definitely going to be needed.

Head held high, tail waving like a flag behind him, Ulrich ran the last few steps to the house, leaped over the railing, and headed back into the bedroom. A shower, a little sleep, a good meal, and he'd be ready for just about anything.

Even a double dose of Camille.

Midnight Man

SHARON PAGE

1

"We were supposed to meet in public, not have sex in public."

Erin's voice, sultry and breathy, wrapped around Michael Rourke—tempting, rich, and classy, like sweaty sex on hot silk sheets. The subtle note of warning in it made him grin—carefully, to hide the tips of his retracted fangs.

He brushed his knuckles against Erin's outer thigh, just below the hem of her skirt. "No, love, I'm not going to make love to you here."

Her emerald-green eyes glinted in the soft amber light of the pub, and he caught the flash of disappointment. She was excited, he knew, despite the way she glanced at other tables to ensure no one was looking their way. "Then what do you plan to do?"

Michael unfurled his fingers to cup her bare leg, her skin warm and satin smooth against his cool palm. His wrist caught the edge of her tailored skirt, lifting it as his fingers crept slowly toward the hot nest between her thighs.

This game of seduction with his intended soul mate was giving him the most agonizing rock-hard erection of his two-hundred-year existence.

She tensed her thigh, and he stroked gently until her leg relaxed at his touch.

In three months of trading steamy e-mails—three months of sharing her secret desires—Erin had laid her soul bare for him, whether she knew it or not.

She wanted adventure. She wanted great sex. But after building a successful private investigation agency chasing adulterers, she didn't believe in love.

And he had to.

"I plan to pleasure you here, Erin." *And I plan to capture your heart.*

"Oh, you do?" She crossed her arms on the table and leaned closer to him, giving him a view down her white silk crossover blouse, a peek at the shadowy valley between the lightly freckled swells of her breasts. Again, he smiled at the trace of confrontation in her tone—even when she so obviously desired him. "And how do you plan to *pleasure* me in public?"

"That's to be my surprise, sweet."

Her brows drew together in an exaggerated frown, drawing a chuckle from deep in his throat. Michael winced at the sound—rusty, unused. How long since he'd last felt the urge to laugh?

"No," she insisted. "Tell me."

She didn't like him to take control, but he found it impossible to understand her complex rules about equality. He was a Varkyre, the damned of the damned, the most predatory subspecies of vampire, and when he wanted a woman, he claimed her.

Hell, he'd always lived outside the rules of human society, even in his mortal life. Michael had no qualms over bringing his intended soul mate to a screaming orgasm in an intimate little curved booth in Bellissima's, the most popular bar downtown.

He had to take Erin beyond her sensual limits, take her beyond the rigid, protective walls she'd erected. He had to teach her to trust.

To trust him.

"I like to start with the neck." *And you, sweetheart, possess the sexiest neck I've found in two centuries.* He lifted Erin's thick auburn hair and pressed his lips to her skin. Flicking his tongue along her peach-soft flesh, he tasted traces of salty sweat and wildflower soap. Delicious.

He drew slow circles on her leg, letting his finger dip down farther over her inner thigh with each spiral. Her nipples puckered, tenting the silk. The draped fabric shivered with her quick, shallow breaths.

"Are you really going to put your hand in my panties here, Michael?"

Her direct question sent a surge of desire through him just as his fangs lengthened and grazed her flesh. Shuddering, he backed off to break the contact before he lost it and sank his teeth in. Before he revealed to her what he was.

Erin's hips rocked, slowly, seductively, and he knew she wanted him to lift his hand higher. By playing his game, she was taking a first step in trust.

Michael took three deep breaths. And for the first time in his cursed existence, his fangs retreated, even as desire burned in him.

Only with his soul mate could he have that kind of control.

"No one can see," he promised. "They think we're just necking in the corner."

"I've never done anything like this before." Her voice shivered with awe and arousal.

He had. In his mortal past, he'd often engaged in public sex at brothels and parties.

"Naughty, isn't it?" he teased. He slid his hand around her upper thigh to cradle her ass. As his fingers encountered soft bare skin, his brows lifted in astonishment, and his cock jerked up against the hard zipper of his leather motorcycle pants. "You're *not* wearing underwear."

"I am," she protested in a whisper. "A thong." Her warm breath coasted over the rim of his ear.

"So your ass is essentially naked."

"Under my skirt, yes."

He laughed at that. Her legs parted slightly, and he knew his breath had played its own magic against her ear. He trailed his fingers back up, over her leg, to the damp, lacy thong nestled between her thighs.

"Have you decided?" their ponytailed server trilled as he flipped out his pad and parked himself with his hip jutting against the table.

Michael stroked his fingers along Erin's hot, wet thong.

She gasped. But her composure returned admirably fast. "I'm not hungry."

"We're fine," he instructed the waiter, breathing a sigh of relief. He had a beer in front of him, barely touched. Since he could consume only blood, he'd used his ability to move faster than human senses could detect to pour it out and make it look like he was drinking.

Bloody ironic. He had finally found the woman who might free him from imminent destruction—if he could convince her to believe in him—and he'd done nothing but lie to her so far. The only topic on which he could be honest with Erin was sex.

As soon as their server left, he bent and nibbled her neck again. This time his fangs remained retracted.

Sex was the way to capture her heart.

She whimpered, bending her head so her hair spilled over him.

He loved hearing her moan with need. Loved the way her auburn waves shivered over her shoulders as she tilted her head. And he adored the throaty melody of her laugh, the honey-sweet sighs of arousal she made at his touch—

"Oh!"

The elastic trim of her thong snapped against her skin as Michael worked to slide his index finger underneath.

Springy curls brushed his fingertip.

He nipped her earlobe gently. "You are so wet."

Her cleft was snug and hot, and he pressed two fingers against her clit. With a moan, she jumped on the seat.

"Relax." His fingers circled over her, and her eyes opened wide. "Trust me."

Would she?

"That's so good, Michael." Her hand dropped to his thigh to brace herself as her head arched back in pleasure.

"Touch me." He kept his voice low and seductive. He wished he could compel her to do as he asked, but he couldn't. He could not do that with his soul mate.

Erin drew her hand up his leg, her touch all the more erotic because he knew it came from her desire.

"I've never groped a man in public," she confided. Yes, she was beginning to trust him, revealing more and more to him. "But writing all those wild, hot e-mails to you—" She pressed her open palm to the bulge in his pants. "Can you feel that through the leather?"

"God, yes."

His hips bucked as her hand slid along the zipper of his pants, following the line of his swelling cock until she found the engorged head stuffed against his waistband. She cupped him with her palm.

His head swam as his blood pooled in his crotch, as his cock grew and grew and grew and pushed urgently with no place to go. Hunger surged with every pulse of his rigid shaft.

Control it. Fight it.

His jaw throbbed, burned even, but, by a miracle, his fangs stayed retracted.

"You've unleashed a side of me I never knew existed," she murmured as she glanced down to watch the motion of her hand coasting over the black leather—pulled taut over the broad head of his prick. Her firm gliding motion almost took him to the brink.

Yes, trust me, Michael almost groaned. "I sensed it existed, love. This is no surprise to me." The lips of her pussy parted for his fingers. He crooked them within her, dipping into her wet heat. Stirring her, he inhaled her scent deeply. Musky and primal, it made him ache with want. He withdrew his fingers and tapped the sticky tips against her clit.

Her green eyes glazed with desire; she looked as needy as he felt. "This is like going to bed with a stranger."

No, don't draw back, Erin. "We've already been intimate, love."

"On a computer screen. Which makes this a lot weirder than I expected."

Despite her words, she squeezed his cock through the leather. Both lust and hope shot through him, a mix so intense he almost exploded on the spot. "Weird?" he rasped. "Are you disappointed, then?"

"In *you*?" Her eyes opened wide in surprise. "No. I mean, to be honest, when I pictured us meeting, I skipped over the getting-to-know-you part—"

He plunged his finger into her pussy. Her flame-hot, creamy walls clamped around his finger as his thumb lightly rubbed the tip of her clit.

Erin jammed her fist into her mouth and moaned around it.

"—and put us right into bed," she finished hoarsely.

"Sounds good to me." He kissed her soft, freckled cheek, tasting a trace of vanilla-flavored lotion, savoring her delightful feminine flavor.

Expertly, he shifted his hand to fill her tight pussy with two fingers, to stroke her snug ass with his index finger, all the while teasing her clit. An orgasm would chip away at her defenses.

"Oh, god."

His cock throbbed painfully as Erin sank her teeth into her own fingers. He saw the bite marks as she moved her mouth away, and his groin clenched.

"You've got to stop, Michael." She lifted her hand from his cock. "This is really hot . . . really sexy, but—"

He silenced her protests by slanting his mouth over hers.

Erin moaned into Michael's mouth as he kissed her. She tried to slide her tongue inside, to taste him even more intimately, but his wouldn't retreat. His powerful body shifted over hers, possessive and dominant, sandwiching her between his hot, hard chest and the warm leather seat. Her swollen, sensitive breasts squashed against him. Her nipples poked into unyielding muscle.

This is one large, dominant guy, her inner voice warned. A *strong*, large, dominant guy.

Yeah, but she could handle a large guy. All those kickboxing lessons hadn't been for nothing.

He smelled so masculine. So erotically of sandalwood and leather and the clean heat of his skin. She loved the hot, wet, minty taste of his tongue in her mouth. Strange—she didn't taste or smell beer on his breath.

He deepened the kiss, ravished her mouth. She'd never been kissed with such hunger, such raw need. As though he'd yearned for this moment for a lifetime.

Erin clutched his leather-clad shoulders.

Suddenly she realized she was sliding back along the booth, pulling him with her.

Her chest was tight with desire, her throat dry with it; her heart hammered against her rib cage. She felt ready to combust on the spot.

Erin now understood why people would risk everything for sex. She was horny enough to do him in public. Which would be a crazy thing to do for a woman who made her living by being discreet.

Dimly she saw waiters race by them, couples pass by, a group of guys in suits leer at them.

She struggled to cool down and sit up.

Just take the man home and screw his brains out. What more reassurance do you need?

She'd run every kind of background check imaginable on Michael Rourke, to the point of trying to follow up his public school records in England.

A raven-haired, totally gorgeous sex god had his hand up her skirt and was kissing her like his life depended on it.

A sex god without a criminal record, an ex-wife, dependents, restraining orders. A sex god with a good job—VP for vam-pire. com, a ruthless vulture company that sucked the life out of failing start-ups, kept the lifeblood, and sold off the shell. He was a millionaire. She knew. She'd checked.

What was the main risk with too-good-to-be-true guys on the Internet, besides the risk of an existing wife or a criminal record? They were in it for the sex. And what did she really want? Not "ever after." Just a sexy guy who got a real charge out of making her come and who conveniently disappeared with the light of day so she could run her business.

Get on with it. Crook your finger, and tell him to follow you home. Or, better yet, lead him by the big, hot bulge in his pants.

He moved his mouth from hers, and Erin almost sobbed at the loss.

"Do you know what I truly want, love?"

His voice flowed over her, deep, compelling, and complete with a sexy upper-crust English accent. In response, her pussy clenched greedily around his large fingers.

This guy was the best British import since Cadbury chocolate.

"What do you truly want, Michael?"

His fallen-angel mouth quirked up into a wicked smile. "I want your first orgasm to be on my face."

Her first orgasm? While she was perfectly capable of multiple orgasms, only she and her lifelike "drawer willies" knew that for sure. Her sexual encounters involved lots of screaming, groaning, and Oscar–worthy cries of delight, but no real pop. She'd never come with a man. Come close, but never actually hit the peak, rang the bell, gone over the edge—

He wouldn't . . . would he? Erin pulled away to look into Michael's eyes. Teasing, glittering eyes. The irises were the strangest shade of silvery purple, a startling contrast to his thick midnight-black eyelashes and straight black brows. "You aren't planning to do that here, are you?" she asked.

Erin moaned at the sudden vision of being stretched out on her back across the leather booth, skirt forced up, legs spread wide while he ate her. Fondling each other under the table while the jazz and low laughter swirled around was wild enough. Naughty, just as he'd said.

But oral sex . . . ?

With the hand that was not stuffed in her pussy, Michael took her hand. He twined his fingers with hers, laid their clasped hands on his thighs. Encased in black motorcycle pants, the muscular length of his leg was like granite.

"What do you want, love? Where do we go from here?"

He held her gaze captive. His fingers slid in and out. She could barely form words.

What she wanted to do with Michael Rourke, Internet lover extraordinaire, meant trusting him, at least for tonight.

She knew exactly where she wanted to take him. A place she could strip him naked and run her tongue all over his buff bod. A place she would finally unleash the do-me-now, sex-crazed vixen inside—the one threatening to burst out of her skin like an alien life form.

"My place."

"Here we are." Erin tried for a light, casual tone as she reached the landing outside her door. She hadn't brought a guy home in a year.

Michael strode up the stairs behind her, pausing at the top as she turned the key. Her century-old apartment building had a narrow staircase with only two apartments to a floor.

As she turned to him, saw him leaning on the banister waiting for her to open the door, her heart leaped to her throat. Her body ached with desire.

Lines from their wicked e-mails flooded her mind.

I want to suck your big throbbing cock.

I want to lick your hot, sweet pussy.

I want to make you explode for me, Erin. I want to make you scream with pleasure.

Goofy, yes. Funny and hot at the same time. Her legs trembled as she gazed down at the man who'd authored all those erotic promises.

Even under the warm incandescent light, Michael's hair was a true lustrous blue-black. The thick, glossy locks drifted over his forehead and brushed his broad shoulders. His leather jacket was so well worn, it looked more of a good friend than an article of clothing. Hanging open, it gave a teasing glimpse of bulging pecs in an open-necked, burgundy dress shirt. He wore an eclectic mix of clothing, the true hallmark of an IT million-aire, and he possessed an elegance that made her heart race.

His sensuous mouth lifted in a smile, and his eyes glowed with unearthly beauty.

He was magnetic.

Gazing into his gorgeous eyes, she remembered what he'd written to her last night. *Don't give up believing in happily ever after, love. I do, and I'm the least likely person with reason to believe.*

"May I come in?"

She gave Michael an answering smile, shaky with desire, and swung the door wide. "Of course."

He stepped inside, made an admiring comment on her place, and closed the door.

An instant later, he was on his knees before her, pushing up her skirt. Erin caught her breath as Michael bunched it above her hips and splayed his fingers over the cheeks of her ass. Her legs almost buckled at the erotic combination of his fingers pressing into her skin and his hot breath blowing across her thong, the heat teasing her lips though the web of pale pink silk.

He was going to lick her pussy while she stood, hand braced on the wall, right beside her front door. For the first time in her life, male impatience seemed a positive trait.

Erin moaned as Michael skimmed his hands up over her hips. His fingers hooked in the sides of her thong, and he drew it down. Down over her thighs, down to her knees, down until her panties were around her ankles and her soaking pussy was exposed to him.

"Beautiful. I love your scent," he murmured. He touched his lips to her curls.

He lifted her, strong hands behind her thighs, so she was on her tiptoes, straddling his face. His hot tongue made exquisite spirals over her hard, aching clit.

As he increased his pressure, her spine went rigid, and she lifted higher on her toes, moving away. It was too . . . intense.

"Relax against me," he urged. "Trust me."

Those words again. When he asked for her trust, she found herself wanting to give it to him. How she could hear him talk when his face was buried between her legs, she didn't know, but she obeyed, and he eased the pressure. Gently his tongue slicked through her cleft. His lips toyed with her nether ones. His tongue gave one quick lick to pry her sticky flesh apart.

It was spectacular.

Erin's eyes closed, her mouth went slack as he nibbled, sucked, laved her. She'd never been eaten this way, with a man's mouth open wide over her, feasting on her.

To think she'd wondered if he could possibly live up to his e-mails.

Michael worked magic over her, delving his broad, long tongue up her pussy. Each plunge sent an answering shudder down her spine. Shudder after shudder after intense shudder.

His tongue licked the bridge between pussy and ass, and she threaded her fingers in his silky hair, cupping his head, stroking him in the same rhythm.

"Oh, god, Michael, I'm going to . . . fall over."

He moved his knees between her legs. She took unsteady steps to let him through.

Erin had never had any man offer himself at her feet and be so intent on pleasuring *her*.

"Sit on me," he urged, his voice soft, compelling.

He arched back, grasped her ass, and lifted her onto his face. Her thighs spread to accommodate his wide shoulders, the worn, smooth leather of his jacket a caress against her skin. His stomach muscles must be straining hard to keep him suspended there, her weight almost fully on him.

He was so strong, rocking her on his mouth. She clutched locks of his hair. She bent forward to watch him, her hair falling forward. Through the screen of it, she saw his eyes, strangely reflective in the faint light, watch her as he took her to ecstasy. All she could see were those glowing eyes, the dark slashes of his brows, the rest of his face buried so hard against her. Could he even breathe?

Enough to keep suckling her clit, to roll his tongue around it, to part the cheeks of her ass and touch his fingers to her puckered entrance, to penetrate just a touch, to take her . . .

Her body tensed, tightened, wound up.

She couldn't believe it.

Oh, yes, please.

Erin's teeth sank deep into her lip, and then her mouth stretched wide into a soundless scream, her orgasm streaking through her. Her hands slid from his head, and he caught her somehow, fingers thick and solid between hers. The pressure of his hands held her upright as she rode every pounding wave. Her body clenched tight, locking around his tongue.

She'd never known such pleasure.

Did he feel every ripple and quiver pulling at him? Did he love seeing her buck and moan and sob?

He must, the way his fingers slid gently between hers, his touch erotic and intimate. He licked relentlessly at her while his powerful grip held her.

Her climax pulsed endlessly. Her body flailed with it, her hair whipped her face.

As it eased, she slumped forward, drained, and he held her up.

"I've never come like that before," she whispered, awed. "Never."

It sounded so trite. He'd changed her forever; he'd let her know what she could have.

Of course he couldn't answer. She was sitting on his face. But she sensed he was pleased.

Michael held her tight, straightening his back. Desire shivered through her as he suspended her on his face.

Suddenly he stood upright, lifting her, balancing her.

"*Michael—?*" Erin clamped her thighs against his face. Her panties dropped to the floor.

His strength was incredible. He supported her so easily. Sure, she'd seen the way his wide, powerful pecs stretched his dress shirt to the limit. And the first time she had touched his hard biceps beneath his leather jacket, she'd marveled at their sheer size and hardness, at the power of him. But she'd never dreamed of *this*.

She prayed he held her tight.

But she was willing to trust him. For this.

Holding her up to the ceiling, he was like the roller coaster of sex, exciting her even as he made her stomach lurch in shock.

Erin rocked her clit into Michael's rolled tongue, wanting more. Greedy for more. Pleasure—mind-numbing, bone-melting pleasure—raced through her with each arch of her hips. Until she could barely think. Until she clung to his hands, fingers locked tight with his.

She ground herself against his hot mouth—she'd never been so aggressive on a man's face before—and his low, throaty moans urged her on.

His tongue gave one more hard, rough rasp over the oh-so-sensitive tip of her clit, and she burst. His name echoed in her desperate shriek. She almost toppled. Her legs squeezed hard; her hands clung to his.

As the last waves died away, Michael lowered her. She floated through the air. His powerful hands locked around her waist to hold her steady.

"Oh, I just want to melt all over the floor." She reached up to caress his cheek, to stroke the sharp planes of his face. As her fingers touched him and stroked warm skin and scratchy stubble, he grinned. Wickedly.

The glimmer of her kitchen light—the one she always left on—spilled faintly over his face.

"Ohmigod." Erin's legs went rubbery. Her heart skipped a few beats, enough for dizziness to swamp her. "Are those fangs?"

2

"Are those *real?*"

In the dark shadows Michael saw Erin clearly as she scrambled back, clawing her skirt down. She gaped at him in horror while her hands struggled to get her hem over her thighs. In her haste to retreat, she stumbled in her high heels.

Michael was behind her in a heartbeat. He caught her and set her back on her feet. Her scream at his touch almost shattered his eardrums. It did lance his heart.

What in hell had he expected?

He'd known this moment would come but had planned to make the revelation with more care.

"Yes, love, they are." He held her a little longer than necessary to make sure she was steady. He used his deep, hypnotic voice to soothe, and her struggling stilled. "I am a vampire." He tried for a matter-of-fact approach. Like he was just talking about a job. "But I promise I don't bite. You must understand that I would never hurt you, Erin."

"*Vampire?*" Erin yanked her hands free of his gentle grasp with surprising strength for a petite woman. But he knew she had a black belt and loved to kickbox. "You must be joking," she snapped.

"No, love, deadly serious."

She groaned at that.

"I am a vampire, and I belong to you."

"*Get out.*"

Despite his pledge of fealty, she took a stance similar to a martial-arts pose.

Maybe now was not the time to call her his soul mate.

Slowly Michael paced around her, backing up until he stood only a few steps from her door. He sank to his knees before her so he had to look up at her to meet her gaze. He hoped to appear less intimidating.

She glared down at him. "I investigated you. How could I have missed this? I help women *avoid* men like you."

"Erin, I'm still the man you wrote to. The man you spoke to. The man who pleasured you. Nothing has changed."

"Thirty seconds ago I thought you were a nice, normal guy who writes software and likes to work at night. Now I know you are delusional. Michael, vampires are *fiction.*"

She launched over to the wall switch.

Light flooded his eyes, and Michael blinked away the instant blindness.

His plan had been to pleasure her senseless, then reveal what he was. Slowly. Seductively.

And then her musky essence had flooded his senses as she came on his face. He had heard her cry out his name in a voice throaty with passion and something more—

Delight.

Pure joy.

Reverence. For him.

He'd lost control and—zip—out slid the fangs.

"Okay, Mr. Vampire, I want your ass and your fangs on the other side of my door, pronto."

"Let me prove to you what I am, Erin." Michael lifted his wrist to his mouth. The sharp points easily parted his flesh.

She took a step back as he held up his arm. Droplets of his blood rolled down his forearm.

Michael ignored his wound and watched Erin's face. He knew the routine. The blood would dry almost instantly and then drop away. Before it fell to the ground, it would evaporate as though it had never existed. The long, straight slice would knit together, change to a shiny pink scar, and finally disappear. All in the space of a few seconds. All right before her eyes.

She stared at him, speechless.

"I'm no myth, Erin. I'm real."

Had he succeeded in convincing her or terrifying the daylights out of her?

Her mouth hardened into a firm line, and one brow arched up. "Oh, come on. I bet any rookie magician in Vegas could do that."

Now he was the one rendered speechless.

"Were you planning on making me your late-night snack?" She cocked her head to the side.

He didn't know what to make of her new, more cynical attitude. Apparently his display had amused her more than it had frightened her. Likely she was *humoring* him.

It wounded him.

Fervent vampire hunters pursued him on a daily basis, and those well-armed warriors quaked in fear in his presence. In his early days, long before he'd gained sufficient control of his hunger, he had rampaged through Regency London, terrifying the populace. Pimps and drug dealers—the scum he tended to prey on now—turned into puddles of whimpering cowardice before him.

And yet a five-foot-five-inch private investigator was studying him as though he were a four-year-old wearing a fake cape with a phony sword in hand.

"No, love. A man does not eat his soul mate. Except in the erotic sense."

He had three nights to convince Erin she was his soul mate—three nights to the next full moon, when he would reach the end of his two hundred year existence as a Varkyre and burn up in a ball of fire. Three nights to have wild sex with Erin and convince her she loved him.

This did not look good.

"Well, you certainly ate me in the erotic sense," she remarked, cool and wary. "And you are exceptional at it, I must say. Now you can just pack up the undead routine and head on home."

Michael bit back a groan.

Once again it appeared he was not going to have a lot of luck putting his life and soul in a woman's hands.

Erin put her hands on her hips and glared down at Michael. She was not afraid of him—six feet-four inches of massive male or not. She knew how to combat a man's strength, and she wouldn't be in trouble unless he was taking serious drugs. He didn't look stoned, but with his reflective silver eyes, it was hard to tell.

Unless he really was a vampire with superhuman strength.

Yeah, right.

"Erin, I do not have to remain a vampire. I have the chance to regain my soul."

His expression became imploring, and she found herself captivated once more by his stunningly beautiful eyes. She loved dark-haired men, especially ones with blue-black tresses and sinfully long lashes. Her traitorous body heated for him even now.

Michael exuded a seductive, primal sexual allure that would be perfect for a suave creature of the night.

If such a thing actually existed.

Given that he fit the part so well, perhaps he'd purchased some wacko cosmetic dentistry to complete the fantasy.

"You can help me, love," he continued.

"I can?" Erin kept her tone neutral, intrigued to hear him out before throwing him out. "This sounds good. How, exactly?"

From any guy, the words *soul mate* would have sent her running as far as possible. They sounded so phony. Just like when her last potential boyfriend had told her on their first date he wanted more than a platonic relationship. His idea of seductively sweeping her into bed consisted of pulling out his electronic organizer to set a date for sex.

From a hunk like Michael dressed in black motorcycle attire—a man with the teeth of a beast and the graceful, predatory presence of a panther—the idea of *soul mate* made her shiver with desire despite herself. It was like being singled out by the leader of the pack.

He looked hopeful. "It involves really great sex and falling in love with each other."

"Sex will help you regain your soul?"

"Really great sex."

Scenes from their e-mails flooded Erin's head. Her cheeks flamed. Resisting the impulse to picture this hot hunk doing those things to her, she tapped her fingers on her arms.

"Okay, right. You're undead, and you need to have sex to regain your soul. So, what happens? We go to bed a few times, and then you suddenly jump up and claim you're cured? Do you have to bite my neck? Geez, I now understand why you're dating on the Internet."

Michael rubbed his temple. "Erin, love, I had no choice. I've roamed the earth for two centuries. I drink blood for sustenance, burn in sunlight, and I spent one hundred years sleeping in a coffin. Did you think I'd find a lot of dates by advertising those things? Would you have wanted to meet me if I'd been honest?"

"I would *never* have sex in a coffin," she cried, without thinking.

"Don't worry, neither would I."

"Wait a minute. Do you actually go around biting necks? Or do you stick your teeth in bags of blood like the nice vampires do in books?" She asked the question sarcastically, but she felt ice cold. Was he just a guy with a weird vampire sex fetish, or did he attack people?

She'd checked his entire past—hadn't found a whiff of this.

"I am a predator, sweetheart. I try to restrict myself to the scum when I can, like drug dealers and pimps. But you can help me change that. You can free me."

Okay, this had gone on long enough.

"I don't really care if you *are* Dracula or a government experiment, a refugee from Area Fifty-One, or a genetic freak. You lied to me. And if there's one thing I'm certain of, it's that men don't change. I doubt *vampire* males are any different. If you are not on the other side of the door in thirty seconds—" She broke off, blinking.

He was standing on the landing outside her door, which now stood wide open, watching her and obviously waiting for her reaction.

How in hell had he—?

In two quick lunges, she reached the door and slammed it in Michael's face.

God, she was exhausted.

As Erin cranked her steering wheel to maneuver into her office parking spot, she jerked her foot down by accident. She shoved on the gas, and her car barely squeaked by a concrete column.

Her third near miss this morning.

She slammed the gearshift into park before she accidentally drove off the edge of the parking garage.

Groaning, Erin slumped forward and rested her forehead against the leather-wrapped steering wheel. Not only was she exhausted, she was freaked out, shaky, and furious that she still wished she'd done Michael before she'd found out how crazy he was.

All night she'd dreamed about him and awoken at least a dozen times from a nightmare, drenched in sweat. Each dream started out wildly erotic, where she and Michael fucked until she was senseless with pleasure. In half the dreams he then plunged his fangs into her neck and sucked her dry. In the other half she slammed a stake into his heart to kill him in self-defense.

Questions kept haunting her.

Did she really buy the vampire routine?

How else to explain the amazing things he'd done right before her eyes?

Should she call the cops?

Was there a law against pretending to be a vampire? For that matter, was there a law against *being* a vampire? Maybe he sucked on only willing victims. A man so unbelievably sexy must have women eager to bare their throats for him. Especially if he started with the mind-blowing oral sex he'd given her. . . .

And the most unnerving question of all: why, deep down inside, did she still want him?

Erin shoved open her car door, pausing at the echoing sound of footsteps. Impatiently ignoring her thudding heart, she swung her legs around and got out. Of course there were footsteps. This was a parking garage, attached to an office building, and while she always arrived at seven fifteen A.M., she wasn't the only person to start so early. Jessica, her receptionist and bookkeeper, for example, began at seven.

Rays of sunlight spilled into the open parking garage, but

the center core of elevators and stairs were shadowy and dark. After locking her car, Erin flipped up the lid of her cell phone to speed-dial her office. She planned to talk to Jessica or someone else for the entire time she made her way from her parking spot to the office reception desk.

"Ms. Kennedy?"

The harsh male voice surprised her, and her fingers slipped off the preprogrammed phone key. It wasn't Michael's voice. She spun around.

A man stepped out of the shadows on the other side of her car and stood silhouetted against bright daylight. Though she couldn't see his face against the glare, and the man was huge, she definitely knew he wasn't Michael. This guy was bulky. He looked like a dark wall.

Slowly Erin's blindness faded, and she recognized the mammoth glaring at her. Dave Phillips. A married construction contractor posing as a single man under the dating name "richandavailable." Yesterday she'd sent a report to Megan Phillips, confirming her client's suspicions about her chronically unfaithful husband

Phillips took a menacing step closer. "Look, lady, you'd better keep out of my private business. My wife isn't gonna leave me—she's wasting your time. We've been down this road before. So I suggest you quit poking your nose into my private life, if you know what's good for you."

Erin couldn't believe the balding brute was talking to her like some second-rate mobster. "Are you threatening me?"

He squared his enormous shoulders. His beefy right hand clenched into a fist. "Take it how you like," he said as he took another lumbering step toward her.

Was he actually going to hit her? Well, he'd get a kick in the crotch before he got—

Something exploded behind her. An incredible force knocked her forward, yet she hadn't felt anything hit her.

She steadied herself and bit back a shriek.

A tall man dressed in a black T-shirt and black leather pants gripped Phillips by the jaw and held him up against a concrete column. Though Phillips had to weigh more than two hundred and fifty pounds, his attacker held him as though he weighed nothing.

Michael.

With a gasp Erin realized that Michael had raced out of the shadows to protect her. Michael looked terrifying, his face contorted with rage, his mouth wide open, his fangs long, curved, and deadly.

Michael wrenched his victim's head back to expose the thick throat.

"No. No, Michael! Don't! Stop!" Erin screamed.

Too late. She clapped her hand to her mouth in horror as Michael bit hard into Phillips's neck.

She couldn't let him kill the jerk.

She launched forward, wrapping her arms around Michael's waist. Michael was rock solid and impossible to move. Desperate, Erin tried hammering on his powerful, wide back, mesmerized by the way his throat moved with every gulp. Phillips had wrapped his arms around Michael, too, and had ceased fighting. He was caressing Michael's back.

Then Michael reared back, plowing right into her. Unsteady on her low heels, she almost fell, but Michael dropped his victim and grabbed her arm. She was astonished to see his bloodthirsty expression was gone. Instead he gazed at her with tenderness and concern.

"Is he dead?"

Michael shook his head. "You stopped me before that point." He looked even more amazed by that statement than she felt.

"What's going to happen to him?"

"He'll heal. And he won't remember what happened to him." Michael drew her close. "Are you okay?"

"Yeah." She pulled free of his grip, realizing he had been holding her gently. "But you didn't have to . . . to bite him. I can look after myself."

"A man goes a little crazy when the woman he loves is in danger."

Her heart leaped. His silvery violet eyes narrowed, the gleam in them hot and possessive, promising he would protect her at all costs.

She'd never had a man look at her this way.

Michael's thick, dark hair spilled across his brow. Dark stubble shadowed his cheeks and jaw, and his powerful body was encased in black. He looked like a lethal panther. A wildcat vowing to pace dutifully at her side.

She didn't know whether to walk into Michael's strong embrace or burst into tears. Never had she been so confused about a man. Coming to her rescue was brave, sweet, and noble. Good. But—

"What are you doing here? Are you *stalking* me?"

"Of course not. I'm not some creepy psychopath."

"Michael, you just drank blood from a human be—" She stared down at Phillips's huge prone body. Snapped her gaze back to Michael. "So, why are you here?"

"I admit I wanted to try to talk to you one more time. I hoped to make you believe in me. I arrived before dawn, waited in the shadows—" He broke off as a band of bright sunlight slanted over them.

"If you are the undead, doesn't sunlight burn?"

She got her answer.

Michael cried out and lurched back.

Smoke curled up from his bare forearm. Erin choked on the smell. Michael's face contorted again, but this time he obviously was in pure agony, his flesh burning where the light touched.

Could this be an elaborate trick? Doubt still fought with faith.

A shaft of sunlight spilled over Michael's pained face. The ridge of his cheekbone instantly turned black. Tendrils of smoke wafted from his arms, his face, his neck.

She expected him to run for darkness and couldn't understand why he still stood there. His arms were bubbling now.

"You can't just let yourself cook." Erin grabbed his wrist and hauled him into the shadows, beyond the reach of the light. "Is this dark enough?"

"For now."

She looked around wildly for total darkness. "How do you get out of here?"

"Could I ride in your trunk?"

Erin gaped. Michael winked and smiled, silver-purple eyes crinkling at the side in the most adorable way. But he winced as his grin plumped up his wounded cheek.

"I can't believe I'm agreeing to this." She pulled her car keys from the pocket of her beige linen jacket. "Do I drive you to your coffin?"

"Don't use one anymore. And I'd prefer your place," his accented voice purred.

She knew exactly what was going through his mind. In truth, she wanted it to, but she just . . . couldn't. Could she? "I don't know. And you're wounded. Do you vamps have hospitals or something?"

"No. But I'll heal." Michael gently encircled her wrist with his large hand. His thumb spiraled sensually on her skin. But despite the erotic skill of his touch, she stiffened.

"I'd never hurt you," he reassured. "Unless you find multiple orgasms painful."

She pulled her hand free. "I'm taking you to heal you, Michael. We aren't going to bed."

He bent down, bringing his face level with hers. "We've already been intimate for months. And I think you enjoyed last night—before the fangs came out."

She couldn't deny that. The man licked pussy like nobody's business. But . . .

"I was intimate with a charming, seductive human named Michael Rourke." She pointed at him. "*You* are a total stranger to me."

He must have been in pain, but he leaned forward and kissed the tip of her finger softly. "With you, I'm just a man. A man who truly cares about you. You once told me I see into your heart. That's still true. I love you."

I love you? Oh, she was so not ready for this. "Look, that means a lot," she hedged. "And I should thank you for jumping in to stop Phillips, but—"

"Thank me?" Michael's black brows lifted. He crossed his wounded arms over his broad chest. "I'm insulted. You can command anything of me, Erin. Ask me to walk out into sunlight for you, and I'll do it." Suddenly he towered over her again, standing his full six-four, as though to show her the power she could command.

"That's the problem," she cried. "You are so . . . intense. I've never had any guy say stuff like that to me. It's hot, but it's so extreme."

He gave an exaggerated sigh. "Two hundred years, and I still have no idea how to talk to the woman I love."

She couldn't help but giggle. "You are two hundred years old?" She hit the keyless-entry button and the trunk lid popped up with a beep.

"Two hundred and twenty-one." Michael opened her trunk as wide as he could. As he hoisted himself onto the edge and swung his long, long leather-clad legs in, he groaned. "This is going to be a tight fit."

Erin shuddered as he dropped himself in. She would freak if she had to close herself into a dark, cramped space like that. It reminded her too much of the times her nanny would make her—the poor little rich kid—stand in her closet for punishment.

But Michael appeared unfazed as he lowered the lid. As it clunked closed, entombing him within, Erin had to lean against the rear fender and gulp several steadying breaths.

She then checked Dave Phillips, who was beginning to regain consciousness, mumbling and groaning. Sure enough, his neck was unmarked.

Erin's legs wobbled again.

She stared down at Phillips, reluctant to just leave, though unsure how long Michael could stay in her trunk. Did Phillips need medical attention?

With cold dread, she thought of Megan Phillips. What would Phillips do if he regained consciousness and went after her in a fit of thwarted rage? Or had he hurt Megan already?

This was not the place to hang around to think about it. As she stepped back, heels clicking on the concrete, Dave Phillips snapped his eyes open. Groaned. His huge hand clasped around his neck, rubbing as though he had muscle pain. "What the hell did you hit me with?"

She was tempted to reply, "My fist," except he would expect bruising. Too bad she couldn't supply any.

"I didn't," she replied. "You fell against the column after threatening me. Now get the hell out of here before I call the cops. Which I will do if you have harmed your wife."

Phillips staggered to his feet. "I've never touched Megan."

"And you'd better keep it that way, Phillips."

With a snarl, Phillips backed away, watching her with respect. She crossed her arms over her chest and tried to look tough. He sneered, turned, and headed back toward his car. His weaving gait straightened before he reached it.

She flipped open her cell phone and called her office.

"Kennedy Investigations," Jessica trilled.

"Hi, Jessica, it's Erin. I'm just calling to let you know I've had something come up." She winced at her own words. Normally she could pretext—lie—much better than this. But normally she was not in the process of discovering that vampires existed. Succinctly she explained what had happened with Phillips—leaving out Michael's part.

"Are you all right?" Jessica squeaked.

"I'm fine, and Phillips just hightailed it out of here. I'm going to call Megan Phillips, check that she's okay, and see if she'd like to have Matt watch her for a while. I'm just a little shook up, and there's something I need to do before I come in. Nothing major, just a personal thing."

Erin hung up and dialed Megan Phillips as she started her car. By the time she was out of the garage, she knew Megan was okay and aware of her husband's anger. Megan insisted Dave would never hit her. How Megan could have that much faith in a man who slammed his fists into drywall and shouted obscenities, Erin didn't know.

"I'll go to my sister's," Megan promised.

Erin sighed. She felt Megan was doing it to humor her. "I'm sending an investigator to watch over you while you pack and to escort you there. His name is Matt Black."

Megan agreed and hung up.

More relieved about her client's safety, Erin concentrated on driving strictly at the speed limit. What if she got pulled over by the cops and they decided to open her trunk?

Not going to happen. Just drive carefully. Her knuckles were white against the steering wheel, her leg almost cramped with tension as she kept her foot light on the gas.

She remembered her reassurance to Jessica. *Nothing major.*

She had an undead man in her trunk, and she was about to bring him home.

This was the most bizarre thing she'd ever done. Possibly the craziest. Could she really trust Michael? Believe him? Take him on faith?

Or should she pick up a stake, a cross, and a garlic bulb on the way?

"What can I do for your arms? And your face? Do you want ice?"

Michael watched as Erin raced from window to window, yanking down her roll-down shades and blinds. Her concern for his welfare was endearing.

"Lukewarm water is better for a burn, I think," she muttered, more to herself than to him.

"Relax, love," he soothed, following her. "I've already healed."

Erin spun around at his statement and stared in astonishment, her gaze darting from his face to his bare forearms. "Already?"

He displayed his arms to her to show they were now smooth and unmarked, the regenerated skin the same golden color as the rest of his forearms—the exact color his skin had been the morning he had become undead.

The relief on her face touched his heart.

She looked so damned sexy standing there, dressed in a beige suit with a slim skirt that brushed her knees and a white blouse that displayed just a hint of the deep valley between her breasts. There was something naughty about fucking a woman who was all dressed up.

Michael clasped her right hand, drew Erin into his embrace to nuzzle her neck. The feel of her skin against his mouth, the thump of her heart against his chest, did not call forth the predator in him; instead, they summoned the man within him, the man who yearned to love.

"Michael?"

"Hmm?"

"Thank you for coming to my rescue."

His lips skimmed up to her ear, breathing in her tempting vanilla scent. His fingertips trailed down her stomach to touch her hot center through her linen skirt. She must feel his hard cock jutting against her. "Let me show you how much I love you, Erin."

Erin reached up to his shoulders. "You know, if you were any other guy, I'd tell you off for a tacky statement like that. I'm just making allowances for your advanced age."

He laughed, pleased she was teasing him now, touching him, not afraid of him.

But her voice sobered. "How could you know I'm your soul mate, Michael?"

"A million reasons, Erin," he told her honestly. "But only one that truly matters."

"And that one is—?"

"That you are with me now. You trust me. Even knowing what I am, you care, love."

A little "ooh" escaped her lips as he splayed his fingers across her firm, slender back, lifting her into his kiss. At the touch of her lips, plump, soft, and yielding, he almost lost control. Almost yanked up her skirt, pulled aside her panties, and slid his prick home.

All their ultrahot e-mails raced through his head, sparking a dozen wild sexual fantasies at once, taking him to the brink of his restraint. Damn, he was ready to take his beautiful Erin up against the wall, but he wanted their first time to be more sensual than speedy.

Slanting his lips, he parted hers with his tongue. Carefully keeping his fangs covered, he teased her tongue with his. Erin melted against him.

He slid his hands down, following the tempting curve of Erin's back to her incredibly scrumptious ass. The best he'd ever grasped. Slowly drawing away from her mouth, he cupped both cheeks, smiled down into her sparkling green eyes, and squeezed. "Gorgeous."

Erin rained kisses along his jaw, her wavy auburn tresses shivering as she traced its ridge. His cock throbbed as her fingers explored his neck, his shoulders, his chest, caressing him with a hunger as intense as his. He pulled her tight against him, clamping her heat to his insistent prick.

She stroked down his shoulders, massaged his biceps, let her hands run delicately down to his healed forearms. She paused. "Sorry."

"Not to worry. They don't hurt," he reassured.

His muscles tightened as he tugged her blouse out of her skirt, fumbling in his haste, and she gave an appreciative murmur as she ran her fingertips over his taut veins.

Michael groaned as he slid his hands under her soft blouse and tailored jacket. "Baby, your skin is like hot silk."

"So is yours." She tugged at his T-shirt, but once she'd freed it, she didn't stroke his back as he'd thought. She dipped the fingers of one hand down into his pants to touch his ass.

He'd never desired a woman so much. Erin was a tempting combination of sensuality and restraint. No virgin, of course—this was the twenty-first century, after all—and she had a damned sexy appreciation of his body, but he understood how she protected her heart. She'd had to know him well before revealing her father had cheated on her mother. She'd admitted she was too cynical after years of catching adulterers to believe in happily ever after.

Despite what he'd said in his e-mail, he'd never believed in happily ever after either. Now he had to, or die. He had to find happily ever after with Erin, even though she'd told him she wasn't looking for love and didn't want to risk her heart.

"God," she moaned, fingers delving between the cheeks of his arse. "You've got a beautiful ass."

He had to grin. He'd never been called God before, though he'd often been referred to as the devil.

"And you don't wear underwear," she noted in surprise.

While she fought to slide her hands between his tight pants and his skin, he drew up her blouse. He unveiled generous breasts cupped by a lacy push-up bra. He sucked his breath in hard. The filmy white cups gave a teasing glimpse of her pale skin and her hardening amber nipples.

Michael opened his mouth wide to take in the whole round nipple of her left breast.

"Wait! Watch the teeth."

"Of course." He gently put his mouth to her bra, sucking in soft lace and skin. While lovingly licking her nipple through the web of cotton, he pinched its twin.

Her back arched, pushing her breasts against him.

He shifted his leg forward and lifted Erin until she straddled the tightened muscles of his thigh. Her skirt rode up as her legs parted, leaving only a white cotton thong between his butter-soft leather pants and her wet pussy. Her rich scent brought out his fangs, made him growl. He slid one hand under her skirt to tug on the thin strap of her panties nestled between her ass cheeks and tightened the fabric until it sawed between her lips, rubbed her engorged clit, and the room filled with her lush sexual smell.

Her hands, fingers wide, clamped tight around his ass, completely captured between his flesh and his pants.

"I must be crazy, Michael. This feels so . . . natural. So right. Or maybe it's just because I feel like if I don't make love with you, I'm going to burst into flames."

He buried his face between her full breasts, knowing that he had to tell her he was literally going to go up in flames if they didn't make love. In two damned days.

But, right now, he hungered to please her.

"Where's your bedroom, love? Because in one minute I'm going to lose control and make love to you, and I'd like it to be in your bed."

"Down the hallway," she whispered throatily. "Last door on the right."

He lifted her to his waist. "Wrap your legs around me."

Erin obeyed. Her satin-smooth, shapely legs slid across his hip bones. One of her pumps landed with a clunk on her hardwood floor.

He didn't race her down the hallway in a heartbeat—her fragile human body might not take it. Instead he cradled her and eased her pussy up and down the leather restraining his swollen prick as he carried her to the bedroom. The deep moans she gave in response sent wave after wave of blood to his hard-on until he sported the thickest, heaviest erection he'd ever had.

"Kiss me hard," she begged, and he complied. He paused at her bedroom door to give her a long, hot kiss. She tasted of her morning coffee and mint toothpaste, of a unique sweetness. Her tongue met his with a tentative tickle.

Slowly he withdrew his tongue. To his surprise, her tongue filled his mouth, touched, then played with, his fangs. She pressed too hard, and the sharp point lightly pricked her. He tasted a little drop of blood. He knew she was safe from the beast he could be, but the coppery tang in his mouth was unbearably erotic.

Added bonus, Michael thought as he laved his tongue over the wound in hers to heal it.

3

Uh-oh. What would Michael do once he tasted blood?

Erin stiffened in his arms, half expecting he would rear back, bare his teeth like a rogue vampire in a bad movie, and sink them into her jugular.

Instead he broke the kiss, kept his mouth hovering over hers, and whispered, "Did you hurt yourself on my fangs?"

She relaxed at his concern. "It was my fault. I should have expected they would be sharp."

And that made her tense all over again. They were sharp for the purposes of—

"Don't think about what I am now, Erin," he murmured, his voice so deep and sensuous her fearful thoughts skittered away. "I want to become a mortal man again. For you."

Erin touched the silvery line along his cheek—the line of healing where the sun had burned him. She cupped his jaw, rough with stubble. "I don't understand how you can become mortal again if you are undead. What does sex have to do with it?"

"Will you trust me enough to let me show you?" He nudged

open her bedroom door with his heavy black motorcycle boot and carried her inside. Her blinds were drawn, and the room was plunged in soft gloom.

Erin saw her furniture spin as Michael lifted her over the bed. She glimpsed her burgundy and gold quilt below her and saw herself in the mirror, captured in his arms. Michael had a reflection. Just as she gasped in surprise at that, he lowered her to her bed.

He joined her, stretching his long, magnificent body beside hers. He completely filled her queen-size sleigh bed; his hair brushed her headboard, and his boots clunked against the end.

Yes, she was willing to let him show her. She couldn't wait to view his unbelievably gorgeous body.

Rolling onto her side, Erin stroked her bare foot along his hard metal-trimmed boot. "Can I see you naked?"

His sexy grin heightened her excitement, sent her heart into palpitations. "Of course, love."

As he sat up and pulled off his T-shirt, she admitted, "I've fantasized about this for months."

"So have I." He tossed his shirt to the floor. "And I've been hungering for it for so long, I'm afraid I might explode before I strip." He paused with his hands on his opened waistband. "Something I've *never* done before."

Erin caught her breath as he unzipped his pants; she put her hand to her rapidly pounding heart. She knew there was nothing underneath his leathers but bare skin. Knew he must be well endowed—he'd felt huge when she'd put her hand on him in Bellissima's, but . . .

Holy s—

He peeled his pants down, revealing a generous tangle of black curls and his hard, thick cock standing straight and tall, dead center. His pants slid down his thighs, and she could see his full, lightly furred balls dangling beneath. He possessed the most beautifully perfect, hard cock she'd ever seen—as wide as her wrist, truly as long as her forearm. The base looked even bigger around than she could grasp. And all that rampant beauty tapered to a firm, helmet-shaped head that begged to be kissed.

She could hardly believe this . . . *this* . . . was hers to play with. To enjoy.

Michael's eyes closed in ecstasy at her touch. His cock pulsated against her closed hand. She gave a long stroke upward, caressing the taut, glistening head. Her hand drew his foreskin up over the ridge.

She moved to keep her hand stroking his length as he pulled off his boots and struggled to slide his pants down his legs. He was moaning at her touch, leaking so much juice into her hand her palm was slick and shiny.

"Now you," he groaned.

To tease, Erin continued to jerk him as he tried to undress her. His fingers fumbled over the buttons on her blouse.

Finally, with a hiss of irritation, Michael tugged. Buttons scattered, some hitting her floor with a clatter.

"Michael—!"

"I'll buy you another," he promised. "I'll buy you a hundred, if you want."

She had to admit, she'd never been with a man so eager to see her naked he'd shredded her clothing. She shrugged off her jacket, and the motion pushed her chest ahead as he unsnapped the front closure on her bra.

Suddenly her breasts were in his hands, cradled lovingly as his thumbs strummed both her nipples in unison. His eyes glittered with feral intensity.

She flung her jacket to the floor beside his T-shirt and peeled off her blouse, arching back to again thrust her breasts hard at him. He kneaded them with a touch both rough and loving, turning her into molten lava inside.

Erin tugged at her skirt. Michael's hands moved under her

hips, lifting her, and he stripped her skirt and her thong away in a heartbeat.

His bare chest flexed deliciously as he moved.

How many times had she fantasized this scene? Hundreds. But even her horny little imagination had never envisioned Michael would be so gorgeous, so ready, so . . . big.

His hot gaze raked her naked body.

"You are beautiful," he murmured reverentially. He bent his head to her breasts.

Her left nipple disappeared between his firm, full lips, and he nudged her onto her back. He lay along her body to suckle her, supporting himself on his bare flexed arms.

She cried out as he drew her nipple and breast into his mouth between his fangs.

Oh, god, she had a *vampire* on her breast. And Michael really knew how to pleasure her. His tongue laved and teased, drawing lazy, wet, tingling spirals over her swollen nipple. She arched with pleasure and threaded her fingers into his hair to capture his head to her chest.

Suddenly he sucked hard, and desire streaked through her.

Erin squealed. Michael glanced up, a naughty smile shining in his eyes. He looked utterly wicked as he flicked his tongue over her nipple. And flicked and flicked and flicked until she struggled for breath and clutched his shoulders as though she were in danger of falling away into space. He licked and sucked and tweaked her breasts, and when he released them, she saw the marking of his attentions in the dark red mottling around her pink areolas.

He was feasting on her, and it frightened her slightly. How closely linked was arousal and hunger for him? In fiction, biting was as erotic as sex, but she wasn't certain she was quite ready to try—

Ooh.

Michael cupped her breasts in his large hands, lifted them to lick in the warm fold beneath each one. She loved the wet, loving caress, loved the way his black hair drifted across her skin as he nuzzled her.

His hands skimmed down, followed her curves, and slid between her thighs. His tongue filled her ticklish navel, and she almost launched off the bed, shrieking and giggling.

Grinning, showing the tips of his fangs, he parted her legs. Erin squirmed beneath him, knowing her honey was leaking onto his hands. His head moved lower. . . .

Yes, she trusted him to be gentle, to be careful with his teeth. . . .

She wrapped her legs around his beautiful, broad, triangular back and massaged his ass with her toes. Such perfect, tight, hard muscles.

He put his face to the curls between her legs. Little moans of pleasure escaped his lips as his tongue slid into her slit. He obviously loved her body.

This was the best ever, but—

Erin broke off with a squeak as his tongue rasped her clit. She realized she'd spoken her thoughts out loud.

Michael blew a hot breath over her wet lips, her hard nub, before he glanced up, eyes gleaming like pure silver disks. "Yes, love?" he asked in a droll voice.

"How can this save your soul?" she asked again.

"How could this not save a man's soul?"

Michael inhaled Erin's sweet, rich arousal.

She was a beautiful seductress, a temptress, lying naked with her legs spread and her sweet pearlescent pussy just an inch from his face, and she wanted to talk about his soul?

He must be losing his touch.

Yes, he needed her to save his soul, and his life, but right now, more than anything, even more than saving his life, he needed to make love to her.

He bent his head, sucked, and tugged on her musky, juicy lips, astonished at his control over his brutal nature. Again it spoke to the power Erin possessed—the power of a mate over a predator. He'd never before made love to a woman without drinking from her, and once a woman was in ecstasy she would willingly offer her neck to him.

Erin's scents and flavors were delectable, triggering hungers he'd not had for a very long time. Not for blood. Not even for mere pleasure.

For love.

Reigning in his desire to give a sensual play nip to Erin's delicate nether lips—nothing that would hurt, but would just tease—Michael tongued her hard clit. Erin didn't trim her bush, and he loved looking up and seeing her curvaceous, flushed body screened by the dark auburn curls on her mound.

He couldn't hold off any longer, and he rose over her, hand on his rigid cock.

"Oh, yes," she moaned. Then suddenly, "No . . . no, wait. I want you to use a condom. Do you have one?"

Panting, Michael shook his head. Since he didn't need one, he never carried one. "As an immortal, I can't get you pregnant, Erin, and I don't have any diseases. We can have worry-free, hot lovemaking."

"*I* would prefer to take precautions." Her voice was definite. Determined.

"Of course," he agreed, cursing himself for being a damned idiot. Any mortal guy would carry a condom with him.

He almost fell off the bed when she pointed to her bedside table. "See that box? There's some in there."

He stared at her in surprise.

"A woman has to be prepared," she said defensively. "And, no, I haven't had the need to use one since we started our relationship."

He flipped open the small jewelry box on her table. On the

red velvet lining sat several small packets, some beads, and a tube of lubricant. He fingered the beads for a moment, knowing how those could be used, before selecting a gold packet. It crinkled at his touch. For several seconds he studied it. He knew what condoms looked like, but he'd never used one.

Not even two hundred years ago, when he was mortal.

"What's the problem?" she asked.

He met her wary green eyes with a sheepish grin. "I've never put one on."

"You're kidding."

"No."

Erin sat up, took the package from his fingers, and tore it open. "Do you want me to put it on you?"

He licked his fangs. "Oh, yes."

"Okay. Now, pay attention."

Michael moaned at her touch as she grasped his cock and pressed the ring to the sensitive head. Slowly she unrolled the smooth sheath.

Watching the gold-colored membrane cover him, he shivered with intense desire. He'd never guessed putting on a condom could be so erotic.

"I don't know," she murmured. "This seems very tight. I don't think there's enough space at the tip."

"Do you have a bigger one?"

"They don't make a bigger one."

Michael's heart pounded. What if she refused to let him make love to her because of his too-tight sheath? But she stroked her fingers along his tightly packed cock, rolled onto her back underneath him, and whispered, "Let's try."

He slid his fingers between her thighs, opening her, delighted at the flood of juice that met his touch. He dragged in a rough breath as her emerald eyes glazed with need.

"Tell me what you want," he urged. "The way you used to write to me."

"Ummm . . . okay . . . put your huge cock in me," she begged, all throaty voice and coy eyes.

He growled at her lusty invitation. Her fiery pussy opened easily for him, slick with her sweet liquid, and he sank right in.

He'd fantasized about this moment, this moment that he needed to stay alive. This first coupling with his soul mate. But, once engulfed inside Erin, his Varkyre nature almost overwhelmed him, and he had to bite down on his own tongue. Had to take the edge off the sudden driving instinct to bite.

The predatory urge faded quickly. After a few long, slow, tantalizing thrusts of his cock into her snug passage, Michael could trust himself. Bracing himself on his arms, he lowered his mouth to Erin's, joining them in a kiss, joining them as intimately as he could without uniting them with his fangs.

Erin tipped her head back, hungrily opening her mouth to him. She was exquisitely beautiful in passion—the green depths of her eyes glowed with desire, her long hair spilled out across her sheets, her nipples were hard, teasing points against his chest.

Buried in Erin's hot, beautiful body to the hilt, Michael knew that all the erotic fantasies they'd poured out over the Internet were tame compared to the fiery heat of being together.

Of it being real.

And when she lifted her legs, locking them around his hips, pulling him tight against her, he had to stop thrusting to keep from exploding. His back arched as she explored it with her hands, as her nails lightly raked his skin.

His very life depended on her pleasure. Not only did he want to make her scream in ecstasy, not only did he want to fuck her until she couldn't walk, he wanted to make love to her until she closed her eyes, limp with exhaustion, and told him she loved him.

Erin whimpered. Michael was teasing her—buried so deep in her, filling her, but not moving. His cock was enormous inside her, splaying apart her tight walls, and she'd never felt so full in her life.

"You feel incredible in me," she whispered, locking her arms around his taut neck.

She bucked and rolled her hips. "Please."

He pumped into her slowly, riding high so his shaft slid along her slick clit with every thrust. He watched her respond to every deep, hard stroke, and the intensity in his shining eyes seared her soul.

Oh, how she wished he had a soul. How she wished he were human . . . or alive . . . or not undead. She wasn't sure what she meant, only that she couldn't imagine giving her heart to a vampire. . . .

Could he be mortal? Be hers?

God, she was so filled. So wonderfully filled by him. . . .

Could everything he'd said to her about his soul be a lie? A way to get between her legs?

What was she doing trusting him? But her instincts told her she could. Michael had written to her every day for three months, talked to her for hours on the phone.

A lot of what he'd told her was lies but . . . he wasn't here just to take her blood.

What was the price of his soul?

Michael shifted, and suddenly one large hand was beneath her ass, fingers flared across her cheeks to lift her to him as his cock slid in. Arching in pleasure, Erin touched her lips to the hot skin of his neck. She licked his throat, tasting sweat—she had no idea the undead could perspire.

She wrapped her legs around his hips to clamp him to her. To hold him tight. She ran her hand up the taut, sinewy column of his arm, over rock-hard muscles. How much was he restraining his incredible strength?

Michael slid into her relentlessly, his thickness gliding over the ridges of her passages, battering deeply into her core. He rocked his hips hard, then harder and faster, until he pounded her, and she hammered her heels against his ass to drive him on.

His hand moved, let her go, and she clung to him. His hand was at his mouth, scraping across his fangs.

She arched back to moan, stilled as his finger approached her lips. Drops of his dark crimson blood welled on his fingertip.

"I can't drink your—" Erin broke off as he plunged so deep she had to scream. "—blood," she finished.

"Suckle it," he urged. She was sure he must be on the brink of orgasm. And strangely, as she took his finger into her mouth, and the unusual sweet, metallic tang of his blood hit her tongue, she was on the edge. She *liked* it. Her favorite chocolates were maraschino-cherry-filled and his skin, his blood, was more scrumptious than an entire box of those.

Fear gripped her heart. Was she making herself into a vampire?

But she knew, if she kept sucking, she was going to come, explode, burst into flames.

He pumped into her, head on her breast, licking her nipple in the same hot, commanding rhythm. Her fingers slid in the sweat on his back. His firm, smooth powerful body was so slick, so wet, so scorching hot—

Aah. Her body arched, her muscles clenched. Her pussy jerked and burned and turned molten.

Pleasure.

Bliss.

Exploding lights blinded her before she tumbled into a hot, velvety darkness.

Gasping for breath, riding each powerful wave, Erin was sure she was truly dead. Or undead. She'd never known such a powerful orgasm. Did this mean that tasting his blood had turned her?

She didn't care. Not if it meant coming like this.

Michael spread her legs wide, her pussy still throbbing

around his cock, and she sobbed as he drove in, deep, deep inside, filling her completely. He moved his hips, slanting them to slide deeper still, to take her into a realm she'd never known.

She'd never clawed a man before—was sure it was a faked thing women did solely to delight men—but as her second climax took her, she drove her nails into Michael and dragged them over his flesh. She growled and whimpered and snapped her teeth into his neck.

He cried out her name against her ear, drove his hips hard against her. His body bucked, his head arched back. He yelled loud. A wild, deep roar.

He burned into her. His come filled her like a wash of fire. She tensed beneath him; how could she feel it so hot through his rubber?

Shuddering, braced on his arms, Michael bent and captured her mouth. He ravaged her mouth before softening the kiss to a gentle caress.

As he began to withdraw, she whispered, "Hold on to the condom," in case he didn't know.

"Okay—oh."

"What?" She pushed up slowly to see. Gulped. The condom was a messy ring around the base of his still large, semihard cock. He'd ripped right through it.

"I'm sorry, love. But I give you my word you have nothing to worry about." He took it off, tossed it to the garbage, but his eyes never left her face. He wanted to hear she believed him.

She did, but she never let a man assume she bought into everything he said. "Not much we can do about it now."

His lips cranked down, his lashes shrouded his dark eyes, and he looked like a chastised boy.

"It's not your fault, Michael. You can't help it if you have a superhuman cock." Erin rested her hand on his thigh beside the softening organ in question.

"Did I pleasure you well?" He stretched out at her side, snuggling close.

"Did you not hear a scream? I distinctly heard one. I think it was me."

His large hand slid over the mound of her right breast, engulfing her tingly skin with warmth. "You made me howl like I've never done before, Erin. I normally never make a sound when I come."

"Really?"

His eyes shut. "Now I must sleep. Sleep in my arms, would you?"

"But it's the middle of the morning—oh, that's when vampires do sleep, isn't it?"

He didn't answer. Curious, Erin watched for several minutes. She saw no sign he was breathing; his chest stayed motionless, his body didn't move or twitch. Even when she put her fingers to his lips, she felt no soft rush of air from his nose or mouth.

He must be okay. . . .

She felt strangely tired, too. Lazy and sated and spent.

Mmmm, would Michael want to sleep all day in her bed? Should she rest up for the coming night?

She reached for her phone to advise Jessica she would be gone for the day. She really needed to investigate vampires.

After three hours of searching the Internet for vampire sites, Erin leaned her head back against her headboard. She'd learned plenty about fictional vampires and ancient legends about creatures that drank blood.

What had she expected? A site dedicated to real honest-to-goodness, certified vampires?

She had reread every scrap of information she had gathered on Michael Rourke. He had a social security number, a driver's license, a college degree, and he paid his taxes, but his records became foggy during his youth. He was reputedly orphaned—which had tugged at her heart when she'd first learned it. The orphanage that had raised him had been closed for years, and she hadn't been able to locate anyone who had been employed by it. The British school he'd supposedly attended no longer existed, and the teachers—called "masters"—were either untraceable or dead.

At school she'd had the qualities of a PI drilled into her head: Be skeptical of the obvious, and develop a sense for the unusual. Learn to sense when something is out of place or not in keeping with the norm. Acknowledge your own biases, and balance them with the truth. Maintain objectivity.

In other words, believe in vampires if you found enough evidence to prove they did exist.

Her cell phone rang, jarring her. Erin fumbled for it on her bedside table, jostling her laptop, which sat on her sheet-covered thighs.

"Hello?" She closed the computer screen with her free hand.

"Erin, darling?"

Oh, god. Mother.

"Are you certain you won't be available for dinner tonight?"

She had an undead man in her bed. Available for dinner? She almost laughed into the phone. "No."

"Hmmm." Erin could hear Linnet's manicured nails tapping. "So, how is Internet dating progressing?"

"Just fine." Erin gripped her computer and carefully leaned out of the bed to lower it to the floor. "But I can't—"

"I looked at one of those dating groups you were talking about," Linnet broke in. "I've never seen so many photographs of naked, er . . . penises in my life. Was size your criteria for deciding which one to date?"

Erin groaned. "I'm not dating a man from an adult chat site."

The thought of her conservative, immaculately groomed mother discovering adult personals brought a nervous giggle to her lips.

"I assumed, darling, that you told me you are Internet dating because you want my opinion." Linnet sounded hurt.

No, I mentioned it because you were threatening to arrange a dinner party chock-full of unattached lawyers. I didn't want to become a lawyer, and I sure as hell don't want to marry one.

"The Internet dating is going just fine, Mother." *I've found a hot, single, unattached vampire.*

Erin turned and glanced down at Michael, sleeping beside her. He lay on his side, facing her, with his eyes closed.

He was so beautiful. His right arm, lightly furred with short dark hair, was folded beneath his pillow. The left stretched across to her, fingers splayed over the sheet. His naked chest, wide and beautifully muscled, took her breath away. Shadows defined his straight collarbone and caressed the underside of his pecs, emphasizing the firm, jutting muscles.

All thoughts fled Erin's head as she let her gaze slide down over Michael's rippling abs to the rumpled edge of her burgundy sheet. It clung to his slim hips, was wrapped between his legs, giving a teasing glimpse of the thick curls near his crotch, but covering his cock.

She longed to reach over and stroke the soft, black hair dusting Michael's forehead. With his eyes closed, his eyelashes black slashes against his golden skin, and his lips pressed together, he looked angelic—merely an exceptionally beautiful, normal man.

As though she'd only dreamed he was a vampire.

Dimly she heard Linnet chattering. "Isn't that the point?"

"Is what the point?" She rolled away from Michael, planning to wrap up the conversation quickly.

Linnet gave a long sigh. "Darling, wouldn't you rather be

doing something more worthwhile than investigating cheating husbands?"

"Like defending them in divorce settlements?" Every conversation with Linnet ended the same way. She hated needling her mother by referring to her father; Peter Kennedy's firm was known for ensuring that male clients got through divorce with their bank accounts intact.

"There are other law firms. Firms more successful than your father's."

Erin sighed. Her parents' breakup was one more nail in the coffin that contained her dying belief in "happily ever after"—the coffin her adultery investigations had pounded shut. "This week I prevented a nice seventy-year-old widow from giving her savings to a con man. That's worthwhile. And I own my own business. I like owning my own business."

Well, the bank owned a considerable chunk of her firm, but there was no reason to disclose that to her mother.

What she needed were siblings to keep Linnet distracted. Alas, she was the only hope for grandchildren, and all of Linnet's friends now had brilliant, beautiful grandchildren.

"But you aren't meeting any men while you're working all these hours in your business. And really, dear, I can't understand how Internet dating is the least bit . . . satisfying."

"Mother, I—oh!" Erin gasped as Michael's hand stroked down her spine. She'd expected he'd sleep, well, like the dead, but hadn't been sure.

As his mouth followed the path of his hand, she knew she'd better hang up fast. Her mother said something she didn't hear because Michael was kissing the base of her spine and kneading her ass.

She stuck her fist in her mouth to keep from yelling in excitement. Desperately she hit the hang-up button without another word and dropped the phone to the floor.

Michael pressed his fingertip to her lips, and she took it in, tasting the rich tang of his blood. She sucked his finger like a cock, drawing in his blood as though she were drinking his come, while he tickled her anal passage with his fingertip.

To her surprise, she felt bereft when he took his finger from her mouth. Until he parted her cheeks and licked her ass.

Michael rolled her onto her stomach, lifting her so his fingers delved into her wet pussy and toyed with her sensitive clit while his hot, wet tongue explored the tingling rim of her rear. The delicious sensations were more than she could bear.

"Oh, god!" Erin cried as she climaxed. Before she'd relaxed from that orgasm, he plunged his tongue deeply into her ass, thrusting it like a cock, and she came yet again. Tears spilled onto her cheeks with the tide of pleasure crashing over her.

This was way better than e-mails.

4

"Are you planning to make me a vampire?" Erin rolled onto her back, floating in a mist of pleasure. She could barely find the energy to speak. Her head pounded with rushing blood, her ass and pussy pulsed in luxurious ecstasy, and she was trying not to panic at the thought that Michael really wanted to turn her into the undead.

Michael levered up on his arm at her side. He looked genuinely confused. "No, love. Why would you think that?" With his free hand he reached over to gently cup her breast, bouncing it lightly with his palm.

Erin wiggled her index finger in his face. "You keep giving me your blood."

"You've merely tasted it," he corrected. "You have to be at the point of death and drink a lot more to be turned."

"Oh." She let her hand drop to her forehead and brushed her damp hair from her face. "Why did you do it then?"

A wicked smile curved his seductive mouth. "To give you a fantastic orgasm. Vampire blood heightens erotic pleasure. It is also why we are renowned for our stamina."

"Mmmm. Well, I've never come like *this* before in my life." Erin splayed her hand over his hot, solid, and deliciously sweaty chest. His heart pounded furiously against the heel of her hand. She gave a long feline stretch, wriggling her toes in sheer pleasure.

He looked so boyishly pleased, she had to giggle.

"I don't want to turn you, sweetheart, I want you to save me."

"Are you certain you want to get your soul back?"

"Most definitely."

"But why would you want to be mortal? Isn't it a male dream to be blessed with a cock that always stands at attention?"

"I want to be mortal to share my life with you, Erin."

Her heart tripped at his words. But most of her clients had promised to love, honor, and cherish.

She was determined to be honest. "What if we discover we don't get along? Great sex is . . . great, but are you sure you want to give up immortality when we barely know each other?"

"I know I am in love with you."

"But I can't say that about you, Michael. I don't know anything about you. Everything you told me was a lie, wasn't it?"

"I never lied. I admit I didn't tell you everything, but I never lied about what is in my heart."

"So are you going to tell me how sex wins back your soul?"

"Not sex, exactly. I must pledge myself to you, and you must reward me with your love. We have to be in love—and it must be true, real, and unconditional love."

"And what happens if it isn't?"

"I burn up in flames."

Erin gaped at his nonchalant demeanor. "You do?"

"Honestly."

Unconditional love? What did unconditional love even feel

like? She didn't know if she could ever give in to a love that powerful.

Hell, did she believe him? Was this just an elaborate story? But even if his story was true . . . "Michael, I can't make that kind of promise."

"I know." His hand slid beneath her to cup her ass, fingers delving in the hot, damp valley between her cheeks. "Did you like what I did with my tongue?"

"Oh, yes."

One finger teased her tight, puckered entrance. "I'd love to do it with my cock." His fingertip circled inside her rim. "Would you like that? You never wrote that as one of your fantasies."

Her cheeks burned. "I was too shy."

"Roll onto your stomach," he directed.

His hand moved away, and she obeyed, sprawling over her sheets. She moaned as his fingertip returned, stroking her rim. He was so large, she was a little nervous, but also sopping wet with excitement at the thought of his huge cock taking her that way.

What was the harm in trying more great sex for the sake of his soul?

He kissed the curve of her low back. "I saw the beads in your bedside box. I know you have many more fantasies you never told me about. I would like to live out every one with you."

"*Every* one? I don't know. . . . Oh, wait, I guess you do have eternity."

"You're teasing me. You don't want to discuss your uninhibited side." His hot breath licked up her spine. "Have you ever used your beads on a man?"

"No," she admitted. "But . . ." Her voice failed. This was so . . . forbidden, secret, personal.

She doubted she'd shock him, but still . . .

"I used them on myself," she mumbled into her pillow.

"The way you would on me?" Michael asked, his voice low and seductive and rich with sin. "Did you slide the beads up your ass, one at a time, feeling the little pop as each one passed your snug rim? Were your legs trembling in anticipation as you did?"

A weak "yes" passed her lips. What did he do? Read minds?

Oh, but vampires did, didn't they?

His breath tingled between her ass cheeks. "Was your pussy dripping sweet, hot honey as you pushed the beads in higher, filling yourself? Did you feel naughty? Did you put them all inside, leaving just a small loop to wrap around your finger?"

"How do you know this? Have you done it?"

"Yes, but a very long time ago. With a string of pearls."

"Did you enjoy it?"

He lay over her. Erin felt his hard cock skate over the valley between her cheeks. Oh, god, she wanted him inside. Her ass was eager, ready.

"Yes," he replied. "How did you make yourself come, Erin? Were you with a man who slid his big cock in your molten cunt?"

"I was by myself. I used a . . ." She stopped, assuming he got the picture.

"A big, fat, long dildo?"

"Yes," she answered. She tipped her head back, sending her tangled hair spilling down her spine. She stared up into his large, reflective eyes, blushing madly. "But not as long or as fat as you. Now, please, please, please, Michael, would you fuck me?"

Michael cradled one plump cheek. His thumb slid in the glistening droplets his cock had leaked over her. He trailed it between Erin's cheeks, tapping it at her entrance as he uncurled his fingers within the lips of her pussy.

So wet for him. So ready.

She handed him a pillow, and he slipped it beneath her hips, so her ass was presented to him like a precious jewel on display.

His breathing was ragged. His cock as rigid as a pistol. Taking his hard shaft in hand, he forced it down to dip between her legs, to stir Erin's wet pussy. She tried to arch down to lead him to the right place, and he stopped teasing her, pressing the big, full head to her anus.

"Oh, Michael," she moaned, circling her ass over his prick, spreading their fluids, preparing to be impaled. The motion sent a ball of fire through his cock, his balls, up his spine to ricochet around in his brain.

He pushed forward. Stopped. "Do you wish me to sheath myself?"

She moaned as though in pain. "Yes. Please, Michael. I doubt it will hold ... but we should at least try." She quivered underneath him. "Don't use too much lube," she instructed quickly.

He'd never had such a request. His brows lifted. "Are you sure?"

"Oh, yes. Just promise to go slow, very slow, and easy at first. I don't want to spoil the friction."

He flipped open her little box. "You are certain?"

"Trust me. As long as you take it slow, slow, slow at first."

"Of course I trust you, Erin." And he was pleased she trusted him to pleasure—not hurt—her delicate ass.

As he ripped open a small package and rolled the sheath carefully over his staff, he saw Erin dig her nails into her bed. He squirted a small drop of lubricant on the head of his cock. He hoped he could readily get his prick inside her in this "overcoat" without tearing the thin membrane again. And he did not want to hurt Erin by pushing in too dry.

As he spread the cool gel over him, he watched Erin wriggle on her burgundy pillows, obviously ready for him to get started.

Michael couldn't believe how perfectly mated they were; she seemed as eager and ready as he to try everything they'd ever written about and more.

He positioned himself between her beautiful, outstretched legs. Opened for him, her pussy's rich scent tempted him. He slid two fingers into her cunny first. Between her previous orgasms and her current arousal, she was drenched with sweet honey, and he put his fingers to his mouth, licking them, delighting in her taste.

She didn't flinch as he pushed his cock to her tight, puckered hole again. She lifted her rump to welcome him in, pumping slowly against him. He stayed motionless, letting her take him inside as she pleased. The tight ring of her anus teased him, refusing him entrance, but he fought for patience, as he'd promised her.

His cock pressed hard, and she hissed. Worried, he started to pull back.

"Oh, it's good," she said quickly. "Give me more."

He pushed ahead slightly, she thrust her ass back, and his cock popped in. Lord, she was scorching fire, velvet softness, and tight as a clenched fist. Instinct demanded that he thrust hard, bury deep, bang his brains out. He had to fight to resist.

Erin stopped moving, moaning deep in her throat. Braced on his arms, Michael lowered his head and whispered, "Is it all right?"

"It's perfect." She tilted her ass up to take him in farther, then gasped and drew away. "It just takes . . . a while."

"I know, angel." And he waited, his body trembling with the need to take her. To keep himself controlled, he stroked down her bare back. He followed the arch of her spine to caress the curve of her cheek. A change of position would make it easier for him to control his depth, and he moved, drawing his knees ahead, taking his weight on his haunches so he was sitting above her ass.

With a soft cry, Erin worked up against him, drawing him deeper and deeper into her hot fire. She began to really rock along his cock. Her butt pumped up to him, and he took a ragged breath, knowing he could now thrust, but still determined to be gentle.

She squirmed on her stomach, trying to slide her hand between her body and the pillow. Sensual agony slashed through his groin as she began to play with her clit while pounding against him.

Still, despite his every instinct begging him to nail her, to possess her completely, he kept his strokes slow until Erin cried, direct and honest and without shame, "Oh, fuck me hard, Michael, I want it hard."

His control snapped. He pumped deep into her, just as she'd requested, one hand splayed over her generous cheeks. He stretched out his legs to get maximum leverage, supporting his weight on one arm braced into the bed. Over and over he lifted to draw the tip of his thick, throbbing cock back to her rim before stuffing himself back in.

"God, yes," she wailed, meeting him stroke for stroke.

He drove his hips into her soft cheeks, feeling his own buttocks flex as he sought to bury himself to the hilt. His body was hot and damp with the exertion; he licked the droplets of moisture off his lips. Her back gleamed with sweat as she drove up to him, rubbing herself with her fingers. She arched her head back to cry out in pleasure again and again. Her hair flew in a wild dance around her head and shoulders.

He loved watching her lose control. Loved releasing the wanton woman he'd known for so long only by computer. Loved the sight of her from behind. And loved her slick, tight, scorching ass.

"Do you like it?" he growled. "Tell me if you like it. Tell me what you want me to do."

He needed her to be verbal, to describe what she felt. He

was so accustomed to being aroused by reading her words he needed to hear them.

And she gave him his wish.

"Oh, yes, give me your big cock," she moaned. "Do it harder. God, I want it hard. And fast. And deep."

Her face was buried in her mattress, her cries muffled as she came up to meet him. She turned her face, gasped for air before begging, "Slam it into me, Michael. Ram your huge cock into me."

He gave it to her, amazed at the pounding she was enjoying. Her hair was a fiery tangle over her face, her eyes closed tight.

"Make me come, Michael. I'm going to—" She screamed and hit the mattress with her free hand, dragging her fingernails along her sheets. "Oh, yes, yes, yes."

She came ferociously, her body bucking beneath him, her passage pulsating tight around his pole as though trying to squeeze his come from him. He fought to stop his own orgasm and was damned glad he did.

In seconds, Erin was working herself to ecstasy again. Amazed, wildly aroused, Michael thrust into her. She exploded around him almost immediately. His fast rhythm and her frenzied motions had him on the edge, but when she flattened down against the bed to enjoy her climax, he staved off his own.

Once again, as her spasms faded, she rocked on him again. She fucked her ass on his cock viciously but only for a few seconds until yet another orgasm ravaged her. He clutched her hips, held her steady, and drove into her climaxing ass until his body arched in exquisite agony, his brain exploded, his hips slammed brutally into her as his come launched deep inside her.

His face distorted as he roared in pleasure, his fangs slicing the air as he bent over Erin's back and found her soft neck behind her thick, silky hair. . . .

*   *   *

In exhausted ecstasy, Erin sobbed into the damp, wrinkled sheets. Michael's weight had forced her into the bed, and she tensed as his fangs scraped her neck. But he didn't bite. She felt his large body shake against her. His cock felt enormous inside, parting her wider than she ever dreamed possible.

Michael must still be coming in her. He rocked his hips into her for what seemed like forever until he stopped moving and levered himself up, gasping for breath.

She fought to breathe, too. Her body throbbed with her pleasure, her ass, her pussy, and her feet exquisitely tingling.

Teasingly, she began thrusting along him once more.

Michael gave a shuddering moan. "No, Erin, love. . . . I'm too sensitive." He collapsed on the bed beside her, lovingly caressing her bare, hot back.

"So am I." With a contented sigh, Erin flopped over and sprawled on her back.

"Are you okay? Was I too rough?" Michael lifted onto his side, and she licked her lips at the sight of his slick, naked body.

"Yes. No." Her heart still hammered. "You were perfect."

"I would like a shower," he suggested. "Would you like to join me?"

"Oh, yeah. But I can't waste this salty sweat." Though she felt like a boneless puddle of pleasure, she grasped his huge biceps and stretched up to flick her tongue along a trickle running between his pecs.

His hoarse groan made her giggle as she coasted her tongue to his throat. *He* tasted good enough to bite. But she didn't dare. Instead she sucked on his corded neck as her hands skimmed over the solid ridges of his abdomen. Large but lean and lithe, he was formed of pure muscle. Not the body of a man who exercised for the sake of it, she realized, but one intended for prowling the night. A body made for hunting. And earth-shattering sex.

Her fingers delved in his wiry pubic curls as she released his delicious neck. "Let's shower. We can make you sweaty again after that."

He threw back his head and laughed, rolling to swing his legs over the edge of her bed. Erin studied him as he stood before her.

Physically he looked twenty-one, with the flawless body of youth and beautiful bad-boy face. His full, soft lips alone made him tempting enough to spend eternity with.

But she could see in his face, in his strange guarded eyes, that he had lived a very long time.

Michael strode to her bedroom door, displaying his tight butt, and Erin was torn between giving him a loving squeeze and worrying about the future. As she got out of bed, worry won out. What was going to happen between them?

Could she really give him back his soul?

Michael held out his hand to her. Her heart skipped a beat at the gentle, tender, and devoted expression softening his chiseled features. He'd declared she was his soul mate, and the possessive gleam in his eyes told her that their hot sex had only intensified his feelings. So where did that mean they were headed? For all she sensed that this beautiful, soulless man deserved to be loved, could she ever love him unconditionally?

It scared her that she was so ready to believe in him. Was she willing to trust a man who had, despite his denials, technically lied to her to lure her into falling for him?

What exactly did unconditional love entail?

Ask him, dummy.

Erin gazed at the tall, dark, and dangerous man waiting for her to join him. One shower couldn't hurt. Why get into the weighty issues of "ever after" right now?

Erin's bottom jutted against his groin as she twisted on the water. Michael glanced into her glass shower enclosure as Erin stepped in. It was a tight fit for two, but he had no complaints as he joined her. Until cold water blasted his back, ass, and legs. He yelped.

Erin laughed. "You're a big, tough immortal predator but can't take cold water?"

"Who can?" Though she'd joked, her voice had held a note of vulnerability as it hesitated on the word *predator*. He wrapped his arms around her waist, pressing into the natural indent, and lifted her around him, turning her so she caught the spray. His forearms cradled her tummy as he drew her ass against his erection. The cool water pounded against Erin's pert breasts. When she squealed and struggled against him, he laughed, slipped his hands underneath to cup her breasts, and held them out to receive the blast.

How long had it been since he'd laughed with joy with a woman? Erin's e-mails, filled with wry humor, enthusiastic sex, and heartfelt emotion had made him smile. He'd known that being with her would be a delight.

"You wanted a cold shower?" he asked, shuddering.

"No. It's just one of the downsides to living in an apartment in an old house. Part of the character."

"Tell me about it," he muttered.

She wriggled away from him. "Let me warm it up."

She ducked under the spray, twisting the knob sharply, and he gave her wiggling bottom a grope. He groaned in pleasure as the needles from the showerhead went from icy to hot. In seconds the shower filled with steam. Brushing his wet hair from his eyes, Michael drank in the alluring sight of Erin drenched.

Water sprayed as she threw her slick hair back in a dark auburn cascade and licked the stream running past her lips. When she stuck out her tongue and let the spray bounce on it, his cock quivered and jolted against his belly. The rivulets racing over her breasts were too tempting. Michael soaped his hands and closed them over her wet breasts. He sighed in pleasure as her hard nipples poked his palms. Her throaty groan sent shivers of need through him as he rubbed frothy suds over her full curves.

Weakening need.

He leaned more heavily against her, resting his chin on her shoulder while circling his hands over her pointy nipples. Tiredness dragged at him. The hot water spilling over his back soothed him until he yearned to give in to slumber.

He slid his soap-covered hands down from her sudsy breasts, followed the flare of her hips to the curves of her legs. As he slid his hands around to Erin's soft inner thighs, desire gave him renewed strength.

"Make sure I'm extraclean," she directed as he lathered up once more.

He worked diligently until her hand was clenched in a fist pressed against the tile.

Clinging to Michael's back, Erin moaned as he washed her legs. He massaged her feet with his strong, soapy hands, and Erin thought she was in heaven. He slipped a wet finger between her pubic curls, and she almost sank to the bottom of the tub. He wriggled her clit until she came, cried out, and smacked her palm against the wall.

As the last spasm died away, she turned shakily to squirt soap into her palms. "My turn."

Michael sucked in a sharp breath as her mouth, glistening with moisture, closed around his nipple while her hands soaped his chest and his prick. Her fingers circled over the head of his cock, and he leaned against the tiled wall.

Her nightlight cast a soft glow in the darkened bathroom. Rendered in warm light and shadow, Michael was beautiful, especially with his face contorted in sexual agony.

Erin held his shaft with a coy smile. She pumped him using

his favorite stroke—just the way he'd described it to her by e-mail.

As she sank to her knees in front of him, he groaned. "You're incredibly gorgeous."

"Especially with you in my mouth," she teased before sticking out her tongue to lick the head.

Hot water ran in steamy rivulets from his ink-black hair and raced down his back, dripping off his ass, his balls, running into her mouth along his cock. A few long, slow strokes had him bracing himself against the wall. Erin took him as deep as she could, about halfway down his shaft. His cock was so thick her teeth raked him. He moaned in pleasure at each scrape as she sucked him in and slid him out.

She released him and turned his hips. He understood, presenting his squeaky-clean naked ass with a flourish. He moaned as she planted a kiss on one firm cheek. His moan changed into a howl as she playfully gave him a big open-mouthed bite.

It felt so naughty to part his cheeks and find his well-soaped, tight little hole. Gathering her courage, Erin slid her warm tongue just inside the rim of his ass, where she knew it was so very, very sensitive. She captured his cock between her warm palms as she slid her tongue in and out and copied the rhythm with her hands along his shaft.

"It's never been this good. . . ." His words died into a groan.

Inspired, she made circles with her tongue. Wet, stroking circles. Michael's butt muscles instantly tightened, turning rock-hard. His legs stiffened. His cock grew huge in her hand.

But he apparently wanted to finish inside her. Panting hard, he swiveled and lifted her, holding tight around her waist as he lowered her onto his ramrod-straight prick.

She moaned as she became wonderfully full. "This is awfully dangerous in a bathtub."

Michael clutched her ass as he thrust into her. "Danger makes it more fun."

"You're immortal. I'm not."

He thrust deep; his heel skidded. Erin's heart stopped. Just when she thought they were going to fall into the tub, Michael regained his balance.

"Okay," he admitted. "Too risky." He took an unsteady step to the side.

Erin squealed. She clung to his neck as he stepped out. Wow. He stayed buried in her the whole time.

Crossing her fluffy bath mat, he staggered to the counter. He seemed a lot weaker. Was that because it was daylight, and he should be sleeping? Was the drawn curtain enough to protect him? As he settled her bottom beside her sink, Erin twisted in his arms to study the mirror.

"You have a reflection."

Michael looked fascinated by the provocative picture they made. "Yes, Varkyres do, because we exist."

"'Varkyres'? What's that?"

"It is what I am. A subspecies of the vampire."

"But what makes you diff—"

She broke off as he spread her legs wide and began thrusting hard and fast. She had to clutch his shoulders to hang on.

Michael fucked her wildly, sending water spraying from their hair to coat the mirrors and walls as they bucked and rocked.

His cock hammered so deep she felt an agonizing jolt of pleasure and pain with each thrust. The pain evaporated quickly, and all she knew was the joy of his cock pumping into her tight, bubbling pussy.

Erin slid her hands into his hair and devoured his mouth. She welcomed him in, held him tight. Her ass bounced on the counter as she moved with him. Her glass and toothbrush toppled into the sink. Her hairbrush hit the tile floor with a crash.

Her nails dug into his scalp as she screamed into his mouth, her brain and body exploding. He bucked into her, coming, too.

She clung to him, and he held her tight, their bodies pulsing and throbbing together, both gasping for air, shuddering through the throes of their orgasms.

Her spine seemed to dissolve. Erin sank back blissfully against her steam-covered mirror and smiled at Michael's tightly closed eyes, his slack mouth. "You look exhausted, too."

His eyes flicked open. "I just need to sleep."

"I thought so. But you should dry off first. Could you get me the blow-dryer out of the bottom drawer?"

Michael handed Erin the dryer and her hairbrush, anticipating the decadence of having her dry his hair. He draped a towel around her for warmth, then he dropped to one knee to let her reach his head.

Hearing her quickly drawn breath, he realized he'd adopted the classic marriage-proposal position.

In two nights, would Erin declare her love for him? Would it save his life?

"Move a little closer," she instructed.

He shivered with pleasure as the brush slid through his hair, lightly stroking his scalp. He loved her touch.

She lifted the dryer, pausing with her finger on the switch. "Why exactly were you Internet dating, Michael? Aren't vampires supposed to be drawn to their mates instinctively? According to books, anyway. Am I not the only woman in the world for you?"

He gazed up at her teasing smile. "Yes, you are, love, but I wanted you to begin to care for me before you had to learn what I am. I was afraid you would never see beyond the fangs."

"But why me?"

"Trolling for compliments?" he teased.

A pretty pink blush touched her lightly freckled cheeks. "I just wonder how you could be so sure before we'd even met."

He leaned forward and kissed her knees. "Because you are tough and courageous but vulnerable, too. Because you care for people, such as your clients, and feel for them, but you are strong enough to be honest. You are as sensual as I am. You like to laugh. There are so many reasons . . . but what matters is that I was obviously right."

"No doubts?"

"You are drying my hair after making wild love to me. I don't have a doubt in the world."

He closed his eyes and let the warmth of the hair dryer and the stroking of her fingers through his hair lull him into a sense of contentment.

He hadn't told her the entire truth about why he had been cyberdating, but he did not want her to know what he really was. What a Varkyre really was. She could never love a beast.

It was why he'd waited so long to try to meet her.

Actual face-to-face dating had not been an option for him. Not at the beginning. Not when he had risked biting into Erin's throat instead of kissing her good night. Physical desire triggered wild, uncontrollable hunger and he could restrain his feeding urge only with a woman he loved. Now *that* made first dates a real bitch.

He'd been afraid he would not be able to control himself with Erin. He'd never had the chance to love anyone before; he had no family, no friends. With other women, women who might have cared for him, he'd fallen into the trap of the curse and fed from them before he could love them, before they could love him.

Erin had been safe from him while he fell for her over a computer screen.

She shut off the dryer and gave his hair a loving ruffle. "There. Do you need to sleep now?"

He smiled into her sparkling green eyes. Reached up to cup her full breasts. "I can wait a little longer. It's my turn to dry you."

Erin opened her eyes with a start. She smelled Michael's essence on her and realized it hadn't been a dream. She had spent the day making love with a vampire, and drained by monumental orgasms, she'd fallen asleep.

A feline smile curved her lips as she remembered how Michael had made her come. When they made love, she felt so connected with him she became a totally sensual being. Reaching orgasm became as instinctive as her heartbeat.

With a soft, contented sigh, Erin stretched and rolled over. Instead of touching Michael's warm back, her hand hit the crumpled sheets. Rubbing her eyes, Erin sat upright.

She was alone in bed.

Where was he?

For a few seconds she thought he might be in the bathroom—maybe even vampires had to do that—until she saw that his clothes and boots were gone.

Turning to check the time on her bedside clock, she saw it was eight o'clock. Past sundown and it would be safe for Michael to go outside.

Her blood turned to ice. Michael must have gone out to feed. To find prey.

Footsteps. Footsteps in her kitchen.

Kicking free of her sheets, Erin stumbled out of bed. Naked, she sprinted down the hallway and skidded into her kitchen.

Seated at her counter, holding a pen, Michael looked up in surprise. A large sheet of notepaper was on the surface in front of him.

His handwriting sprawled across the page, but she couldn't read it upside down.

Meeting her gaze, he shrugged and turned the page.

I'll be back soon, my love.

"No, Michael, please . . . you can't go out and drink someone's blood."

5

Erin's heart pounded in her throat as Michael stood up from her kitchen stool. He paced toward her like a magnificent predator. She couldn't tear her gaze away as his powerful body moved through the silver-blue streams of moonlight slanting through the room.

The buckles on his jacket and boots glinted. His eyes glittered at her, mirrors that told her nothing.

He was so badass sexy he took her breath away.

"Please, Michael—" Could she truly ask a vampire not to feed?

"It's what I have to do to survive."

Erin gaped at his cool tone. "But you can't just go out into the night and claim an innocent victim."

"I try to choose those who are not so innocent, love."

She wrapped her arms across her bare breasts, feeling vulnerable in her nudity while he was fully dressed in his biker leathers. "I want to change you back. Can we try now?"

A slow smile curved his sensual mouth. "Erin, love, I'm

willing to risk burning rather than have you hate me for being a Varkyre."

She clapped a hand to her mouth. "I don't want you to burn," she mumbled through her fingers. "It has to be true, real, and unconditional love, right?" Dropping her hand to her side, Erin almost dissolved into tears. Even if she believed love could change him . . . "Oh, Michael, I'm just not sure. I have no idea what love should feel like. I've only ever loved my parents, and believe me, what I am feeling for you is a totally different thing. I don't want to condemn you to death, but—"

He reached out for her hand. She started at the surprising coolness of his skin.

"If it's what you want, angel, then I won't feed," he promised.

"But won't you be starving?" Was she crazy to keep a starving vampire at home? She couldn't force him to fight his need for blood forever.

"I can survive a night or two."

Okay, now she had a time limit. "A *night* or two? To discover if we are in love? I can't do that." Hell, her parents had divorced after twenty-five years together. She'd need a lifetime.

She struggled to find a solution. It was noble he was denying his instincts for her, but was she asking too much?

As though he knew she was searching her soul to understand how she felt about him, he grasped her chin and drew her into a hungry, hot kiss. His big, solid thigh pressed between her legs, and she parted them, letting him slide her up along his leg. She loved when he did that. Her breath hitched into his mouth as his hardness rubbed her clit.

His cock wasn't affected by his hunger. It straightened as soon as she walked her fingertips down the fly of his leather pants.

He slanted his mouth over hers and slid his tongue in and out, mimicking the sensuous rhythm of sex.

But suddenly, beneath her fingers, his body arched, stiffened, and he broke the kiss, letting out a strangled cry. The spasm eased just as quickly, and his mouth moved to hers again.

"Wait," she cried. "Are you in pain? Does it hurt you not to feed?"

"When I crave blood, it's excruciatingly painful."

"Oh, god. I'm asking too much of you, aren't I?"

His gleaming gaze moved over her face, his expression tender. "You can ask anything of me, remember?"

"I can't ask you to do the impossible, Michael."

"Your caresses ease the pain. That is the power of a soul mate."

"Really?" She placed her hands on his chest, underneath his open jacket. She found his nipples beneath his shirt and gently squeezed. "This helps?"

He groaned. "Oh, yes."

"Sex distracts you from pain and saves your soul? I thought vampires combined their feeding and sex. Of course, my reference material on this subject is books, but—"

"Only your caresses protect me from the pain." His voice, smooth as velvet, sent a shiver of desire through her. "Only sex with you would have that power. You don't believe me, Erin, do you?"

Michael pressed his mouth to her neck.

Erin whimpered as he sucked along her throat, aroused, yet frightened. Wasn't that just a little too much temptation to dangle before a hungry vampire?

"Well, I think sex is better than food. What do you think?" she tried to joke as his licking and nibbling grew more enthusiastic.

"Sex with you is better than anything, love," he agreed. "And I understand that you aren't ready to believe in me. All I ask is that you trust me."

She shivered as his teeth toyed with her earlobe. God help

her, she wanted to trust him. It scared her—the yearning to believe in him. She was fighting to stay objective. To protect herself.

"You must be hungry, Erin. *You* should eat." He rested his hands on her upper arms, holding her as his tongue licked her inner ear.

His mouth promised heaven.

"I did," she managed. "Nuked leftover lasagna. Ate it while you slept. Now what about you?" She gave him an exaggerated sultry look. "Do we have sex?"

Michael laughed. He slid his hands down Erin's slender, naked arms and took hold of her hands. He loved her so. She was willing to accept him. To help him.

When he'd first seen the horror in her eyes, his heart had almost stopped. The sensation had been like bleeding to death. His body had grown icy cold just as it had that morning when his blood had seeped out onto the cold dueling field where he'd lost his mortal life. With every passing second, he'd known what was happening wasn't good.

To have her offer to free him had been a gift he'd not expected.

He led Erin into her living room. Then frowned. He'd forgotten her apartment had the smallest living room he'd ever seen. A sofa, a love seat, and a coffee table filled it completely. "The floor isn't going to work."

She pulled him toward the petite lipstick-red sofa.

As he stretched out on it, her eyes widened. "Wow. You completely cover that thing. Do you think it might collapse?"

His head bumped awkwardly against the arm. One booted foot hung over the other end; the other rested on the floor. "Come sit on top of me."

It was the most erotic sight, watching her scramble naked on top of his legs. Her curves glowed in the moonlight, pale and silvery. Her bare ivory legs straddling his black leather was one of the more seductive things he'd ever seen.

Damn, he almost wished he'd put on his bike gloves, just to see the contrast of black fingers cupping her round, pale breasts.

Erin pressed her hands against his chest and sensuously ground her naked pussy against his clothed thigh. Her auburn waves danced around her shoulders as she rocked on him.

His breath caught.

"I want to know everything about you, Michael," she whispered, her voice as soft and light as the moonbeams spilling in from her kitchen. "How you became a vampire. How you've lived. What your mortal life was like. I want to understand you. I want to love you."

And if he told her, she wouldn't love him.

"All that matters is our future," he said. His future of just over twenty-four hours.

"No. I can't do that. I have to know." She moved her pelvis in a milking motion, skimming her nether lips along his thigh. "Don't you trust me?"

"Yes," Michael said, even as he knew she would never accept what he'd been.

"What is a Varkyre?"

"Not exactly a vampire."

"*Not* a vampire?" Erin rose and slid forward, continuing her seductive rocking motion until she was astride his crotch, but her glistening pussy barely skimmed his bulging cock. "You do a pretty good imitation of one, Fang Boy."

"Fang Boy!" But he laughed. Settling his hands on her hips, he tried to press her against him. Erin scurried back.

"If you want more, you have to tell me."

Strangely he wanted to confide in Erin. Wanted her to judge him knowing everything about him. His every sin.

And if she loved him then . . .

Unconditional love.

Now he understood.

Michael searched for the words to explain, and he apparently took too long. Erin scooted farther back.

Delicious blackmail.

"I surrender." He grinned. "Now come sit on my cock."

She waited, innocently batting her lashes.

"Okay. Varkyres are very similar to vampires. We drink blood and hunt at night, but we have to take human prey. We're more predatory than most vampires, and we can't choose to just drink blood from a bag or use other means to avoid biting human necks."

"Why?" Erin teased him by rubbing against his thigh, not his aching, insistent cock. Her pussy was wet fire against his leg, even through leather.

"The folklore is that it is because we all stem from men who tried to gain immortality but who were cursed by druid priestesses in the name of the trio of Celtic goddesses—Morrigan, Epona, and Brigit. Punishment for enforcing the patriarchal society brought by the Romans. The men became demons and drank the blood of the invaders, but eventually discovered they could change people into demons like themselves. The priestesses conscripted warriors to destroy the demons, but some escaped."

Or so Cymon—the two-thousand-year-old Celt warrior and arrogant vampire elder assigned to babysit him up to his destruction—had explained.

"So you were made into a vam—a Varkyre by one of those men?" Taunting him, Erin lowered her bare breasts until her erect nipples stroked his shirt. His throaty plea for mercy only made her smile. "Tell me more first. I want to know everything."

"I was made by a woman who was created by one of those men, but because she was a woman she carried the curse within her—in a dormant state, the way some humans are carriers of disease but are never affected. She had the power to make those she turned either Varkyre or vampire."

"But it sounds like there's really no difference."

Michael groaned as she swayed her breasts back and forth, a seductive pendulum over his chest. "True, there's really no difference. Varkyres don't have all the same powers. We can't read thoughts, for example. . . ."

And Varkyres were not immortal.

"What else?"

It was as though Erin could read *his* mind.

She bent over. His heart lurched; his hips bucked as she licked his leather pants up the fly, tracing his hard-on.

At the waistband, she gripped the zipper with her teeth. "Tell me more and I undo your pants," she promised.

"With your teeth?"

She nodded.

His chest rose with his deep, quick breath. "That is something I'd like to see."

She dragged the zipper down an inch. "Then talk."

For that, he would give her anything. "The reason Varkyres are called cursed is that we are not immortal."

Opening his pants one more inch, she asked between her clenched teeth, "What about the two centuries?"

"Our existences are limited, lasting only to the night of the full moon two hundred years after we are turned."

She dropped his zipper. "But you said you're two hundred and—"

"I was turned two hundred years ago."

Understanding dawned in her huge green eyes. "And the next full moon is—?"

"Tomorrow night."

* * *

"You're supposed to die tomorrow night?" Erin jerked upright, gaping down at Michael's shadowy face. "How could you not tell me this?"

He looked apologetic all right, but how could he have kept this from her?

"The truth? I never found the right time."

What a guy answer, she fumed. "We could have met earlier. Gotten to know each other. Fallen in love. Why didn't you try to meet me weeks ago? Months ago?"

"It would not have made any difference. Would you have loved me out of pity? Out of the desire to save me? Would you happily have met me if you'd known I was a vampire destined to die? I wanted you to know and love the man first, Erin, by getting to know me through e-mail."

His voice soothed over her through the shadows. A beam of moonlight slanted in to dance across his face. The silver stream hit his reflective eyes, dazzling her. And she knew the truth: if he'd tried to coerce her to meet, she would have refused. He hadn't had a choice.

"Are you only here because you are going to die?"

He frowned. "There are two ways to break the curse. One is to find my soul mate. Find the woman I love, pledge my heart and soul to her, and declare my love for her before my destruction. If my soul mate declares her love in return, and her love is true, I regain my soul. I become mortal again." He stroked along her arms, found her hands braced against his chest. "If you love me, you can free me, Erin. But I came to you because I love you. Because if I had only a few more days to live, I wanted to meet you before I lost you forever."

"What is the other way to break the curse?"

Michael shook his head. "It doesn't matter. It's not something I plan to do."

"Tell me."

"The woman who made me offered long ago to take me over and make me a vampire. But I turned her down."

"Why? And why didn't she make you into a vampire in the first place, if she could?"

His wry look hid a lot of pain, she could tell. She desperately wanted to know. She bent, heart hammering, and opened his pants. Heard his deep, needful moan as she released his erect cock.

It looked harder, bigger, thicker than she'd ever seen it. She pressed her lips to the taut head, slid her tongue over the silkiness of it, then stopped. "Please, Michael. Stop hiding things from me."

"You're going to hate the answer."

Erin gave a long lick to the sensitive rim where the head of his cock joined the staff.

His hips bucked up. "For more of that, I'd tell you anything."

She flicked her tongue again, then drew back. Waiting.

"She condemned me to die because I betrayed her love for me."

"Did you do that for any particular reason?"

But he couldn't answer for moaning as she stuck her tongue in the little eye where his juices leaked out. Erin backed off again to give him a chance to explain.

He was right, though. Learning he had betrayed another woman didn't exactly thrill her. But she and Michael couldn't *have* a future anyway.

Could they?

Do you love him?

Michael lifted his hips, obviously in hope.

She shook her head. "No, babe, you have to pay to play."

"Yes, ma'am." He growled. Teasingly. "I was young, angry, wild—impossible to tame. She was a beautiful woman—voluptuous, skilled, elegant. She had lived for a thousand years and possessed experience I couldn't begin to understand."

"So you loved her?" Erin asked softly.

"No. I didn't love anyone, didn't care about anyone. Not even myself. I was all piss-and-vinegar arrogant, willing to die, and I screwed every woman who offered herself to me for desire or money—I didn't care. This was England, just before the Regency, and I lived like a dissolute god, spending my days gaming, drinking, fucking, and fighting. I didn't understand that Mrs. White—I never called her by any other name, had no idea what her real name was—was waiting patiently to turn me."

"So she could have you for two hundred years?"

"No, she wanted me as her boy toy for eternity. She promised me immortality; she lusted for me, but I learned after she turned me that she didn't love me enough to forgive my sins. She punished me in a way she knew would torment me. I had wanted to live like a gentleman; she made me into an animal."

Erin grimaced at the stab of hot jealousy. It hurt to know he'd been with so many women. But at least he was being honest with her. Brutally honest.

She gently eased his cock into her mouth, swirling her tongue against his rigid silkiness. Needing to hear more, she gave him a series of quick, encouraging sucks.

How she loved his taste.

She felt Michael's shudder of pleasure tear through his entire body.

Erin sucked him in, carefully opening her throat to give him the sensation of being taken deep inside. His silver-purple eyes widened as she swallowed him up to his curls and his balls. Unfortunately she then gagged and had to let him right back out. She tried again and again until tears rolled down her cheeks.

He brushed them away. "You're unbelievable, love."

She loved hearing that.

Slowly she released his cock. "But why were you so angry? Why were you willing to die?" She bent and nuzzled his balls, drawing in his earthy, erotic scent.

There was definitely something more—something worse—Michael was not telling her.

With exquisite care Erin drew his delicate balls into her mouth. Her tongue toyed with his large sac. She gave a light suckling that drew a groan of hunger from him.

"Come up and sit on me, angel. *Please*."

She dropped him out of her mouth. "I asked you a question, didn't I?"

"My mother was a prostitute."

A bastard, then. Which wasn't his fault. But his hands were tightly clenched into fists at his side, and his jaw was tense. She knew that he was angry remembering his past. He deserved to be given what he wanted.

She rose over him, and he held his cock upright. Slowly she settled on him, drawing him into her welcoming body down to his fist. To her surprise, he didn't move his hand, and she sank lower, letting her soaking lips envelope his hand as far as she could.

The sensation left her gasping. He released his shaft and slid his hand to stroke her clit, and she swallowed his cock way up inside. It shoved apart her snug, sensitive walls. Struggling to find her voice, she asked, "How did you end up with Mrs. . . . Mrs. White?"

"She bought me. From my mother."

So, in essence, he'd been sold into sexual slavery. "How old were you?"

"An infant."

She stopped moving on him. Her shock registered plainly, and his uniquely beautiful eyes narrowed. Even though his reflected eyes appeared so guarded, so secretive, she could read the pain in them.

Michael's hands gripped her hips, and he tenderly moved her up and down on his cock.

"My mother decided she didn't want me. She was only thirteen—though I didn't know that until years later. Caring for me was impossible for her. Most times she was starving or fucking brutal men who abused her. I don't know exactly how old I was—not much more than a few days—when she took me to the Thames. She planned to drown me."

Oh, god.

"It happened. Often." He shrugged even as he thrust into her. "I probably would have died soon anyway of hunger, neglect, or disease. Mrs. White stopped my mother a moment before she tossed me into the river, discovered I was a boy child, and purchased me on the spot for a guinea."

"But she didn't want you as a son, she wanted you as a—"

"Shhh," he broke in. "Just make love to me, Erin."

She wanted to do him until he hollered. Wanted to wipe out his pain and make him forget the future with the wildest fuck he'd ever had, but she stopped on her next thrust. She ached to go crazy on the huge cock filling her but realized what he was doing.

He was trying to distract her. He didn't want to talk about his past, and while he had every right not to want to go there, she wanted him to open his heart to her. She wanted this connection with him. She felt a tightening in her own soul, a depth of feeling she'd never known before.

This might be the way to keep from losing him forever.

She might be falling in love with him.

She leaned over, and he parted his lips in anticipation. Reaching between her legs, Erin wet her finger with their mingling juices and traced the shape of his lips with her sticky fingertip. "I'll give you the ride of your life if you tell me what you did that angered Mrs. White so much."

Michael licked his lips, grinned. "We taste delicious, don't we?"

"That's all you're going to get unless you talk." She playfully teased him by clenching her muscles around him.

"Okay. Story time first."

But he rocked his hips with a maddeningly sensual slow motion that made her cry out in pleasure.

He was taking control—giving her what she wanted but making her pay now.

"I met a woman—an opera dancer. She was exquisitely beautiful and selected her lovers from the most powerful men in England. I didn't love her, but I felt like a king when I made her beg for me in bed. Her protector, a marquess, called me out. Pistols at dawn. When I got to the field, I was still drunk from the night before and confident I wouldn't miss. Next thing I knew I was on the ground, watching the sky turn pink and gold, and my blood was gushing into the earth."

His eyes changed from purple to pure silver as he spoke. Erin arched forward and kissed his cheek. He seemed to be reliving the moment, for his expression showed astonishment, then wonderment, then resignation.

"Mrs. White came and sent everyone away," he continued. "They all thought I was done for, so they obeyed. I'd been hit point-blank in the chest. Luckiest shot my opponent ever had. When I was ice cold and about to black out, she plunged her teeth into her own wrist and held it to my lips, spraying her blood into my mouth. I could barely gulp it down fast enough. But she cursed me as I drank."

"But if she was willing to save you, why condemn you to die now?" Erin whispered.

"She thought she could claim my loyalty still. I admit, I was an unfaithful, selfish bastard, and I'd put her through hell for years. She told me she could change me from Varkyre to vampire if she wished, as long as I would commit my heart to her."

He thrust upward so violently, Erin found herself lifted right off the couch. She had to grab his shoulders to hang on.

"She made me into an animal, and I hated her for it."

His eyes had turned to dark, swirling pools. Unfathomable. Frightening.

Clinging to his body with her hands and legs, Erin panicked. What had she unleashed?

"After I was turned, I was angrier, wilder than ever before." He fucked her so wildly, Erin could barely focus on his words. He rammed into her brutally, yet she'd never felt so joined with him, so much a part of him.

"I discovered what I was after I ripped apart a groom in Mrs. White's stables the first night. A rabid animal. It was the worst at first. She had to chain me up to keep me from running rampant across London." Michael's eyes glowed with triumph at the wild animal sounds she was making. "I want to take you beyond your control, babe."

Pleasure arced through her; she was on the brink of something spectacular. She struggled to speak. "Why . . . why didn't you let her turn you?"

Oh, he stopped moving, leaving her suspended seconds away from climax.

He reached up to cup her breasts and strummed his thumbs over her nipples. "I was bitter and angry. Once I had enough control that she could release me, I left her. And she let me go. It was from someone else—a vampire elder—that I learned there is another way to break the Varkyre curse."

Her breath caught as he grasped her hips and launched his cock into her over and over.

"If *you* love me, you can free me. Now come, love. Come all over my cock."

Screaming, shattering, surrendering to his will, she did.

He'd revealed his heart to her because she'd asked for it. Gone into the past he hated just for her.

"Erin!" He cried her name, drove his fingers hard into her hips, and impaled her on him as he shot up into her.

Heart pounding, she wrapped her hands around his wrists, holding him as he mercilessly ground into her and yelled with ecstasy. As it ebbed away, as he relaxed, she collapsed, melting over his chest.

He wrapped his powerful arms around her back and whispered against her ear, "You are the only woman I've ever known I loved."

Erin's head was spinning, her throat dry, her heart racing out of control.

It was so early—so much had happened, and she was still wrapping her head around the fact that Michael was for real and that he wasn't at all the man she had thought he was.

Tilting her head up, she caught her breath at the tenderness in his expression, exposed in a slant of moonlight.

"Thank you, Michael," she whispered.

"For the orgasm?" he teased.

"For trusting your heart to me." She nibbled on her lip, thinking. "Mrs. White is still . . . alive, isn't she?" *Alive* was not the right word, but she thought Michael would understand.

"She's immortal."

"And after wanting you and turning you, she would just let you die?" She sat up and put her hands against his chest, gazing down at his shadowed face. Would Mrs. White pursue him? Want to claim him now?

"I would imagine, after two hundred years, she no longer gives a shit about me."

His stark tone startled her. One interpretation of his cold bitterness stared her in the face. Her body was shadowing him, and she shifted to try to throw light on his features. "Did you love her, Michael? Did you hate her only for what she did to you, but you loved her before that?"

"I don't love her, Erin." He shook his head; his hands rested over hers, stroking lovingly.

"But she raised you and cared for you and—"

She broke off as the moonlight vanished, leaving her feeling lost. Michael's hands tightened over hers, giving her reassurance.

"She didn't care about me." His voice was a whisper in the dark. "She purchased me. That was all I ever was to her. Bought property. She tutored me to be what she wanted. When I was a boy, I cried once over my mother, and Mrs. White beat me until I promised I never would shed a tear again."

"I'm so sorry." Erin bent and kissed him gently on his lips. Her parents might have been distant, but at least they loved her in their own way. They had fired the nanny who put her in the closet. She couldn't imagine how frightening it would be to have no one to turn to.

"That is how I know I love you," Michael whispered into her mouth, "when I've never known love. I've never had anyone touch me the way you do." He moved back, gazed intensely at her, his eyes brilliantly silver.

She felt her forehead crease in a frown. "I don't understand this curse. You have to find your soul mate now, two hundred years after you became a Varkyre? What if . . . what if you had found someone to love before . . . what if your soul mate had existed a long time ago?"

"I don't have to wait until the last night to break the curse. I could have freed myself at any time, Erin, *if* I had found true love. But if I'd tried to break the curse and had failed, I would have burned up anyway. I never wanted to risk trying before. I didn't believe I was loved."

She bit her lip. "That's what I mean, Michael. Maybe you don't love me. Maybe you want to believe you do because you've run out of time."

"I truly love you, Erin. I've never understood what love is, but I know now." His lashes dipped to shroud his eyes. "I know I love you because you give the man inside me the strength to conquer the beast."

Her heart felt oddly swollen in her chest. Yes, she was falling in love. . . .

But she definitely needed more time.

How could she commit to Michael by tomorrow night?

6

Michael was creative. They'd made love in every possible location in her apartment and were now back in bed.

Sighing in blissful exhaustion, Erin reached down to ruffle
his silky hair. He lay between her legs with his arms wrapped
around her thighs while his tongue made lazy circles on her clit.
She'd never felt so completely sated in her life, too tired to do
anything but giggle and whisper, "I just can't come anymore."

Michael obviously took her words as a challenge. He suddenly flicked his tongue, whipping her pussy, and as she screamed
and gripped his head, he proved her wrong.

When Erin next opened her eyes, she was snuggled against
Michael's chest, her lips pressed against the dark, sweaty curls.

"What time is it?" she asked.

"Almost dawn." His large hand stroked her shoulder in a
gesture both protective and tender.

She'd never had a man touch her so reverently. Purring like a
cat, she stretched. Her breasts rubbed along the ridges of his taut
stomach. Her tummy pushed suggestively against his crotch.

"Then you'll sleep? You're hungry, and I can see how you are becoming drained."

"Yeah, then I'll sleep."

She fought to wake up, but his caresses lulled her back to drowsiness. "Can't you sleep now?"

"Not until dawn, love. I can't sleep at night. Even if I am weak from wounds or lack of blood, I can't rest."

"Wounds?"

"We do get hunted." He flashed her a wry smile.

"I want to make love to you until you have to sleep," she whispered, then bit her lip. She didn't say what else she was thinking. She wanted to love him as much as possible today because by tomorrow he might be dead.

And it would be her fault.

Shaking off her tiredness, Erin sat up. Smiling wickedly, she cupped her breasts. Her nipples hardened as she pointed them at Michael's face. As his brows lifted, he licked his lips in anticipation.

Playfully she lifted her left breast and flicked her tongue at the swollen pink peak. She couldn't reach, of course, but his hoarse groan told her he didn't much care.

She wriggled down his body until his soft cock rested between her breasts. Even flaccid, his member was remarkably long, and it belied the myth that a long cock didn't grow much more when it hardened.

Erin squeezed her breasts together, trapping the shaft between. Popping out from between her breasts, the head was huge, swollen, adorable.

She rubbed the dewy valley of her cleavage along his length. "Do you remember the e-mail you sent two Fridays ago?"

He swelled and straightened before her eyes, and she let out a whistle of appreciation that made him laugh. She marveled at his responsiveness. He'd had more erections in one night than she could count.

"I thought I had a damn good imagination," he said. He hissed as she grasped his cock and drew circles around her nipples with the wet head. "I could never have invented anything as hot as this."

When she pulled the weeping eye of his prick open more and pressed her nipple to it as though trying to put it inside, he widened his eyes. The silver depths were erotically charged, shooting sparks of lust at her.

This he obviously liked.

Ooh, this erection wasn't going to last long, she vowed.

He lay with his head propped on his folded arms and let her rub her cleavage rhythmically along him. But, in minutes, he grasped her breasts, pulling roughly on her nipples as he pumped his cock between them.

"Touch yourself," he ground out.

She didn't need further encouragement. A few expert strokes of her clit with two fingers sent her to heaven.

"Yes," he hissed. And he joined her in the unbelievable moment. He shuddered with his intense climax, eyes shut, hips bucking to send his come spraying over her breasts. Instead of tensing over the entire messy experience, as she normally would, Erin gloried in his wild shooting orgasm, testament to the pleasure she'd given him. She slid her hands up to join his on her breasts.

As his moaning and groaning died away, he rasped, "I love you, Erin."

Her hands froze on her wet and sticky breasts. She'd never asked how they declared their love or what they must say to break the curse. But she couldn't say "I love you" back. She wasn't certain yet. Wasn't ready. He needed her to love him, needed her love to be true. . . . "Michael, I—"

He pressed two fingers to her lips, silencing her. "Erin, no. Don't say anything."

Tears suddenly welled in her eyes. She wasn't a woman who operated on faith. Now, or a mere few hours from now, she wouldn't be able to say she loved him and be sure.

Was it going to be enough to say the words when she wasn't sure? The thought of losing him brought a lump to her throat, an ache to her heart, a wash of agony through her body. Was that enough to free him? How much love did the curse require?

How could anyone be certain their love was true until they'd spent a lifetime together? Had kids, built a future, shared both joys and sorrows?

If there was some all-powerful being out there who could judge love, Erin wished she—since it had to be a woman—would give a hint.

Michael woke tangled in Erin's sheets. He opened his eyes to shadows. Erin had kept the blinds down.

He felt . . . haunted. Dreams—nightmares—had pursued him in his sleep. Hell, given the weird images flitting through his brain in the last—he checked the clock—four hours, he was damned glad he hadn't had a nightmare for two centuries.

Instead of falling into his normal deep sleep, his rest had been light, fractured. Yesterday lust had kept him wakeful, and sex with Erin had kept his intense hunger in abeyance. Now it cramped his body.

Michael heard the ringing of Erin's phone, knew that sound had woken him. The phone stopped. He concentrated to hear her voice.

She didn't sound happy.

"I'm taking a couple of days off for myself, Matt. Personal time. It's no big deal, considering I haven't had a vacation in about three years. Megan Phillips is okay, and everything else is under control. I realize it is kind of sudden—"

As Michael sat up, his head swam. Damn, he felt mortal already. Weak and powerless. Groggily he got out of bed, assessing the damage. His limbs felt like lead, his throat was parched, his head pounded.

He paused at the closed bedroom door, memories of the night flooding him. Very pleasant memories, immediately dispersed by the one he could kick himself for.

I love you, Erin.

He'd said those words as he came. What had he been thinking?

He had just exploded all over her lovely breasts and hadn't been thinking at all. At least he'd had the presence of mind, the instant he heard her hesitate, to stop her from answering.

He hadn't told her everything. Once he declared his love at orgasm, at his moment of vulnerability, he'd begun the process of reversing the curse. If Erin had answered . . . if Erin had said "I love you" and her love wasn't true, he might be charred ashes by now.

He'd seen love over two hundred years, had seen other Varkyres regain their souls. Erin's very doubts told him that her love would be powerful and strong, the passion of a lifetime. Michael knew Erin would give nothing less once she committed her heart. But did she have to recognize her feelings for the curse to vanish? Did she have to accept that she loved him—believe in the words?

That he didn't know. All he knew was they must join in the most erotic sex imaginable and declare their love together at climax. If their love was true, the curse would be broken.

Damn, he should talk to Cymon. The snotty vampire elder knew everything, especially his folklore.

Shaking off his tiredness, Michael staggered to the kitchen doorway. Erin stood with her back to him, arguing with Matt. Michael knew he was weak—normally he would hear the other man's responses to Erin. Today he couldn't.

She slung one arm over her chest in a defensive gesture. She was also dressed, breathtakingly lovely in a soft, pale green, silk tank top and matching short skirt. His cock propelled upright at the sight of her hem skimming over her shapely legs as she paced around her kitchen.

She paused, then complained into the phone, "No, I am not freaked over Dave Phillips. I'm *fine*. This has to do with my private life—" She broke off, listened for a while. Finally she laughed—the light, joyous sound Michael loved. "Argh, you are worse than family!" she cried and hung up the phone. She cocked her head and spun around. Surprise widened her dazzling emerald eyes. "You're up?"

In more ways than one, and she could see that for herself. He stood proud and naked as her heated gaze slid over him.

"Your employee?" he asked.

Grimacing adorably, she nodded.

"He's worried about you." He laughed at her frown. "You are a well-loved woman, Erin Kennedy."

That comment seemed to astonish her. "I suppose so—despite the fact that I've totally disappointed my parents. And my employees are great—happy, content, and there's no hideous office politics."

He couldn't believe her family could ever consider her a disappointment, and he told her so. "You are a successful, strong, beautiful woman."

Again the cute grimace. "But not a lawyer. My parents can't deal with the fact that I preferred to be a PI and have my own firm. My father is a divorce lawyer, famous for ensuring that men don't get carved a new one in the settlement. My mother insists on complaining about my father to me and telling me stuff I really don't want to hear. But I understand why, and I want to be there for her. Strangely she hopes I will at least marry a lawyer. And here I am, dating a vampire." Her smile faded suddenly, and sadness touched her eyes. "Do you really have no one who cares about you, Michael?"

After two hundred years, why did the answer to that question hurt so much? He was a human's worst nightmare. He prowled the streets to slake his bloodlust—he was not the kind of creature to worry about touchy-feely things like friends.

"Elder vampires," he answered. "Not that they care about us, but they have to ensure that Varkyres are kept under control. And other Varkyres—comrades of a sort . . ." Not friends. Fellow hunters. Sharing the common bond of being damned. Not the sort of people you'd sit down with to share coffee and hugs.

His heart wrenched as Erin's moist lower lip trembled. She crossed to him in one floating, graceful step, arching on her toes with her arms outstretched.

He almost moved to step out of her embrace, knowing what she would learn, but he wanted to hold her.

Erin gasped as her arms slid around Michael's narrow waist, and her skin touched his cold flesh. "You're like a block of ice." Panic shot through her. "It's because you need blood, isn't it? Just sleeping is not enough."

"I suppose. I've never gone without before."

The full implication hit Erin cold. Every night for two hundred years, he had hunted, he had drunk someone's blood. "Could you feed from me? Just a little, I mean."

He considered her question, staring deeply into her eyes as though searching her soul. She tried to look confident, even as her heart thudded, and she put her hand nervously to her throat. Was she certain she could do this?

Finally he nodded. "Thank you, sweetheart. I wouldn't have to take much."

She read the appreciation, the depth of his thanks in his face, even as his glimmering, mirrorlike eyes hid his emotions. Shutting her eyes, she tilted her head back and waited to feel his mouth on her throat. Would he touch her with his lips as though kissing or just plunge in his fangs? Her shoulders cramped with tension.

"The bite won't hurt, Erin, love. I will be very gentle." She heard his voice, soft, deep, and hypnotic near her ear. A shiver fled down the back of her neck.

"Will it be like when you bit Dave Phillips, the man in the parking garage?" She opened her eyes to assess his expression.

"No, it will not be like that. I was driven by rage then. But with you, Erin, because you are my soul mate, I could never hurt you."

She read honesty, an intense seriousness. Her hand strayed to her throat again. What had she done? She'd almost passed out at her last blood test. "And you definitely can stop?"

"Yes."

She smothered a cry of shock as Michael touched . . . not her throat . . . but her breasts. With his hands. Lovingly, with slow, spiraling caresses. Even through her silky tank top, her nipples puckered at the iciness of his fingertips.

Her eyes opened wide. "Do you want to bite my breast?"

He winked. "The offer's tempting—I've never drunk from a breast."

"Where does it hurt the least?"

"Your neck, for that is the quickest. The artery here." His finger coasted up her tingling skin, tracing a line.

She inhaled his scent, male and erotic, and it flooded her like a drug. Her fear receded, replaced by arousal, by wet, hot need.

His lips parted, and at the sight of his fangs sliding out over his lips, she caught her breath. Her breasts tightened, her pussy throbbed. "Are you going to do it now?"

"Not yet." Scooping under her bottom, he lifted her and carried her to the living room. He set her down carefully on her feet. "Take your clothes off for me." Pure hunger radiated from his quicksilver eyes as he issued his command, and desire tore through her, exploding between her legs.

She spun, presenting her ass to him. Wriggling it, she slowly unzipped her skirt.

She was no exotic dancer and had absolutely no clue how to dance sexy, but she gave it her best shot.

She only hoped he wasn't smothering laughter.

Keeping her legs tight together, she jutted her rear to the side as she slid her skirt down.

Michael let out a low whistle as she caressed her bare ass. Apparently she was doing it right.

Hooking her thumbs into her panties, she peeled them down. They caught on her heel, and she almost fell over.

She turned, expecting he would be grinning at her clumsiness.

Instead he was breathing hard, massaging his leaking fluid over the head of his cock.

She could not wait any longer. She tossed her tank top. His hypnotic eyes held her as she unclasped her bra and shrugged the straps off her shoulders. Her pale mounds jiggled with her movement.

"Beautiful." His velvety voice ached with sensual approval. "Come here."

Erin breathed in his scent, even more sexual, more alluring. She knelt on the couch, and he rose quickly, covering her from behind. He clamped one large hand on her breast, the other between her thighs. His thick finger pressed between her nether lips, sawing back and forth.

"Are you ready, Erin?"

"Yes."

He picked her up gently, laid her on the couch on her back. Erin arched up, brushing aside her hair to expose her neck. A tremor shivered through her every nerve ending. A wet fire raged between her thighs. The same fevered excitement controlled him, she knew, as she opened her legs to let his heavy erection slide between. She ached to complete the dance of predator and prey.

God help her, she wanted to get bitten.

Michael pierced her—with his cock, sliding it deep into her soaking passage with one animal thrust as his teeth grazed her neck. He didn't bite, but the blended sensations—the pure bliss of being cleaved apart by his cock and the yearning for his bite—brought a scream from deep in her throat. A cry that morphed into a growl. She'd never growled for sex before him.

And what he gave her made her roar.

He gripped her bottom to clamp her against him, to take his onslaught as her sofa banged hard against the floor. Each thrust teased her swollen, tender clit. She was so slick, so molten, she took his pounding and begged for more.

A take-no-prisoners climax ripped through her. In the fiery solar flare that consumed her, he sank his teeth in. Pain and pleasure merged; she gripped his head to push his teeth deeper. The throbbing of her blood flowing into him was intensified a dozen times in her pussy as it clenched around him. She never wanted to release him.

As he drank at her neck, he plunged his prick in and out. Erin cried out at the pressure of him inside her, filling her, parting her, reaching her soul. Then she reclaimed her senses and realized his cock was thickening within her. Growing. With each gulp at her neck, his prick expanded inside.

What had started as huge was now colossal; if she'd known this, she might have offered her neck during their first time together.

He moved with pure grace, sending her head arching back with the ecstasy delivered by each long, hard stroke. She wrapped her legs tight around his hips, pushing him into her with her heels. She didn't care how much blood he took. She clung to him, lifting to him out of sheer sexual hunger. He panted against her neck, groaned into her flesh with each hot breath he took. Erin roamed her hands over his naked back, coasting her palms over smooth, firm skin. His body was growing warmer to her touch. His thrusts sent her whimpering for mercy, and she drove her fingernails into his flesh. Like spurs to a horse, her gouging drove him. Raking his back, she urged him on and on and—

An explosion seared her, racing from pussy to brain. She sobbed with it. Beat his butt with her heels. Shook and shattered and surrendered once again.

This time into blackness.

"Erin, can you hear me?"

Dreamily, Erin giggled at the concern in Michael's deep, sexy voice. He must be afraid he'd killed her.

If she could die from extreme orgasms, then he almost had.

She'd fainted. Something she'd never experienced as a side effect of sex.

"You didn't tell me about the side effect of drinking my blood." Tentatively she touched her neck where he'd bitten her. She felt only smooth skin—no cut, no scab, no scar. Her wounds, too, had magically healed.

"What?" He still sounded scared witless.

Erin opened her eyes and smiled at the sight of sweat on Michael's furrowed brow, haunting ragged pain in his eyes, and grim tension in the set of his mouth.

He'd been terrified at the thought of losing her, and she saw how much he cared.

"Your cock grows when you feed. Did you know that?"

He shook his head, sending a lock of inky-black hair falling across his eyes. "The feeding is sexually arousing to me, but the other urges are so powerful I'd never realized . . . that . . . before."

"Well, it does. And after tonight, it won't anymore. . . ."

He ducked his head, his forehead resting on her collarbone, fangs lightly pricking her flesh.

"When you're mortal," she continued. Was she promising too much? There was so much she wanted to know about him, to know before giving her heart. She touched his face, fingertips tracing the defined line of his high cheekbone. "If you were raised by Mrs. White, Michael, why is your name Rourke? Was it your mother's name?"

"No. It was the name I chose for my latest birth certificate." He shrugged. "I liked it."

Her brows rose, but she remembered the information she'd found from her search of his records. "You have new birth records created?"

"I don't have any other option. Hard to explain why I'm two hundred and twenty-one years of age." He lifted his head. "That's why you did not discover what I am, even though you investigated me. Because we are hunted, we have an extensive network of well-paid servants and informants. They create appropriate identities and paperwork for us. And if anyone digs into our histories—well, we find out about it."

Unsettling as that was, she understood the need. "But there's so much I need to know, Michael, since I presume everything I learned about you was a lie."

"Not everything. And none of those lies were relevant to how I feel about you. To how much I care about you. Ask me whatever you wish."

"Do you work?"

"Yes, but I don't need to. I'm a man of means. As you already know." He winked at her. "If you'd like to retire, I can keep you in luxury."

Erin flushed. "That wasn't really what I meant."

"But it's good to know, isn't it?"

She laughed. "What is vam-pire.com really? Is it a business?"

"A network for the undead. A way to communicate, to protect, to survive in the mortal world."

"How could vampires require help surviving?"

"I think you can guess. You've dealt with the DMV." He shuddered.

She chuckled at the beleaguered expression on his gorgeous face—as if vampires were poor, caught-in-the-headlights individuals. "But how do you have a Web site and yet keep these things secret?"

"Everyone just thinks we're playing on our name." He grinned. "We use the cover of being a company that sucks the lifeblood of less powerful firms, and any references to vampires are considered tongue-in-cheek."

"If you weren't facing death, would you want to become mortal again?"

His answer came without hesitation. "To spend my life with you? Yes."

Before Michael, she'd never had her heart do somersaults in her chest over any man, but she thought of the many divorce cases she'd worked on. They'd all promised "until death us do part," and some had not lasted even a full year.

And her parents. Twenty-five years together and, according to her mother, they'd never found true intimacy.

Doubt crept into Erin's heart, cold and constricting. Sure, he knew he loved her when his only option was destruction, but what about after that?

And what about her? She'd taken a leap of faith to believe in him, a bigger one to give him her blood, but could she really promise him the rest of her life?

She was offering her heart to him, and the sweet, uncertain quality of her words went right to *his* heart. Michael knew he needed to talk to Cymon. If Erin was still uncertain . . .

How different her touch was now, he thought, as she wrapped

her arms around his neck. There was no fear or hesitation. Her fingers stroked him with the tenderness of a longtime lover.

She had nothing to doubt. All he had to do was convince her.

He parted his legs, opening Erin's wide. He slid his cock into her, his hips sinking tight against hers. Taking her hands in his, he held her arms up and apart, trapping them against the couch. He felt her tense and then slowly relax. Totally under his control, she surrendered her last vestiges of uncertainty, trusting him with her pleasure—just as she had trusted him with her very life.

When Erin climaxed, she sank her teeth into his shoulder. Before she caught her breath, he coaxed her to wrap her legs up around his neck.

She obeyed, and on a sob of pleasure, she whispered, "You are in so deep I feel you are stroking my heart."

"You own my heart, love," he responded.

Each time he plunged into her, he went right to the hilt. Sweat poured over him; droplets landed on Erin's slick body. She opened her mouth to let a drop hit her tongue. And came again.

The instant her fiery walls clutched at his cock, Michael climaxed, too. He cried out her name—she was his savior, his life.

He had never given anything other than his body to sex.

He felt he gave a piece of . . . of *something* to Erin with every orgasm. His heart? Couldn't be his soul.

Damn, he loved her. But he held back the words.

Was it too much to hope that he could have life and the woman he loved?

"So, are you having wild, passionate sex with your soul mate in your last few hours?"

Standing at the window of Erin's bedroom, Michael held his cell phone against his ear and frowned at Cymon's question.

Curled up on her side, Erin waited for him to return. A dreamy smile played on her full lips, and she lazily drew circles on the crumpled sheet beside her.

He was letting her rest. She could barely walk after all their lovemaking.

"None of your damned business."

The vampire elder had been pissed at being woken up—until he'd heard Michael's voice. Michael had bristled because he knew, despite Cymon's sardonic humor, the vampire pitied him. Being hours from destruction bought him sympathy, and he hated it.

It had taken him two hundred years to find the woman he truly loved, but he didn't want anyone's pity. He wanted Erin's love. He remembered her words. *Maybe you don't love me. Maybe you want to believe you do because you've run out of time.* But he knew, in his heart, he had only now found his soul mate.

"So what do you want, Varkyre?"

"As much as I hate asking advice from a prissy vampire, I need to know exactly how to break the curse." "Prissy" would irritate Cymon, and Michael could deal with anger instead of pity. Michael often used the insult to deflect empathy. *Hell, I might not be immortal, but at least I don't suck blood out of a bag like a prissy vampire.*

"Your existence depends on it, and you never bothered to learn the details?" Cymon's voice dripped condescension.

Gritting his teeth so hard his fangs punctured inside his lip, Michael asked, "When my soul mate declares her love, it has to be true love?"

"Yep. Otherwise, *whoosh,* ball of flames."

"Yeah, thanks for the visuals. Now, does she have to know she's in love with me? Does she have to be aware of it?"

"All joking aside, Varkyre, unless she's accepted her love,"

Cymon responded, "it won't be strong enough to break the curse."

Blasted curses—always required the impossible.

"She has to know and accept it," Cymon continued. "That's the deal. You have to explain what you are, how you can be freed, and the fact that you will die if it doesn't work. Then you—"

"Yeah, I'm clear on the rest of it. We have to join in the most erotic sex imaginable and declare our love at the moment of climax, and our love must be true."

"You do realize that if it is not, she dies also."

"*What?*"

"The flames that destroy you will kill her also. You *both* die."

"You're fucking kidding."

"Nope."

The phone rattled against his ear as he shook with anger. "You goddamned vampire bastard. Could you not have mentioned this before?"

"Must have slipped my mind," Cymon retorted. "But there's one more thing, Michael. I was entrusted with your chance to regain your soul. That means that your life mate will always be under my protection, but I can't save her from the flames."

"Well, that's just freaking fabulous."

"Good luck." Cymon hung up.

Flicking his phone closed, Michael fought the temptation to crush it and shove it through the closed window. He didn't want to scare Erin. Instead he ran his hand over his jaw, the stubble rough against his palm. He should have known there would be one last evil twist to the curse.

Whether Erin believed she loved him or not, he couldn't let her risk her life for him. All he'd wanted was to survive and have Erin, but that was an impossible dream. He couldn't bear the thought of her dying if they couldn't break the curse.

And if loving Erin meant sacrificing his own life to know she was safe and happy, he'd sign up to be a six-foot-four-inch flaming torch in an instant. He was going to walk out of her life, and dying wasn't going to seem so bad. Not now that he'd actually experienced love. Too bad he didn't have a soul to continue on to an afterlife—a soul that would never forget Erin Kennedy and her beauty, her sensuality, and her love.

Glancing back to the bed, his heart jumped into his throat. Erin's beautiful green eyes met his gaze. She threw back the sheet, displaying her satin skin, her curvaceous femininity, the body he adored.

"The most erotic sex imaginable?" she asked.

"As curses go, not bad, eh?" His smile died quickly. His heart felt like a chunk of lead.

"If I say I love you, but it isn't the truth, you die, right?"

"Apparently I flame up into a fireball. Not pretty."

She flinched. "Is that why you were so angry?"

"Sorry, Erin, but I—"

"I care about you," she interrupted. "I know it. But love— it's so soon, and I'm . . . I'm a cautious sort of person. I can't guarantee I love you. I just don't know. But we can try to break the curse, can't we?"

"No."

Her eyes widened in surprise. "But you'll die anyway if we don't try. And if I do love you but just don't know it yet. . . ." She reached for his slumbering cock. His stomach tightened as her fingertips skimmed it, ran along his shaft, then cradled his balls. "I want to try, Michael."

Reluctantly he drew her hand away and sank down on the edge of her bed. He'd found two days of heavenly bliss in this bed—two days that had made a two-hundred-year existence worthwhile.

He had to tell her. At the critical moment when his lips

parted to speak the words, her stomach growled. Embarrassed, she pressed her hand over her tummy.

"How about dinner?" He held out his hand. "You need your strength for experiencing the most erotic sex imaginable. There's a lot of pleasure I want to pack into a few hours."

Michael held out a box of chocolates with maraschino-cherry fillings.

"I take it you like these? There are five boxes in the cupboard."

Her secret sin. Erin averted her eyes. "Well, a little."

He bit into one, then held the chocolate over her breasts, letting the sticky pink fondant drizzle over them. Little droplets sprayed over her curves and clung to her nipples.

She held up her breasts, knowing he liked it, but she couldn't reach the candy with her own tongue. His eyes glowed with an unearthly sheen as he watched her attempt to put her nipples in her own mouth.

He offered her the opened chocolate, and she scooped out the cherry with her tongue.

Letting out a moan of agony, Michael dropped to his knees and licked the sweet zigzag pattern on her breasts. Alternately giggling and groaning, Erin bit into another chocolate and rubbed the cherry over her nipples until they were coated with sticky syrup. She popped the cherry into her mouth.

Michael cleaned her with his finger, put his finger into her mouth, and she licked him clean.

Then she jumped onto her kitchen counter and parted her legs.

Never had she imagined placing maraschino-cherry chocolates between her legs, but it seemed the perfect idea for dessert.

And Michael was delighted to draw them out of her with his tongue and feed them to her.

"Mmmm, sticky. I wish I could eat . . . I'd love to try a chocolate that tastes like you." He sighed, licking her juices from his lips.

"I know what I want to try." She slid off the counter. "Turn around and bend over."

As she parted the cheeks of his ass and placed her favorite chocolate right on his puckered entrance, he exploded.

She shrugged, bent, and gobbled her dessert off his tight butt anyway, delighted when her busy tongue got him hard again.

On his second climax, he sank to his knees.

"Should I open another box?" she teased, feigning innocence.

"Okay, you discovered my secret fantasy. Chocolate-covered cherries. Now tell me yours," Erin whispered.

Michael bent over and kissed the top of her head. All their sweaty sex had left Erin's hair in a mass of waves and curls hanging down her back. Clad in the sheet and quilt pulled from her bed, they stood hand in hand, staring out her living room window at the night sky and the huge full moon.

"You as my wife. And children."

He heard her gulp, knew she was fighting tears. He didn't know where the words had come from, but they were true. Up until tonight he'd only thought of her love and his survival and freedom. Now, with Erin, he wished he could dream of the sort of future a mortal man could have.

"Oh, you meant sexual fantasies," he teased, fighting to keep his voice light. "Hmmm. You know, that full moon makes me think of this one." He let go of her hand and tugged at the quilt wrapped around her. When it fell away, he grabbed her bottom. Which meant his sheet also hit the floor.

She squealed. "Michael, with the kitchen light on, people can see us."

"Does that make you hot?"

"Uh . . . oh! Is this your fantasy?"

She turned so fast her hip smacked against his jutting erection.

"It could be."

"It must be. You are rock-hard. A fact everyone can see."

"Only the people in the apartment building across the road."

"Are you accustomed to a bigger audience?" she asked teasingly.

"In my mortal past, I entertained a few fairly large crowds in brothels."

Her auburn eyebrows arched up. "Are you trying to frighten me away?"

Though he hadn't realized it, Michael saw that was exactly what he was doing. Trying to push her away from him, trying to make the choice to leave him to his fate so much easier for both of them. But hearing the pain in her voice, he knew he couldn't stand dying without her knowing how much he truly loved her.

"That's the man I once was. Not the man I am now."

She bent down and picked up her quilt, holding it against her breasts so the drape concealed her body.

"Hmmm." She pierced him with a searching stare, reached out, and grasped his hand. His heart leaped in delight as her fingers twined in his again. Strange how holding hands felt as intimate as sex.

"What if we were to have children?" she asked and bit her lip. "*Can* you have children once you're mortal again?"

"I would like very much to have children." That, at least, was the truth. He wished he could have babies with Erin. "And, yes, if I am mortal, I can."

"But if we do, what do we tell them about your past?" She studied her window, frowning, obviously considering the problem. "Some people won't even tell a child he or she was adopted. How do we broach the issue that Dad was once a vampire? That you were born two hundred years ago?"

"I don't want my children to know what I was."

She looked back at him, eyes wide. "You want to lie."

He saw how much that bothered her.

"But we would have to lie about everything," she continued as he opened his mouth to say something, anything, because it didn't matter, as he would never have kids.

"Erin—"

"We would have to lie about your parents and your past. We would have to create fictional grandparents—basically, a whole fictional heritage. We can't do that to our kids. I mean, I admit I have absolutely no idea how we would explain this. I might pretext for a living, but I cannot lie to my children."

"Do you think they would be happier to know I was a vampire?"

"I don't know." She laughed wryly. "They would likely think we are insane and eventually try to have us committed. And my mother would assist them, if she ever found out. I would plummet from mere disappointment to unspeakable family embarrassment. But—"

She stopped, adjusted her quilt, which had bared her left breast. He said nothing, waiting.

"You're determined not to talk about it," she said finally.

"No." He shook his head. "I would want us to decide together what to do. To make the choice together."

"Oh. You do." Her face lightened, and he saw that, while they hadn't resolved the problem, his answer had been good.

Michael wrapped his arms around her, marveling at the joy of holding her in his arms. He kissed her until they both were breathless.

Her eyes sparkled up into his. "We have to try for the most erotic sex imaginable, right?"

"That's the way the curse is worded."

"Well, if you've done all those wild things, what would be extraordinary sex for you?"

Anything you want to do with me.

"I mean," she continued, "who judges it? Is there some goddess up there with a scorecard?"

He cradled her cheek and admitted, "I don't know."

"Didn't you ask?"

"Hell, yes. But curses are always a bitch. Apparently it is something the couple is supposed to figure out for themselves."

Her hand closed over his, soft and warm. "So we try everything we can think of and hope we get it right?"

Yes, but I won't say the words. I can't risk your life. Make love with me, Erin, but I have to let you go.

"How long do we have? Until dawn?"

"Midnight."

"That's all?" She chewed her lip. Then took his hand away. "Okay. Wait here."

He turned his back to the window to watch her walk down the hallway. He wanted to enjoy the sight of her full hips swaying as she walked; he didn't want to stand there and gape at the moon and remember what awaited him. His body thrummed in anticipation at what she might have in mind. Hell, she made it a lot easier to forget about death.

He closed the drapes to give them privacy. He was about to find out what Erin considered the most erotic sexual experience ever.

"Wow," he gasped when she returned. "I had no idea you were into toys." She held out the double-ended dildo like a weapon, her fist wrapped around the ribbed handle between the two long cocks. She was no longer completely naked; she'd donned a black garter belt and filmy black stockings. She perched on high-heeled black shoes.

Stunned, he asked, "So what do you like to do with that, and why didn't you send me any e-mails about it?"

She winked. "I put it to good use reading your e-mails."

"So you like double penetration?"

She met his gaze frankly. Then blushed. "Yes."

Michael took her reply as a sign of growing trust and his heart ached. He sat his naked butt on the arm of the chair beside the window. "Would you like to put on a show for me?"

He licked his lips as she held the toy so the twin pricks rubbed against her perky nipples.

"I have a better idea." She gave him a grin both wicked and shy, then turned the dildo upright. Slowly she licked it, then drew one head into her mouth while the other bumped in her cleavage.

He'd asked for a show, but the way his cock pulsed as she teased him was absolute torment.

"So do I." He groaned as she let the dildo pop out of her mouth.

"You first," she urged.

"Okay. Mine involves a motorcycle."

7

"You know, I've always wanted to do it in the backseat of a car."

Michael paused, gripping the car-door handle. They had driven to where he'd left his bike—on a side street near the parking garage where Dave Phillips had attacked Erin. Erin had just parked behind his bike.

"You've never done that?" he asked, surprised.

"No," she admitted. "I know—hasn't every twentieth-century high school kid done that? Not me; I was always a good girl. Well, a relatively good girl."

In the driver's seat, Erin slid her loose, silky skirt up as she spoke. The sight of her stocking-clad legs being revealed inch by tempting inch held him captivated. Excitement coursed through him because he knew she wore nothing but the stockings and garters underneath. When the hem was at the apex of her thighs, showing off the ivory-white satin skin of her legs above the black mesh, he was ready to lean over, plunge his head between her legs, and devour her.

She looked ravishing in the long blue sundress she wore—swirls of midnight and silvery blue on almost sheer silk, like water on a moonlit night—and he ached to ravish her.

She took his hand and guided it to the hot nest between her legs. "It would be so sexy to steam up all the windows."

With a naughty grin, she glanced outside. "Is the idea of doing it in the car public enough for you?" she teased. "Or would you prefer we go lie down in the middle of Bank Street and bring four lanes of traffic to a screeching halt?"

Michael looked around. There was a corner store open, and a few people were walking down the street. Just enough audience to make backseat sex a little shocking.

He grinned. "I'm game." He swung open his door and was about to jump out and move to the backseat, when Erin poked him in the back. Turning, he gaped when he saw she'd pulled out the double-ended dildo and a small tube from the blue silk bag she had stowed under her seat.

"When I join you," she said, green eyes flashing hot fire, "I want you to slide this up . . . er . . . inside you."

"Don't be shy, baby," he challenged playfully. "Tell me exactly what you want me to do. Vividly."

Her cheeks turned a fetching pink once more. Remembering her kinkier e-mails, he found it sweet that her good-girl side couldn't talk about the wild things she so easily invented.

But she met his challenge. In a sultry voice she painted a sensual picture that seared him. "Lick the head first," she purred, "then use a little lube to make it all wet to go inside you. Lie back and push the dildo between the cheeks of your ass. Rub it against your tight little entrance until you get all open and ready, and gently work it inside."

"Yeah, I'll be gentle," he said softly. "I've never had a cock up the arse before."

Delighted to hear her sharply drawn breath at his blunt statement, he grabbed the dildo and lube, and got out of the car.

But by the time he stretched out on the backseat, his body was on fire at the thought of what she was requesting he do.

"So I found something you've actually never done?" She sounded thrilled.

He understood. She was trying to find something so wild, so exotic, so kinky, it would have to be the most erotic thing he'd ever done.

Erin got out and sashayed around to the passenger's-side door as he pulled off his boots. Taking off his leather pants proved a challenge on the narrow seat. He watched Erin watching him. She leaned on the door, blocking the view as a couple walked by. A light breeze sent her skirt fluttering and plastered blue silk against her breasts.

Fixing his gaze on her parted lips and wide eyes, Michael touched his tongue to the head of one cock. He held the shaft of the other in his fist.

Her eyes sparkled like brilliant emeralds. "You are so intensely . . . male . . . that watching you do that is *sooo* hot."

That turned him on. To really thrill her, he slowly spread a layer of gel over the head and lifted his hips to push the residue in his anus. He tentatively touched the tip of the rubber cock to his entrance. Staring at him, Erin slid her hand between her thighs, rubbing herself through her skirt. She worked herself lazily, seductively. Michael felt his anus open as he stroked the head against it. He had forgotten how sensitive he was there, and he groaned, surprised at the intense mounting pleasure centered on his ass. His muscles relaxed and took the head inside with a *pop*. God, the feeling of being penetrated. . . .

Erin climbed into the car and closed the door. She clambered on top of him, facing him. He rocked his hips to deepen the penetration, taking more and more inside. He pushed too hard, yelped, and yanked it back until the pain subsided. His body quickly accommodated the tool inside him, and his own prick went harder with every inch the dildo slid in.

With a hungry moan, Erin pulled up her skirt, lifted his cock, and sat down hard on it, sucking it into her fiery core. His heart hammered as her eyes closed in bliss, her lips parted on a moan. Having his cock engulfed and his ass invaded was taking him to the biggest explosion he'd ever known.

Erin lifted and sank on him, then she twisted at the waist, reached down, and grasped the other end of the dildo. He almost cried out as she pulled on it, forcing it to push against his tight passage. She lifted the other head against her own ass, stroking the hole he knew was so sensitive, so made for pleasuring.

Never had he made love with such an inventive woman.

Using slow caresses, she teased her bottom while taking his cock deep, then releasing it. Again and again.

She let the dildo go and bent over until her mouth was against his ear. "Fuck yourself, Michael," she urged.

Obeying, he pounded his butt into the car seat, driving the shaft deep inside, thrusting up into her molten core. She rode him fast, teasing herself, curls flying around her face. Death awaited him, but he didn't care. He was pierced from the back, held in passionate fire at the front, experiencing a wild pleasure he'd never known.

He drove his fingers into the car seat, felt the fabric tear. Nearing ecstasy, he reared his head back. Felt his fangs rip at his lower lip.

Pure fire shot through him.

A searing white light exploded in his brain.

His body bucked, his head flailed, and he yelled her name.

Say it, say it, say it.

Say it.

I love—

No.

His senses returned, and he felt Erin come on him. Heard

her agonized cry as he fought not to say the words and let Erin try to free his soul.

He braced his arms against the seat as Erin jolted wildly on him. She melted all over him in the aftermath, gulping for breath against his chest. "I love you," she whispered. Her words were soft, fragile, and dissolved into a moan.

Then she straightened, opened her eyes slowly. "Ooh." She dropped her head back. "Oooh." She ground her hips against him; the pressure on his still throbbing cock drew his growl of blissful agony.

"Oooooh." She reached out and traced her fingertips through the steam on the window. "Wow, we really did fog them up."

Michael saw her write on the mist. *Erin and Michael.* Then, with a smile, she wrote, below, *forever.*

This was his forever—a few more hours of heaven before he completely ceased to exist. With no soul, there was nothing for him beyond this one last night.

"That was the most erotic sex I can imagine," Erin breathed. Her shoulders trembled as she shivered. A soft, sated smile played on her lips. "And you really got off. But you didn't say it."

Trapped in the tight space, he tried to shift from beneath her but couldn't. His cock was still firmly buried inside her, the dildo deep in him. Reaching down, he eased her toy out. "Not yet. Not here. And. . . ."

He didn't want to tell her now. But he should. Why wait?

He wanted a little more time with her. An hour or two. Then he would send her away.

"I wanted to make love to you by the river. There's a beautiful spot there I love—a lookout."

"Okay." She slid back along his legs, letting her skirt fall over her as she moved.

"I'll ride the bike," he said. "I'll meet you there."

She gave him a glowing smile. "Right. Your fantasy involves the bike."

Water lapped gently at the shore. Moonlight shivered across the ripples. The breeze was stronger along the river's edge, spilling over them like caressing hands. They were both naked, clothes discarded on the sand beside his bike.

Erin had never expected to be terrified looking at a beautiful full moon.

She turned from the shore to watch Michael. He stared at the black water as if lost in another world.

Or, more correctly, another time, she guessed, remembering that he could have died by drowning in a river.

Erin choked on the lump welling in her throat. Tears burned her eyes, and she tried to blink them away. He'd been a baby— completely helpless. Had he been crying in his mother's arms, sensing something terrible was about to happen? She couldn't bear to imagine a baby wailing desperately for a mother's protective embrace, when that mother planned to . . .

It was so horrible.

To break the spell, to reach him, she walked in front of Michael, her feet sinking in the soft sand. She wrapped her hands around his naked waist, felt the tautness in the muscles of his back. "Let's go sit on the bike."

He embraced her. She felt so adored when captured in his strong arms.

"Yes, I want to make love to you one last time."

Confused, she pulled back against his grip. "Last time?"

A grim smile touched his perfect mouth. "Maybe I've just blown the chance of even that."

"What about regaining your soul?" she asked. "About soul mates and our future together?"

He unhooked her arms from his waist, gently forced her to step back. "I haven't been totally honest, Erin."

Her blood went cold. "You've got one last chance to try, Michael."

"I just learned from Cymon that the curse has a twist. If we try to break it and fail, we both burn to death. I didn't know this before tonight."

"Both of us?" Astonished, Erin stared at him. What if he wasn't really in love with her? What if—

"You told me you couldn't guarantee you love me, Erin. Be honest. Can you do it now?"

Was she certain enough to put her life on the line? Was he? He'd bowed his head, and she couldn't read his expression in the shadows.

"It doesn't matter, Erin. I'm not going to let you do it."

"What if I want to? Isn't this my choice to make?" she demanded, heart thumping.

"Like hell. I refuse to let you sacrifice yourself for me." He stepped back, away from the water.

She followed. "*You* refuse? I don't think so—"

He turned and stalked toward the bike. He was so breathtaking with the moonlight highlighting the planes of his back, the lines of his muscles, the curve of his beautiful ass.

He picked up her dress. "I want you to leave me here, Erin. Go home."

She stared at him. "You're afraid because you aren't certain that you love me."

He shook his head. "I love you so much, but I can't bear to put you at risk. You must have accepted your love for it to be strong enough to break the curse . . . but you aren't sure."

The night was beautiful. Was she willing to risk never knowing such a night again? But would any other night—or day—ever seem beautiful if she let Michael die?

No. The answer was clear, definite.

Erin ran across the sand to him. He was putting her safety over his own life. He was willing to die to protect her. She was willing to risk her life to save him. Wasn't that proof their love was true? Wasn't it proof they could survive?

He was stubbornly throwing away his last chance. She wouldn't let him do it. She reached him and pointed at the inky-black stretch of water behind them. "What if we make love in the river? How could we burn in there?"

Michael had his butt planted on his bike seat and her clothes and shoes in his hands. He held out her stuff to her. "That would be a technicality. As far as I know, the fire begins on the inside, in the abyss left by the lost soul. And nothing can quench it. Please, love, go—"

"Michael."

A woman's voice rose from the dark. A sensual voice, elegant and rich, like a treasured musical instrument.

Erin froze, then jerked her head up. Michael had swung around on the bike so she couldn't see his face as the woman stepped forward and the shadows fell away from her. Tall and slim, the woman moved with an exacting step, like a model. A long black jacket and trim black pants clung to her lean body, and her breasts were full and prominent in the tight-fitting coat.

A petulant expression played on the woman's stunning face.

"Michael, my love, I've searched the world for you, and you cannot even smile for me?"

"Did you come to watch me die?"

At Michael's cool answer, Erin understood. This woman must be Mrs. White. Jealousy stirred Erin's gut. Physically this woman was a goddess. And she read the woman's desire plain— as a female, she knew exactly when another woman wanted her man.

"I came to offer you immortality, Michael, dear." Mrs. White swept her gaze over Erin. Erin flinched, crossing her arms over her bare breasts. Being naked made her feel exposed and at a distinct disadvantage.

Mrs. White moved to Michael's side in the blink of an eye, and she draped one long, slim hand on his shoulder. "Who is the little mortal?"

"The woman I love," he answered.

Erin's heart soared at his words, at the abrupt way he pushed the woman's hand aside.

"Oh?" Mrs. White gave a throaty laugh. "This little human wants to try to break the curse? How sweet. And how stupid."

The woman had the charm of a ferret.

"How many human women have you screwed, Michael?" she continued. "Did you ever love any of them? This one will only bore you. You are deserving of so much more."

Mrs. White splayed her hand on Michael's chest, long fingers curving right over his heart. He yanked her hand away.

"I've waited two hundred years to have you, Michael." The vampiress trailed her hands suggestively along the jutting shelf of her breasts. "I want to offer you immortality. To make you into what you longed to be—a vampire."

"You're wrong. What I want is a mortal life." He got up from the bike. Erin realized both she and Mrs. White had let out low, appreciative hisses as he stood to his full, naked height.

Erin's head swam as he coolly and deliberately rejected immortality. For her.

Mrs. White chided, "Foolish boy—"

"I'm not a *boy*."

"I want you back, Michael." Mrs. White's elegant voice slipped into a whine. "I love you—I always have. I've spent two centuries of agony missing you."

"Then you wasted a hell of a lot of time."

Erin frowned as his maker spun and pointed accusingly at her.

"You are going to throw away immortality for this . . . this insignificant human?"

Insignificant?

"I forbid it," Mrs. White snapped. The woman's mouth wrenched open, and her head jerked back. Erin gasped at the sight of long, vicious fangs. . . . Before she caught her next breath, she felt arms wrap around her, crushing her. She smelled flowery perfume, saw Mrs. White's contorted face right in front of hers.

She struggled hopelessly, but suddenly the woman's body was pulled away. Stumbling back in shock, Erin saw Michael wrap his hand around his maker's throat. He lifted the tall woman off the ground, squeezing so hard her eyes bulged out. Mrs. White clawed at his hands, but Erin saw Michael tighten his grip. Relentlessly. Ruthlessly.

"Try to hurt Erin again, and I'll kill you. I'll rip your heart out without a thought."

Mrs. White trembled—whether in fear or rage, Erin couldn't tell. Erin's heart thudded so loud, she was certain both Michael and the vampiress could hear it clearly. She clapped her hand to her mouth in horror. If Michael became mortal, Mrs. White could claim him still. Attack him with her power and strength, and kill him. Or kill her. How could they fight a vampire? Did Michael intend to destroy his maker? Could he?

Michael's breath came in ragged gasps, and his face grew as red as Mrs. White's. Now she understood—he was experiencing the pain he was inflicting. His arm began to tremble.

Erin reached out to him, too far away to touch him, but he turned at the movement. His face looked so horrible.

"Michael, no, don't," she whispered.

Slowly, his arm shaking and jerking, Michael lowered his maker. Mrs. White swept back, even though her stiletto heels sank in the sand. "I made you. How dare you?"

His voice was deep, dangerous. "You can't force me to serve at your side. The only tie that can bind is love. Find your soul mate, Mrs. White. Find a man who will love you." He spoke softly now. Gently. "It truly is better to die than not to know love. I've discovered—" He turned. At his tender smile, another enormous lump lodged in Erin's throat. "—that love is the only thing worth existing for."

Contempt twisted Mrs. White's exquisite features. "I wonder if you will still feel the same way when you fight over the pitiful things mortal couples fight over. And when you have to watch her die."

Erin's heart lurched as his intense gaze never left her face. "I think it is worth the gamble."

"Yes, it is," Erin agreed. "*You* are worth any risk, Michael."

"So it speaks," Mrs. White sneered. "How can you prefer that uncultured little creature over me?"

Michael stayed silent so long Erin wondered if he was having second thoughts. When he spoke, his voice was quiet but charged with an undercurrent of intense desire.

"Erin is the woman I'd wait an eternity for. She's made me understand how important it is to have a soul, because she searched hers to care for me."

"How much does she know about you? She probably expects a tame, faithful husband. I know what you are—"

"You know what I was," Michael corrected.

Erin struggled to breathe around the stupid lumps in her throat; she could count on one hand the times she'd cried in her life. But Michael was vowing fidelity to her, promising he had changed, promising his love.

And she knew—enough to stake her life on it—that she loved him.

Mrs. White's kohl-rimmed eyes blinked. "If you try to break the curse, you'll never survive. Have you any idea what an ordeal it is? The silly girl will not have the courage to see it through. How old is she? Twenty-five? She knows nothing of true passion—"

"I know about true love," Erin broke in, fed up with this condescending woman. In several centuries, had no one kicked this woman's ass? She was sorely tempted to be the first. "Michael didn't want to let me try to break this damned curse because he was afraid for me. He was willing to go to his death just to protect me."

Eyes wide and flashing silver fire, the vampiress spun around. "Is this true? You would burn to keep her safe?"

"That's what love is about, Mrs. White," he replied.

"Rachel," she said. She looked at him pleadingly. "My name is Rachel. Oh, Michael, I've yearned for you for two centuries and—"

The woman stopped and reeled back as though she'd been slapped. Erin saw why. Michael was looking at his maker with pity.

"If you die, Michael, I can destroy her any time I wish. Even if you are mortal, even if you become one of the hunters, you could not stop me killing her."

The lump of tears in Erin's throat morphed into a knot of fear. Truly, the best way to protect Michael would be to let him become immortal. She took a step forward. "Michael, I think you should become a—"

He smiled at her, a beautiful smile that set her heart aching. "Shhh, love. You have nothing to fear." He snarled at Mrs. White—Rachel. "You can't touch Erin. She has the protection of an elder. Of Cymon."

Erin gaped at Michael. She did? Cymon, the vampire Michael had phoned? What exactly was going on?

Whoever Cymon was, he had clout. Mrs. White stared at Michael, fury mottling her perfectly made-up face. "You . . ." Her lips clamped shut as her shimmering eyes narrowed. "Fine, Michael, I leave you to your fate." Mrs. White gave him one last seductive smile. "But what a terrible waste for that beautiful body of yours to go up in flames."

Erin's heart soared as Michael held out his arms to her.

Sticking her nose in the air, Mrs. White stalked off across the beach, then vanished into the dark.

Erin stepped into the warmth of Michael's embrace. How could Mrs. White not even care that Michael would die? The stupid woman believed a man's heart could be bought or blackmailed or captured. Erin could barely control her anger. No wonder it had taken Michael two hundred years and the threat of destruction before he'd searched for love. The two women who'd held his soul in their hands had betrayed him: his mother—though she may have had no choice—and Mrs. White.

Now she held Michael's soul, and she longed to give it back to him. She didn't even care if he walked away from her afterward.

"Are you certain you don't want immortality?" she asked, brushing her lips against his wide, solid chest.

He bent his head. "I told you what I want. You. And children with you."

"Then you'll let us—"

"No way on Earth will I let you put your life in danger for me."

Erin pressed her breasts tight to his chest and wriggled sensuously. "Then you'd better be planning to ride away right now, because I want to make love once more, and I'm not taking no for an answer."

She slid her hands up his long, hard naked thighs, bringing them around to cradle his cock as it grew stiff against her palms. "Get on the bike, Michael."

"No—"

"Don't you want your fantasy?" She smiled into his unearthly, gorgeous eyes. Stubborn eyes. The tightness in her throat was rapidly dissolving into tears that ached to spring forth. "Just one last time," she whispered.

He swung his leg over the bike. For a moment, sexual desire

and the powerful need to express her love overwhelmed everything else. Seeing Michael nude on the motorcycle was intensely erotic. He leaned over, lifted her as though she weighed
nothing, and put her across the bike in front of him.

This was much better than even riding behind him would
be. As she wriggled toward him, he lifted her again and slid his
cock into her wet sheath, slowly lowering her to his hips.

Erin cried out as he filled her, as she reveled in the look of
sensual hunger on his handsome face.

Then she saw something remarkable.

His eyes . . . the silver—the strange reflectivity that guarded
his deepest emotions from her—vanished for a moment. But,
shadowed, his eyes were still hidden, still mysterious.

Physically she knew exactly what he wanted as he cupped
her breasts and began slowly pumping into her. She moved
with him, perfectly joined, perfectly mated.

"If you are willing to give up eternity for me, you must love
me," she whispered, "just as I couldn't imagine living for an
eternity without you."

"Don't." He groaned. "You're opening my heart—making
me hope. Don't. Just make love to me."

"No, not this time." She screamed at his hard thrust, so deep
it seemed to pierce her heart. "Oh, I understand!" she cried.
"The curse! The most erotic sex imaginable is joining with the
man you love." She wrapped her arm around his neck. "Anything we do together is spectacular and special and incredible.
Anything is worthy of saving your soul. . . ."

He captured her mouth, thrusting powerfully, taking her to
the brink.

At her climax, she pulled her mouth free.

"Ooooh. Yes."

She shattered. Saw the stars above spinning around her.
Then gasped in horror. She had forgotten to say it.

Michael was still hard in her.

"I want more," she demanded. She gripped his shoulders and rode him hard, plunging ferociously onto him to pleasure him so much he lost control and came, too.

His skin grew fiery hot under her hands. Surprised, confused, Erin looked up at Michael's face. Her heart tripped in her chest. His face was contorted by pain, a pain she saw must be worse than burning in sunlight. She had to yank her hands away—his flesh burned like fire, searing her skin.

How could this be happening?

Erin almost toppled over, and she realized he was trying to lift her off the bike. She wrapped her arms around his neck, despite the heat, despite the fear ripping through her.

She rode him, slapping down against his balls, grinding her clit against his groin. Terrified, she worked faster as she saw his body glow and turn golden in the bathing moonlight.

No.

She pumped wildly on him. Drove him. Felt him tense, heard him pant, knew he was about to come.

Lost herself to the joy of making love to him.

She took him to ecstasy.

"I love you, Erin!" He tipped his head back and yelled the words to the sky. He held her, rocked her on him, gazed deep into her eyes, and whispered it. "I love you so much, Erin. But don't say it. Don't risk your life for me."

She'd taken him beyond his control, forced him to believe in their love as she did. Yes, she loved him. Trusted him.

An orgasm screamed through her.

"I love you, Michael."

She yelled it again and again, to make sure. Over and over with every wave crashing through her.

No—his body was getting hotter. The smell of burning flesh turned her stomach. Pain lanced her hands where she touched him.

It wasn't working.

He cried out in agony.

Ignoring the heat, knowing she was about to die, Erin pressed her body hard against Michael's. Horrified, she realized he was going to die without a soul. There'd be no eternity for them together.

It wasn't fair! He deserved to know love. He deserved happiness. Even fifty or sixty meager years of mortal life, so they could enjoy every day.

Michael dragged her hands from his body, pushed her back with such force her shoulders hit the handlebars. Shocked by the pain, she stayed motionless as he slid out of her, fell off the bike, fell back onto the sand.

He was trying to protect her.

Erin jumped off, dropped to his side. Saw the glowing of his body fade away.

Scalding tears poured down her cheeks.

Did it mean he was gone? Was she going to die?

Then his eyes snapped open. Again, they were no longer silver. As she watched, unable to breathe, his eyes stayed dark and human.

Slowly, as though it was agony, Michael lifted his hands, tentatively stroked his chest and arms. "It's cooling now. The pain is going." His head dropped back against the sand. His chest rose with a choked laugh. "Thank you, Erin."

He'd whispered it, but she heard it.

She lay down on his chest, felt the thump of his heart against her cheek.

Three magical words. Now so easy to say.

"I love you."

He held her tight.

Erin wrapped her arm around Michael's waist to hold him up. She saw how weakened and drained he was. He would tense his entire body as a bolt of pain shot through him. But she saw that the pain receded faster, and each time it came it was less strong. Drained and weak, Michael leaned on her as she helped him to her car.

"I think I'll live." He gave a weak grin.

"You'd better."

He wrapped his hand around hers, lifted it to his lips. "Will you take me home, Erin?"

When she felt his fangs brush the back of her hand, she clapped her hand to her mouth.

He shook his head. "It might take time. . . . I don't know."

"Do you need blood?" she asked as she bundled him into the car.

Groaning as he lay against the seat, he seemed surprised by her question. And more astonished by the answer. "I have no hunger."

Erin raced around to the driver's side, heart in her throat. As she drove she kept looking at him. He was so quiet. At a red light she realized something astonishing.

He was asleep. At night. His head was tilted toward her. When he let out a gentle snore, she giggled. Then she slumped over the steering wheel with relief. Her dashboard clock read twelve-twenty.

It must have worked.

She couldn't wipe away the tears fast enough. Thankfully there weren't many cars on the road so late—she could barely see where she was driving.

She'd never known such joy in her life.

To think, after all her years of caution, she'd given herself in faith to a vampire. And found complete happiness.

Michael opened his eyes. Goddamn, his cell phone was ringing. He heard the tune "Cravings," written by a Varkyre, playing out of his pants—which were lying on the floor. Stretched out beside him, a goddess in slumber, Erin mumbled and buried her face deeper into her pillow.

He launched out of bed, fished out the phone quickly so he wouldn't wake Erin. She needed rest.

He stopped dead. Let his tongue rove around his mouth. *No fangs.* But he didn't have time to appreciate it.

"Who in hell is this?" he snapped into the phone.

"Congratulations, Varkyre."

Cymon, of course. Who else would have the audacity to call at six in the goddamned morning after the night that was supposed to kill him? His anger immediately faded away.

"Not anymore," he said. "I'm mortal now. Guess that means I'd better keep my neck away from you."

Cymon laughed ruefully. "Just blood in a bag for us prissy vampires. And you know I am pledged to also protect you as well as your mate."

"Yeah, well." Michael rubbed the back of his head. "I'd say thanks, except I know you don't have a choice."

"I'm an elder, mortal; I always have a choice. As do you."

He knew Cymon was referring to the choice he now faced to hunt his own kind. "I haven't thought beyond this morning. I plan on taking Erin out for brunch. Then we'll go for a walk along the river to enjoy the sun—"

His voice caught. A day spent in the sunshine. Erin's special gift to him. *Almost* the most precious gift imaginable. The most precious was her love.

Cymon gave an exaggerated sigh. "Brings a tear to my eye."

"I always knew you were sentimental."

"Right. Well, enjoy your mortal life, Varkyre."

Was Michael wrong, or did he detect a genuinely wistful tone?

"Maybe a hundred years from now," Cymon continued, "I'll

meet your great-grandkids." He gave an exaggerated yawn. "Night-night, mortal. Time for us vampires to get into our coffins. I'm overdue on my rest."

Laughing, Michael hung up. He glanced at the bed with relief. Erin was still sleeping.

He walked to the window. Hesitating for one moment, he made a decision. He raised the blinds a few inches, let the light spill into the window and onto his bare chest.

It hit him, enveloped him, covered his skin.

But didn't burn him.

He lowered the blind and parted the slats at eye level. He stood for ten minutes, staring out, marveling at the beauty of the early morning sun.

"Good morning."

He swung around, caught his breath. Smiling joyfully at him, Erin radiated happiness.

He smiled back at her.

"I saw you open the blinds," she said softly. "Can you?"

Michael nodded, drawing up the blinds to drench them both with light. He remembered thinking—in the parking garage, before his arm had caught fire—how beautiful she had looked in sunlight. Remembered thinking her hair shone like fire, all red and gold, her skin was peachy perfection, her green eyes more beautiful than the lush English countryside in spring, a sight he'd always loved.

This morning he saw he'd understated her beauty.

In an instant he was back in bed with her, cradling her against him as she caressed him. Awed, he told her, "Do you know how perfect it was to spend the night sleeping in your arms?"

Before she could answer, he put his fingertips to her lips. She kissed them.

"I'm the luckiest mortal man alive to have found you as my

soul mate." He was afraid his voice might break—something highly embarrassing for a man who was once a big bad vampire. So, he grinned to cover up how close he was to losing it.

He was rewarded with a glowing smile.

"No fangs!" she cried.

He rolled her onto her back.

"Wait—"

Not hiding his impatience, he cupped his hand over Erin's hot, moist pussy and gazed down into her magnificent sparkling eyes. "Yes?"

She stroked her hand up his neck to cradle his jaw. "Who exactly is Cymon, my protector? How is a vampire supposed to protect me? And what did . . . Mrs. White mean about you becoming a hunter?"

"You know, you ask a lot of questions. And all I want to do is have sex. In daylight. With you."

"Michael, this is serious."

"Okay," he surrendered. "A little Varkyre history, then." He sat at her side and watched the sunlight bathe her body in gold. "Long ago, some Varkyres who regained their souls became hunters of vampires and other Varkyres. They were the only mortals who knew vampires' weaknesses, who knew how to destroy the undead. And once they became mortal and had families whom they loved, they were determined to protect their families from evil. To keep the converted from destroying vampires, the elders—such as Cymon—chose to make the hunters and their descendents off-limits as prey. Any vampire who defies the rule is destroyed. A Varkyre who becomes a hunter loses the protection."

"So, you won't hunt."

"No. And you don't have to fear vampires." He groaned hungrily, climbing over her. "I want to make love to you, but I have to ask you a question first."

Curiosity heightened the deep green of her eyes. "Shoot."

"Are you certain about having children with me? Do you think your family will like me?"

"A charming, gorgeous millionaire? My mom and dad will adore you." Her smile was teasing, but tears welled. "And, yes, I want to have babies with you. We can make it work and be honest. Somehow."

"We can, love. I know it." He arched his hips to stroke her tummy with his cock. "Now can we make love?"

With a giggle Erin parted her legs to welcome him in, but when he sank into her to the hilt, she surprised him by frowning again.

"What's wrong, angel?"

Her fingertips gently traced along his cheek. "You have the most beautiful eyes. I've never seen such a gorgeous violet color. But, you know, in a way, I'm going to miss your sexy fangs."

Laughing, Michael lifted her legs gently and brought them up until her ankles rested on his shoulders. Then he made love to her, long and hard and wild, so she would know that some things never changed.

Night Pleasures

KATHLEEN DANTE

1

Alana ran headlong through the dark woods with supernatural swiftness, drawing on the tall oaks' green strength to speed her feet. Their sap was slow with the advent of winter and the New Year, but they lent her enough power to stay ahead of the simulacra at her tail.

Dry brush parted before her and snapped back into place behind her to block her unnatural pursuers, but the flimsy barriers wouldn't hold them for long. If she was caught, she doubted she could escape a second time, though the consequences didn't bear thinking about.

The shrill creaks of breaking rafters still filled her ears, loud with the memory of their destruction. Her beautiful cottage gone! She clutched her malachite brooch, its magical warmth an assurance that she still had it.

A large rock rolled into her path, fuzzy with torn moss. She leaped it, her thin sandals slapping against her heels, the ends of her ponytail lashing her back through her thin blouse. In her haste to escape the ruins of her home, she hadn't been able to grab a sweater.

The cool night breeze whipped hair across her damp face, caressed her nearly naked butt under her short skirt and her bare legs. She wasn't dressed for a dead run through the brush, but, then, she hadn't expected to be here. Despite the full moon, even wood mages avoided the groves on Samhain Night.

Alana ran on, desperately searching the shadows for an end to the trees. She must have covered more than a few miles already. How much farther to the Pleasure Quarter? She had to get there. It was the one place during Samhain where she might find safety. There, she knew the gardens, and they knew her. Out here, on this one night, Bryce had the upper hand.

As she ran on, bushes rustled and shook behind her. Wandering spirits or the simulacra still intent on her trail? A frisson of fear chilled her at the reminder. Bryce had turned to necromancy, used his earth magic to wrest souls from the spirit world to create simulacra. They wouldn't stop until they'd fulfilled his command to capture her.

White lights finally pierced the thin canopy. That had to be the Pleasure Quarter! Her heart lifted at the prospect of people around her. About to step out of the trees, Alana froze. A mob of púca spilled into the clearing, blocking her path, keening and chittering, their voices shrill with malice. If they saw her, she'd be lost for the rest of the night; worse, Bryce might be able to compel them to bring her to him.

Long, harrowing moments passed before the mob left. Alana waited some more to make sure the púca were gone, straining her ears for the sound of their presence and of pursuit. Her heart still pounding from the near disaster, she darted toward the beckoning lights just beyond a line of shrubbery.

The tall hedge of holly twisted at her touch, allowing her to reach the sidewalk without snagging on its spiny leaves. Past it, the Pleasure Quarter spread before her in all its raucous, brilliantly lit glory, its wide streets filled with boisterous throngs of merrymakers, promising safety.

She drew a deep breath of relief at the sight, her knees nearly turning to water, shaky after that long run.

But as the hedge sprang back to place, a simulacrum entered the moonlit clearing behind her. They were right at her tail! Fear held her motionless for a heartbeat. With all the sexual energy in the Pleasure Quarter, surely Bryce's simulacra wouldn't be able to enter? Fire magic countered earth. Light opposed darkness. Life versus death.

But she couldn't depend on that happening. If they weren't stopped, she had to lose them.

Alana threw herself into the crowds, hoping their life force would hide hers. Somehow she had to keep the brooch out of Bryce's hands. She couldn't let him win.

Leaning back in the leather recliner, Colin drank in the frenetic emotions in the air. Samhain Night was truly the best time to enjoy the Pleasure Quarter. On Samhain Night, all the rules of propriety were suspended, giving way to the most basic celebrations of life. The festival of sex to propitiate the gods and spirits walking the Earth encouraged amateurs to step up to the stage and bare all. The resulting excitement and pleasure made for a heady brew for fire mages.

Onstage, a particularly busty blonde was finishing her turn, slinking off her minuscule bikini to flash the men around her feet to a flourish of drumbeats. A cheer went up as she writhed playfully, making the most of her bountiful assets.

Putting down his glass, Colin added his claps to the applause. The healthy lust radiating from the floor was better than a straight shot of single malt whiskey. Raw power bubbled through him, rich and intoxicating, so full of fire and sheer audacity. A final charge to hold him through the dark of the New Year. He really didn't need anything stronger.

The next contestant, a tall brunette numbered twenty-seven in the line-up, was more to his taste. Leaning forward, he surveyed the athletic slenderness of long, long legs bared by a short skirt. And nary a knobby knee in sight, praise Belanus. She was— He caught sight of a gaudy brooch on her hip.

Alana! Her sable locks were gathered in a simple ponytail high at the back of her head, rather than the usual braids of womanhood. High color stained her alabaster cheeks. An emerald-green satin blouse clung to the gentle slopes of her breasts, deepening the hue of her eyes. The plaid skirt that displayed most of her lissome legs was quite unlike her usual khaki slacks. But that malachite brooch was unique, its baroque lines totally unmistakable.

It was Alana MacArdry standing on the stage.

Colin hadn't expected to see his lovely neighbor tonight, not when she had a steady lover to keep her occupied. He grinned, anticipating her performance. Normally, he wouldn't think of poaching on another man's preserve. But on Samhain Night, anything could happen: the pretty florist was fair game.

The music started over, hidden ceiling speakers piping out an aggressive sensual beat led by a baritone fiddle and supported by guitar, electric harp, and drums. Alana was apparently caught unawares, freezing for a heartbeat before she started moving her hips.

Colin frowned. The unease he sensed from her clashed with the excitement and pride of earlier contestants. If she hadn't wanted to strip onstage, why'd she sign up?

She looked over her audience, wide-eyed, her motions stiff. Stage fright, perhaps? Then she looked his way, and her high breasts rose visibly, her large jade-green eyes widening almost in entreaty.

Maybe all she needed was encouragement.

Taking a deep breath, Colin returned her gaze, imagining those long legs wrapped around his hips, squeezing him in her need, holding him close as he rode her to the heavens. A familiar fantasy after all these months, but his response to it remained unchanged. Heat shot through him, a blazing flame ardent enough to melt platinum. He sat back, allowing his desire to play across his face, showing her how much he wanted her.

Alana licked her lips, staring at him. She swayed in place, her muscles loosening, her nipples beading. Every move an invitation, like he'd fantasized over the past few months. Without looking away, she slowly ran her hands over her body, cupping her high breasts as though offering herself to him. She danced as if he were the only man in the room, so complete was her focus on him.

And damned if he didn't buy into the fantasy, the wolf whistles from the other men fading into the background. *Just you and me, darling.*

Stroking his fingers over his tight fly, Colin urged her on with a nod. He was rewarded by a flare of desire from Alana and a lessening of her dread. He settled back, gliding his palm over his hard-on, savoring the sweet ache. *Show me what you've got.*

Almost as though she'd heard his thought, Alana played with the snaps of her blouse, turning away then back as if undecided. She peeked at him over her shoulder as she ran a hand up her thigh and under her skirt, flipping it up to tease him with a quick glimpse of a pale rounded cheek and leaving an impression of bareness.

Shaking his head, Colin gave her a slow grin at that bit of sauciness, his cock twitching in approval. Obviously, she was hitting her stride.

When Alana turned around, two of her snaps were undone, the edges of her blouse revealing then concealing a narrow triangle of skin as she undulated to the music. The game seemed to fan the flames of her excitement, which sent a burst of raw power roaring through Colin.

He could taste it in his mouth, a nutty flavor that would go well with cream—her cream, in particular. He licked his lips, anticipating that moment. Tonight, he'd finally have her for real.

She did a few slow turns, her hips swirling in erotic mimicry, her breasts raising sharp peaks beneath the thin satin. The hem of her blouse flapped as she danced, rising and dipping with her motions. Each turn revealed another snap undone, until a triangular slash of pale skin ran to her waistband, baring a trim belly.

Colin stared at the rippling muscles, wondering how it would feel to brush his lips over their smoothness. He intended to find out. Tonight, there was no stopping him.

With a knowing smile on her full lips, Alana flirted with him, drawing aside a thin lapel just far enough to hint at pink flesh before restoring her modesty. Staring at him, she snuck a hand under the emerald fabric. Her eyes shuttered as she fondled herself, her lips parting as she swayed to the music. From the way the satin bunched and flowed, he could tell she was tweaking her nipple; the kiss of power he felt confirmed it.

His fingers twitched, wanting that privilege for himself. He glared at her in silent demand. *Take it off, damnit.* He dug his fingers into the arms of his seat, tempted to rend the satin shrouding her body, needing to see what he'd fantasized about for so long.

Alana finally flung it off, flaunting her high breasts, her ruby-red nipples playing peekaboo, half-hidden by her low, strapless bra. She played with the tight peaks, her reckless delight skipping like sizzling beads over Colin's senses.

She liked that, did she? He made a mental note to take his time teasing her nipples.

The bra apparently hindered her, since she doffed it soon after, then returned to her game. She stroked her body, drawing his gaze from her hard-tipped breasts, over her sculpted abdomen, down to her plaid-covered mound, her eyes closing as she gave herself over to sensation.

Colin hissed in a breath at the sensual picture she made. So natural in her hedonism. He wanted her exactly that way, on his bed, her dark hair spilled across his pillows, begging to be taken. Begging for him.

His cock jerked at the image, need blazing through him in a firestorm of lust. By the Son, he wanted her with an intensity that went bone-deep. He cupped his swollen shaft, copying the way Alana touched herself as she swung her hips, all carnal temptation wrapped in one slender form.

She released her skirt, allowing it to slide down. It caught at her high buttocks, as though reluctant to be parted from her, then slipped off as she rolled her hips. It left her standing in a minuscule excuse of a G-string that scarcely covered her pubes.

Staring, Colin swallowed with difficulty.

Bright Belanus, she was perfect. Just enough curves to save her from boyish coltishness and smooth out bony angles, but none of the plump voluptuousness or the pillowy cleavage a man could suffocate in.

While he watched, she traced the edge of the cloth, then up to the thin strap low over her hips. She turned around, flexing tight buttocks as she spread her cheeks and stroked the narrow fabric between them. A roar of encouragement nearly drowned out the drums when she made as if to take it off, her hand dipping the strap down, then pulling it up.

The music ended with Alana still undecided, her thumb hooked on the cord of her G-string. She blinked at the applause and renewed wolf whistles, a wave of color licking the alabaster slopes of her breasts up to her cheeks.

The noise came as a shock, snapping Colin out of their mutual fantasy world. He found he was relieved she hadn't stripped completely. He wanted his first time to see her nude to be in private.

Trying not to gasp for breath, Alana tugged her bra into place, then closed the snaps of her blouse. Her heart still pounded from the crowd's enthusiastic reception; not that it meant much, it being Samhain Night. There was so much sexual pheromone in the air that they'd probably applaud any woman who displayed even a little skin.

She twitched her skirt higher so it didn't pinch her, patting her brooch to confirm it was still pinned on. Thank Flidais she hadn't made a fool of herself onstage. If it hadn't been for that man with the russet hair, who looked so much like her jeweler neighbor, Colin Sheridan, she might have frozen during her turn.

She vowed to herself that when this was over, she'd look for that man, maybe take him up on his silent offer. After all, she'd been intrigued by the yummy Colin, who lived across the street from her shop, but had ignored the attraction out of loyalty to that earthworm Bryce. Colin might not have indicated any special interest in her, but his rougher-looking double here most definitely had. The scorching looks he'd sent her had her so aware of her body she hadn't dared strip completely lest she embarrass herself by revealing how wet he'd gotten her.

She shunted away wistful thoughts of triggering a spontaneous orgy; as delightful as it sounded, she didn't have time for that tonight. First, she had to catch her breath; then she had to move on.

Watching the next contestant onstage, she sipped tart pink punch to wet her parched throat, needing it after the long run through the woods and her performance. She blinked in admiration as the woman performed a salacious bump-and-grind, teasing the men at her feet with her heart-shaped fleece and a glimpse of pussy.

Wishing she could stay longer to pick up pointers, she eyed the corridor to the restrooms where—hopefully—there would be a service door she could sneak out through. She had to keep moving, to weave her psychic scent through the throngs so Bryce's simulacra couldn't find her.

2

The hairs on Alana's arms stood on end. One of Bryce's simulacra blocked the end of the narrow alley, unmoving, the ill-defined lines of its dark, loamy body unmistakable in the bright moonlight. It was alone, but that didn't mean anything.

Somehow, despite all her efforts, they knew she was here.

Backing up gingerly, she closed the door and locked it. Leaning her forehead on it, she tried to think of a way through the problem instead of just reacting blindly. All her nebulous plans refused to gel. How could she fight a simulacrum when hitting it didn't do any damage? She found herself circling back to her original solution: stay away from them.

Tiptoeing through the dark storeroom, Alana returned to the public area of the HardWood. She'd chosen it for its name, thinking it auspicious, but it didn't hurt that the strip bar was one of the busier—and therefore more potent—establishments in the Pleasure Quarter. But now it looked like she might be trapped there.

That infectious sexual music playing over the speakers flowed into the corridor as she approached the dance floor, a siren song urging her body to move and sway, to let loose and forget all her worries. If only she could.

Crowds of cocky revelers toasted her fellow amateurs mingling on the floor, who in turn encouraged even greater liberties. This late in the night, more than one table hosted groups venerating life through the ultimate primal ritual.

The moans of pleasure calling to the deities made her envious. She wished she could take part in the festivities, just as she'd had in previous years. After all these months of tepid sex, she'd planned on having an orgy. Except now she couldn't, not if she wanted to stay out of Bryce's hands.

That deprivation was one more grievance to be laid at that earthworm's door. Hardly fair, but after the way he'd duped her and played with her heart, she was in no mood for fairness.

Edging her way around preoccupied merrymakers, Alana headed for the front door. If she could just evade the simulacra until dawn, Bryce wouldn't be able to do anything. Once the sun rose, she could report him to the garda. She clung to that hope desperately, knowing she couldn't hold off Bryce by herself—not when he had five simulacra to aid him.

The boisterous crowd shifted, giving her a view of her destination.

Alana stopped in her tracks, a shiver of dread sending shards of ice through her veins.

Another simulacrum stood framed in the entry, just beyond the bouncer, rocking on its legs as though something was pushing it back while it attempted to move forward. The bouncer stood with his back carefully turned to the restless simulacrum. If it made to come in, he wouldn't stop it. On Samhain, when spirits walked, no one got in their way, especially when the spirit was obviously the product of illegal necromancy.

She scanned the floor for other exits. One led to the champagne rooms, another to dance rooms for customers who wanted privacy. Neither area had windows or an exit, and the door behind her led only to the restrooms, the back office, and the storeroom—which was not an option. That left only the stairs to the private rooms for those who wanted a bed and more time, but there was no other way down from there.

The simulacrum turned in her direction, all but facing her, as though it knew she was watching it.

To evade detection, she spun around, hoping to duck into one of the alcoves along the walls, and ran smack into a solid, leather-clad chest. Mobile, sensual lips filled her vision while large, hot hands caught her shoulders as she stumbled back, rebounding from the impact.

"Going somewhere?" A mellow tenor with the deep rumble of a hungry lion.

Her hands flat on hard, broad muscle, Alana stared up at the man who held her, unable to believe her eyes. It was the man who'd bolstered her nerve during her turn onstage, who'd encouraged her with a show of his desire, who'd openly caressed his erection in time to her dance.

Up close, it was obvious he was Colin, but a very different man from the sleek, clean-shaven jeweler she remembered. This Colin had the look of a dangerous hunting cat, dark cinnamon stubble giving him a roguish air. The way he stood, he seemed much larger, surrounding her with male heat, taking up more space than he should.

"Actually—"

Laughter rang out, reckless and somehow desperate. Revelers grew even wilder, their actions more blatantly sexual. The disturbance spreading out from the entrance reminded Alana of her danger. She was supposed to be hiding, not ogling men! She scanned the area on either side of her, but no other bolt-hole presented itself. She'd just have to improvise and hope she blended with the crowd.

"How about a lap dance?" Praying to Flidais that Colin

wouldn't object, she pushed him into the seat in the alcove and straddled his lap, her knees sinking into soft cushions. Her breath caught as the position dropped her silk-covered mound flush against a hard ridge.

Unabashed by his palpable arousal, he grinned, slow and sultry, the corner of his lips lifting in a sportive quirk. "Can I touch?" As he lay back, his yellowish-brown eyes glowed with a golden light, like an eagle sighting prey.

Heat bubbled up inside her at the intent look on his face. Could this really be happening? "Nothing too rough," she managed to answer around the tightness of her throat, unable to believe the sudden turn of events.

Almost before the words left her mouth, he took her buttocks in his hands, kneading and spreading them possessively, the motion rubbing her groin against his erection. His hard palms were hot on her bare cheeks, the contact branding her and sending shivers of awareness through her that tightened her nipples to aching buds. "Too rough?"

Catching her breath at the friction, Alana shook her head, releasing the snaps of her blouse while swaying to the music. "That's okay." The thrill that shot through her when she bared herself to him this time was even more potent, sending a spurt of heat trickling from her sex.

Making her body available. They both knew where this was leading, what had been offered and accepted. Even if nothing happened tonight, a boundary had been crossed, and there was no going back.

Humming along with the electric harp, she rubbed her cleavage against Colin, the suede of his jacket clinging to the tops of her breasts. His gaze was like live coal on her skin, searing her wherever it fell.

"Like what you see?" she whispered into his ear before sucking on his lobe and tonguing it, all the while wondering if

Bryce's simulacrum had entered the club. Would she have any warning, or would her first indication of its approach be the smell of cold swamp?

This close to Colin, Alana got a whiff of spicy cologne, something that called to mind fire and summer heat and male strength. A seductive scent. She wanted to wrap herself in it and hunker down, forget the world existed until Beltane and the return of growth in the forests.

"Bright Belanus, yes," he murmured against her breasts, his breath a warm caress, his stubble leaving tiny prickles on her sensitive skin. His callused hands wandered under her blouse, rough pads tracing her spine and the muscles of her back, then coming front to span her ribs, spreading shivers of awareness wherever they touched.

"Surely you can tell?" His narrow hips rose slowly, almost lazily, an unhurried flexure of his body that pressed his undeniable erection against her wet nether lips, yet nothing in his expression suggested any resentment at his carnal response. Only then did she realize Bryce considered sex a distraction to be handled with expediency.

Leaning back, she smiled at Colin, the knowledge of his easy acceptance of her feminine power almost heady enough to make her forget her danger. As she rose to her knees, a placket on his jacket snagged her bra, dragging it down and exposing all of her breasts. "Oh!"

Colin claimed them swiftly, his palms hot, hard, and rough, his thumbs flicking over her pouting nipples. He lifted them free of her bra, plumping them between his cupped hands and rubbing his bristly cheeks against them with an approving growl. "Lovely. Just lovely."

She shivered at the toe-curling sensation, closing her eyes when he plucked the tight tips, trapping them and rolling them between his fingers. Heat streaked down to her core, a flaming arrow that left burning embers in its path. Swift Flidais, he knew how to use his hands.

"Glad you like them." Raising her arms to give him better access to her breasts and burying her fingers in her hair, she rocked her hips over him, moving to the music. The pleasure coursing through her body seduced her, loosened her muscles to supple limberness. It coaxed her into caressing Colin's body with her own, using fluid, undulating strokes.

Fearful, choked-off shrieks behind her had Alana stiffening and stealing a glance in that direction. Above the crowd, she could just make out the dark head of a simulacrum. It was inside the club! Bryce was getting stronger if it could do that.

A sharp tweak on her nipple sent an arc of pure electricity crackling through her body to lash her creaming sex, wrenching her attention back to the man between her thighs.

He stared up at her, a frown knitting his level brows. "Surely you can do better than that?"

That reminded her: she was supposed to be giving him a lap dance as camouflage from the simulacrum's search, maybe even protection from its presence. Resolving to do better, she forced a smile in apology. "Sorry, I got distracted."

Pulling her ponytail over her shoulder, she fanned the ends along his neck, getting a thrill when the strands grazed her bare breasts and from how closely she skirted propriety by using her unbraided tresses this way. "Better?"

He hissed a breath as she feathered her hair over his skin in teasing strokes. "Naughty."

Too right. She wouldn't have dared on a normal day. "It's Samhain," she reminded him, leaning down to trail her hair over his belly and the bulge at his fly. "Live a little."

Colin reached down, recapturing her breasts, his tanned hands dark against her milk-white skin. "I intend to." He fondled her lightly, his touch like lightning to her senses—breathtaking and electric, raising wild sparks everywhere he touched.

Her nipples must have had a direct link to her core: even the slightest twitch of his thumbs showered glittering delight through her belly. Was he using fire magic on her? She wouldn't have thought it possible before, to be so thoroughly aroused with so little effort.

Bryce had never learned to do that in all their months together. Or maybe he simply hadn't bothered to learn.

Determined not to let thoughts of that earthworm ruin this stolen moment, she lunged forward in blatant mimicry of the act she wanted to share with Colin, stroking his swollen length with her crotch. She could feel him against her naked cheeks and nether lips, the silk covering her sex a barrier barely worth mention. The steady friction called more heat to her belly, heavy with promise.

She threw herself into the lap dance, hoping the gods in their approval would see fit to protect her from Bryce's simulacra. She undulated over Colin, running her fingers through his short hair while she used her entire body to pleasure him—and herself.

"Much, much better," he murmured, placing a hand on her hip as she rolled her pelvis, urging her lower until her sex was flush against his, no matter how she moved.

Alana's eyes fluttered shut at the delicious sensations as she gave vent to a soft, disbelieving moan. She could feel every jerk and twitch of his cock sliding against her wet labia, the roughness of his pants against her cheeks, the hard buttons of his fly pressing on her clit. By the Lady of the Forest, all that from a simple lap dance?

"Oh, yeah. That's it." Colin's breath warmed her neck, his stubble scraping her collarbone, then his lips closed on her shoulder. A hot, stinging counterpoint to the creamy sweetness between her legs and the downy suede of his jacket against her breasts. His fingers continued their delicate plucking and strumming, playing her body like a stringed instrument and making it hum.

Rolling her hips to his rhythm, she let her head fall back, losing herself in carnal hedonism, moaning when his hips rose to partner hers in their rocking, swaying dance. Swift Flidais, she didn't want it to end.

"Faster," he growled into her ear, his teeth nipping her lobe, only to soothe it with a gentle swipe of his tongue.

She cried out at the slight pain and moved faster, caught up in the rising spirals of breathless delight. His fierceness was like a fire licking at her heels and threatening to flare out of control.

His hands were firm on her hips, anchoring her against him, fondling her tight cheeks and laying them wide. His body worked beneath her, thrusting and rolling, his cock grinding against her mound and teasing her throbbing clit.

Pulling him closer, she rubbed her swollen breasts against his cheeks, getting another sizzle when his prickly jaw rasped a distended nipple.

What would it feel like if he used his stubble all over her body? A frisson of excitement washed over Alana at the thought. Perhaps she'd find out tonight.

"Bright Belanus!" Colin stared up at her, his glittering eyes narrow, his skin taut over his high cheekbones. Surging beneath her, he matched her lunges, move for move, so in tune with her body, as if he could read her mind.

His breath warmed her breasts, his chest a hard, broad wall she clung to in their wild dance. His body was tense, his thighs like solid oak against her calves. He'd come soon, would take his release from her attentions.

She wanted that for him, needed to see his golden eyes turn inward, dark with rapture. After the way he'd encouraged her tonight, she wanted to repay him with ecstasy. This wasn't about her pleasure.

Bending down, Alana stroked him with her breasts, wishing his jacket and the turtleneck he wore under it weren't in the way. If this night was all they'd have, she wanted to feel his bare chest against her own. She continued to roll her hips, relishing the jerks of his cock against her nether lips.

Colin groaned, his jaw set, a heavy flush across his cheeks, his lips red.

It would be soon. She could tell he was close to the edge.

A scream erupted behind her. She ignored it, intent on bringing Colin to completion. A simple lick of his ear might do it. Or a line of kisses along his neck? Maybe teasing him with her hair? He seemed to enjoy that game.

Another shriller—and much closer—scream shattered her concentration, made her falter.

Hissing, Colin shuddered under her, his hips shaking between her thighs like tree trunks battered by gale-force winds. His face contorted with grueling effort, hardly the look of a man in the throes of ecstasy—more of one dragging himself back from the edge.

The disturbance was spreading, shocked exclamations quickly hushed, coming closer. The chill scent of damp loam freshly turned reached Alana, heavy with danger. She gripped Colin's arms, fighting not to look over her shoulder toward the source of the scream.

"Expecting someone?" Colin's eyes narrowed; gold glinted through his lashes. "Or are you avoiding someone? Alcott, perhaps?" Despite the roughness of his voice, he looked remarkably lucid for someone who'd just stopped himself from coming through sheer willpower.

The questions added to the coldness inside her. How did he know? Was he in league with Bryce? Impossible. Bryce couldn't have known she would come to the HardWood; she hadn't known herself. But how did Colin guess? "In a way."

"You'll have to tell me about it." His gaze darted to something over her shoulder. "Later."

Giving in to the urge prickling the back of her neck, Alana checked behind her.

Just a few feet away stood one of Bryce's simulacra, a distinctly unnatural presence, moaning low and wordless, in the middle of the busy strip bar. Its malformed head swiveled in all directions as if searching for a scent, though it didn't seemed to notice her astraddle Colin's lap.

This close, she could make out coarse sand grains on its dark, humus-rich skin. Dried leaves stuck to its body while brown tufts of weeds dotted its shoulders and head. It stank of rot, the noxious stench of decaying plants and other things.

Its touch was slow death, leaching life from its victims.

She shook, unable to look away, praying to Flidais it would continue to ignore her. Lady of the Forest, let it pass her by.

"Shhh, it's okay." Colin pulled her head down into a kiss, his lips feathering over hers, sweet in their unexpected solicitude. His tongue tangled with hers in a teasing dance of enticement and conquest.

Alana tried to lose herself in his embrace but couldn't forget the simulacrum close by. She shivered, the skin on her back crawling at its proximity, certain it couldn't miss her.

He broke off the kiss suddenly, glaring up at someone behind her. "Leave us alone." If vehemence was all it took to command obedience, his scorching delivery would have routed a horde. But it wasn't a horde behind her.

By the time she'd twisted around, the simulacrum had a hand stretched out to her, reaching for her brooch. She flinched away from it in horror. "No!"

At her cry, Colin snatched up a glass and flung its contents at the simulacrum. Drawing her away with an arm around her back, he gestured with his free hand, his teeth bared in a fierce snarl.

Flames splashed on a sandy chest, catching on sere leaves and dead weeds. With a sudden *woof*, the simulacrum was engulfed in pale, blue-green fire like an enormous torch. Staggering back, it screamed—the uncanny wail of a soul in torment.

"Upstairs. Quickly, now! That won't hold it for long."

Alana found herself on her feet with Colin surging out of the recliner, the simulacrum howling behind her.

He dragged her with him to the stairs, his arm like a solid ironwood bar wrapped around her waist as he scaled the flight two steps at a time. "Why is it after you?"

"My brooch." Struggling to keep her feet under her, Alana clutched the piece, a prized memento of the great-grandfather who'd raised her. She couldn't lose it again.

At the top of the stairs, he released her. His eyes darted to the clenched fist at her hip as he shifted his hold to her free hand. "What for?" He pulled her along behind him, not waiting for an answer.

Bryce's treachery fresh in her mind, Alana wasn't sure she could trust Colin. She countered with her own question: "Where are we going?"

Colin threw her an impatient look over his shoulder. "One of the private rooms."

A frisson of excitement surged through her at his answer. She quashed a wild wish that they could use the room for the purpose it was meant.

Of course, one of the rentals—they were the only rooms on the upper level—but how would they escape from there? She bit her lip to hold in her questions, her heart still racing from Colin's use of fire magic and the mad dash up the steps. He had to have a plan; after his quick thinking with the simulacrum, they couldn't have come upstairs only to be trapped.

He led her down the corridor, past several occupied rooms, their footsteps barely audible on the wooden floor. Behind the doors came muffled groans and voices crying out in pleasure, along with rhythmic thumping from the walls.

"Is it safe?" Alana asked Colin's broad back. "He can move the earth. He did it to bring my house down." The memory of her little cottage collapsing around her turned her cold. She'd survived only because the heavy beams had contorted to protect her.

He shook his head, his hand squeezing hers reassuringly, warming more than just her palm. "This is the Pleasure Quarter. There's too much life around. He can't do that here, not even during Samhain."

He sounded so certain she wondered if he was blowing smoke. "How can you be sure?"

Colin flashed a thin smile at her, that golden predatory light back in his eyes as he took stock of her décolletage. "The Army trained me. I know what I'm talking about."

3

Wards sprang to life as Colin shut the door, a momentary flash of reassuring light that faded into the woodwork. Intended to ensure patrons' privacy, the wards should be able to temporarily stave off the chilling specter from his all-too-recent past. The wards would buy him time to find out what was going on.

But to do that, he had to soothe Alana, preferably with sex: bring her to orgasm as quickly and as often as possible. After her performance downstairs, he didn't think she'd object.

That it would have the added benefit of recouping the power he'd expended went without saying. If that stinking abomination was a sign of things to come, he'd need every bit of fire magic he could draw.

He backed her against the heavy door with indecent haste, the motion plumping up her pretty breasts above her displaced bra. Breasts he wanted to taste and suck, but doing so wouldn't get him the rapid recharge he needed. And right now that had top priority.

"I can't wait," Colin growled, hurrying to release the buttons of his fly. Freed from his pants' constraints, his cock thrust out, thick and florid, its round head wet with pre-come and aching to the high heavens.

He wouldn't last long the first time, not after the way she'd swirled her pussy all over him during that lap dance. He'd already backed off once; he didn't think he could do it a second time, not with his climax condensing in his tight balls.

Thankfully, Alana seemed just as impatient. "Don't wait," she insisted, pulling his head down for a searing kiss, yielding her mouth to his exploration. Sweet.

Grabbing the panel of her G-string, Colin pulled it aside, his knuckles grinding against her slick pussy. The fabric tore like wet tissue, leaving her open to him.

Gasping, Alana arched her body, driving her flesh onto his fist, the power from her delight refreshing to his magic sense. She hooked a leg around his hip, anchoring her heel on the back of his thigh.

He dipped a finger into her, testing her readiness and finding her melting with welcome, her pussy soft and clinging. A deeper thrust got him a throaty moan, replete with desire and warm, vibrant energy.

"Colin! Take me!"

He aimed his cock, gritting his teeth when the sensitive head brushed her creamy, pink lips. A quick lunge seated him to the hilt, enfolded him in warm, willing woman. Bright Belanus, she held him like a snug velvet glove, squeezing gently. It was almost enough to distract him from the blast of excitement his action provoked in her.

Catching her ass with both hands, he raised her to get a better angle on her clit. Two solid thrusts, and his control burst like a flooded dam, molten pleasure boiling up from his balls and shooting up his spine.

Alana convulsed around him, quick rhythmic pulses that caressed his cock in flowing, mind-rolling waves. Another rush of power and pleasure blew through him, trailed by her breathless scream. Praise Belanus!

He continued pumping her, hoping to make up for the bad impression he'd made with his short fuse. Though it was Samhain, he had hopes of convincing her to see him during more normal conditions. He was rewarded by a gentler surge of energy and a long, low moan as her pussy spasmed around him once more.

Panting, Colin dropped his forehead to the door, pillowing himself on Alana's soft breasts, confident that he hadn't left her wanting.

It hadn't been enough to replace all the power he'd expended downstairs, but it was a start. Hopefully, he'd have a few hours to make up the difference and absorb more. He'd need it if he was going to neutralize the threat to Alana.

Trapped between solid oak and Colin's hard body, Alana didn't have any breath left to complain. Not that she would have; her attention was fixed completely on the tremors that continued to shatter her core.

As another surge of pleasure rolled through her, it occurred to her to wonder if his performance was normal, and not a special effort for Samhain. If she hadn't been so blind to that earthworm's machinations, she could have had this sooner.

When the aftershocks passed, he pulled out of her gently, his flaccid cock dragging sweetly on her inner membranes. "Sorry about that."

"Hmmm?" Alana forced her eyes open, bemused by his comment. Her legs felt like they were permanently locked around his hips, disinclined as they were to release their grip. Maybe she could spend the rest of the night in this position?

"I didn't mean to tear your panty."

Oh. That. She found she couldn't muster any outrage for the damage wreaked, counting it well worth the cost. "'Sokay."

He cradled her against his chest, the downy suede of his jacket teasing her softening nipples with every breath he took. "I'll last longer next time."

With that tantalizing promise, Colin carried her to the bed, a simple affair comprising a large mattress, fat pillows, and clean sheets. He set her on it, and she finally had to release him, unhooking her uncooperative legs gingerly. When he stripped down to bare skin, she left on her blouse but took off her bra, not wanting to appear unfriendly but unwilling to get naked when Bryce's simulacra were still hunting her.

He stretched out on his side beside her without commenting on her dress, propping his head on his fist—a pose that made his biceps bunch attractively. Beneath the leather jacket and black turtleneck, he was all lean and muscled male with a light fan of cinnamon hair on his chest that trailed down his flat belly to a thicket around his cock. His strong legs were similarly dusted with hair.

"Now, what's going on?" The lambent gaze he directed at her demanded she make a clean breast of everything. "Why's Alcott after your brooch? And how's he involved in necromancy?"

At his question, Alana reached down to grasp her lucky piece, rubbing her thumb over the smooth whorls of the green center stone, uncertain how much to reveal. Colin had helped her escape Bryce's simulacra, but after how easily that earthworm had duped her, she couldn't be certain her neighbor didn't have an ulterior motive of his own.

He placed his other hand on top of hers. Rough yet gentle, powerful yet protective. She wished she could trust her impressions of him.

"How can I help if I don't know what's wrong?" He leaned forward to press firm lips and a bristly chin on her shoulder, left bare by her open blouse.

She shivered with awareness, wondering if he was trying to

distract her. It would be so easy for him to take her brooch: a quick snatch and all her wood magic would be useless.

Colin smiled against her skin, his lips a smooth contrast to his chin. "Take your time. Alcott can't get to us just yet."

His mouth started to wander down, meandering to the tops of her breasts, dispensing licks and kisses amidst prickles. He spiraled around one mound, circling around and around, each kiss and lick just a little closer to her nipple.

Alana swallowed a moan at his slow progress, her attention focused on the bud straining for contact—the slightest graze, the merest of caresses. She caught his head, her fingers raking the short, smooth strands of his hair as she urged him closer, but he made her wait, stretching out the moment.

So long as he didn't make any move toward her brooch, she didn't have to worry so much.

"You're a tease. You know that, don't you?" Giving in to temptation, she allowed her hand to explore his broad shoulders, wondering why a jeweler had such well-developed muscles. The army training he mentioned? Jewelry work didn't seem the type to involve heavy labor.

He laughed softly, his breath a faint stirring of air that warmed her skin. "Good things come to those who wait. Besides," he bestowed a quick, unexpected lick on her other nipple that sent a sharp thrill through her, "you can't say you aren't enjoying it."

He returned to the breast he'd been teasing for the past several minutes, finally reaching her areola. Then he carefully traced its border with his tongue—still not touching the pouting nipple!

"Demon wretch!"

Smiling down at her, Colin fondled her other breast, tweaking its nipple to similar aching tightness. "You'll have to bear with me. I've been wanting to do this all night, ever since you flashed these pretties at me."

Alana made a doubtful face at his words. Many of the other contestants had bigger and better. Just then, he finally took her nipple into his mouth, and her objections fled her mind.

Heat enveloped her body, radiating from her breast to sear the very tips of her curling toes. Along the way, it kindled a fresh blaze in her core, a crackling fire lively with delight. How could she want him so much so soon after the last time?

He wielded his tongue like a whip, lashing her with electric thrills while his stubble prickled her tender mound. Glory to Flidais! He suckled on her, devastating in his sensual sorcery, devoting long, breathtaking moments to tormenting her sensitive bud while his hands explored her body.

Golden lights flashed around her in time to his hard suction, shimmering sparks that gilded the walls with splendor.

Pure lightning streaked through her, crackling with erotic power and leaving tingling pleasure in its wake. Helpless to resist, Alana arched her back in response, clinging to Colin as she offered her swelling breasts to his lips, craving more of his loving care.

He transferred his attentions to her other mound, licking its neglected tip with enthralling solicitude, unstinting in his carnal attentions. He took it into his mouth, applying strong pressure as he swirled his tongue over the aching nub.

Writhing, Alana moaned as his lips sparked another flash of carnal delight that sizzled through her veins and seared her core. Lady of the Forest! How could he know how much she loved having her nipples sucked?

Colin laved them, his hands fondling her with masterful skill. "By the Son, I love your breasts."

Alana mewled as another sparkle of sensation fizzed through her, setting off fireworks at every nerve. She loved what he could do with his lips on her breasts.

He devoted endless breathtaking minutes on her bosom,

wresting cries of bliss from her, showered her with so much pleasure all thoughts of the simulacra hunting her faded—lost in a haze of satisfaction.

His hard hands traversed her belly, then his lips followed, laying a line of prickly kisses down her torso. He nibbled on her stomach, the ticklish sensation making her laugh. Then she gasped as a wet tongue darted into her navel, teasing the sensitive skin.

"Do that again," Colin urged, his tenor rough with arousal.

"Do what?" Alana barely had wits to think, much less talk.

"Laugh," he ordered, his stubble grazing her belly as he scattered titillating licks and caresses over it, sending shivers of awareness up her spine.

Despite the heat pooling in her core and the cream flooding her sex, she couldn't restrain her giggles. He seemed to take unusual delight in lavishing butterfly kisses on her stomach for no reason she could see.

His hand continued below her waist, trailing heat from every finger. She squirmed, welcoming its descent, wishing he'd move faster. She parted her legs, needing his touch on her hungry sex.

Colin slipped his hand under her skirt, coming to rest on her mound. He stroked her once, then stilled, his palm like a burning brand where it rested on her bare flesh. "Oho!"

Bracing her feet on the mattress, Alana lifted her hips to press herself against his hand impatiently, wondering at his exclamation. What could be so important that he'd stopped?

Flipping up her skirt and the torn panel of her panty, Colin turned back to investigate the smoothness beneath his palm. Alana's pussy was naked, completely shorn of modesty, leaving her pink lips bare to his gaze. He slid down the bed for a better view, spreading her thighs to make space for himself.

Fine like alabaster from the very top of her notch, all the

way through to her round, firm buttocks. Totally, brazenly shorn, with not a curl left to distract him from her flowering sex. Just pure, unembellished woman.

"This is a surprise."

He traced her tender petals and parted them. So smooth and pink and creamy. He breathed in her sweet musk calling to him, nectar for the gods. It definitely was a good thing she hadn't stripped completely for the contest. Something like this was best unveiled in private, given a connoisseur's attention.

"Like it?" She arched her back, spreading her legs wider, lifting her pussy in wanton offering, her clit standing at proud attention.

"What do you think?" Unable to resist any longer, he licked her glistening flesh, taking his time to savor her taste. "Ummm, better than crème brûlée."

Alana snickered at his description, a sound that was cut off when he swirled his tongue over her impertinent clit; then her breath hitched, a delightful sob of gratification that was matched by an equally delightful burst of vibrant power. Ha! Given her responsiveness, he'd have his magical reserves recharged in less time than he'd expected.

She caught his head, pulling him closer, her short nails digging into his scalp. Her long legs wrapped around his back, her heels snug against his shoulder blades as she held him in place.

Obedient to her urging, he lapped her sweetness with a will, the heady scent of her pleasure mingling with her own uniquely feminine perfume. The exquisite smoothness of her bare lips slid over his tongue like so much almond jelly.

He wouldn't mind doing this for hours; in fact, he could do this all night. Not that they had all night but hopefully long enough for him to soothe the ball of suspicion Alana harbored, so she'd confide in him. And perhaps long enough that he'd absorb ample energy to take on Alcott and win.

He couldn't forget that she had a simulacrum dogging her

heels. That bit of illegal necromancy was just a minuscule step from death magic. If Alcott was reaving souls from their rightful reward, how much longer before he took to stealing power from the living?

A husky purr of delight recalled him to the pleasures at hand. Beneath him, Alana writhed in voluptuous enjoyment, her pale body flushed in honest arousal, her dark pink nipples stabbing the air. The tension in her was more sexual now, the fear and distrust he'd sensed earlier leaking away with each surge of gratification.

He caught her clit between his lips, nibbling gently as he ground his face into her wonderfully smooth pussy. She screamed hoarsely, a shout of such joyous disbelief that he added a deep hum to his courtesies, making sure she felt it. The subsequent rush of power blew through him in a firestorm of tingling energy, raising the hairs on his arms and taking his breath away.

He'd bet that necromancer had never given her that much pleasure in all their months together. He grinned to himself in self-satisfaction. The flaming idiot. That boded well for any confrontation between them.

A wave of yellow flickers lit up the walls almost as though protesting his thought. Alcott was testing the wards again. Not that it would do him any good just yet. Alana was beyond the bastard's reach for the moment and enjoying herself.

Her fingers tightened on his hair as she came in a gush of hot sweetness that flooded his tongue. He screwed a finger into her depths, coaxing more cream from her welcoming flesh as he licked and teased her swollen lips. Definitely enjoying herself.

Colin basked in her rapture, her desire like a glowing furnace filling him with vibrant power—power he needed to take on a simulacrum. But that was for later.

His cock twitched with renewed interest, ready for another bout, but not quite yet. He didn't mind prolonging the wait, not when his partner was as responsive as Alana. This was his chance to make up for his initial haste, to change whatever bad impression his ham-handed first time might have made.

He thrust another finger deep into her, smiling as her muscles clasped him eagerly. He pumped her slowly, noting which twists and strokes elicited a groan of approval, learning what pleased her most. By the Son, she was so sensual, full of pent-up desire, tinder for the bonfire. She was giving him this much energy, and he wasn't even pounding into her yet!

"Faster," Alana demanded in her husky contralto that never failed to make him hard, a voice that had haunted his dreams for months on end.

His cock came to aching attention the way it always did whenever he heard her, a reflexive reaction he couldn't control. He gave her faster, lapping up the cream from her pink lips, teasing her clit with his tongue and chin. Reaching up, he tweaked her nipples, remembering how much she enjoyed that.

She mewled in delighted welcome, accepting his caresses with a breathless eagerness that spoke of deprivation. Alcott must have been a niggardly lover to have left her wanting.

The more Colin learned about the necromancer, the more he looked forward to showing him the error of his ways.

He lavished pleasure on Alana, reining in his hunger to bring her to ecstasy with his hands and mouth as many times as he could while his body recouped its strength. Not exactly a selfless undertaking, since each orgasm flooded his enervated senses with added vigor. But the flashes of light dancing on the walls warned he had to make the most of it.

Arching nearly off the bed, Alana came with another gush of sweetness, her fingers biting into his shoulders, celebrating her rapture with another husky, wordless scream of exultation. She gave extravagantly of her pleasure, the swift rush of heady power she radiated bringing him to rampant, swollen readiness.

Savoring her enjoyment, he strung out her transport, encouraging the aftershocks that convulsed her eager pussy in fluttering waves and sent fire magic roaring through his veins. Rarely had he had a more responsive partner; he wasn't about to end their play any time soon. Not when he needed every erg of life energy for the coming battle, and his reserves could still take much more.

Moaning, Alana writhed against the pillows, craving more of Colin, wanting him filling her. But with that last orgasm, her urgency was less, her hunger temporarily sated. Now she could think of other things, like running her hands over his hard body. Samhain might be the only chance she had to do so.

"Wait. I want to see you." Her voice sounded oddly hoarse, her throat raw from all her vocality.

Colin levered himself off her, his forearms braced on either side of her hips. "Look your fill." He grinned, licking his wet lips, her juices smeared across his mouth and stubbled chin. "I'm not hiding anything."

She ignored the obvious reference to his naked state and her lack of the same. "Lie down, then."

Grinning, he complied without demur, stretching out on the bed and clasping his hands behind his head, throwing his pectorals into prominence. He displayed the same confidence that had caught her eye last Beltane when he'd first opened his shop. She hadn't been able to pinpoint what about him attracted her attention back then, but now she knew: it was his carriage, that absolute confidence in the way he bore himself and now allowed her to look her fill.

Sitting up, she smiled, taking pleasure in Colin's nudity and his unabashed arousal.

He was lean yet well-built, with none of the obvious beefiness of burly men—so different from Bryce. She'd never suspected this was what hid beneath the businesslike shirts of her jeweler neighbor, never noticed just how wide his shoulders were. What else had she missed?

He was Bryce's opposite in almost every way: from his easy tenor to his lean physique, the elegant line of his jaw—now shadowed with stubble—and straight, sharp nose to the smooth russet hair and the light, unbroken tan of his skin. Even the soft dusting of hair on his chest.

She couldn't resist putting her hands on him, needing to replace the lackluster memories of Bryce's lovemaking with those of Colin's fiery expertise.

His muscles rippled under her palms, his belly a warm board of resilient cobbles. A remainder of his stint with the Army, perhaps? Bending down, she rubbed her cheek along the faint arrow of soft hair pointing south, bisecting his chiseled abs, mindful of its guidance. She rejoiced in the differences between the two men, grateful that Colin was so much more.

Her ponytail spilled over her face, blocking her view of her destination. Impatient with the interruption, she tossed her head, sending her hair back over her shoulder.

The motion unveiled his straining cock, its round head thick and ready. She skirted his sex, blowing on his shaft as she passed it on her way to his furry balls. She nuzzled them gently, delighting in their size. Down here his summer scent was much stronger.

Colin caught her head, fiddled with something at the back. "If you're going to do that, I want this off." He held out the silver twist she used to put up her ponytail as her hair cascaded across her shoulders and down her back.

His eyes widened, probably recognizing the piece; she'd bought it from his shop during the festival sale last Lughnasadh. "You have good taste." His grin was full of devilment as he laid the clasp by the pillows.

"I wish." If her judgment was so good, Bryce wouldn't have duped her that easily. Maybe she wouldn't have waited so long to act on her attraction to Colin.

"Sorry, I didn't mean to distract you." He ran his fingers

through her hair daringly, fanning them across her shoulders, then settled back on the mattress. "Please, proceed with what you were doing."

His nonchalant offer was so courteous Alana felt driven to shake him. Spurred on by an imp of mischief, she dipped her head, licking the length of his cock like a piece of hard candy, nibbling and sucking up and down his shaft.

She was rewarded by a sharp intake of breath and a low groan; then Colin buried his hands in her hair and pulled her closer. "Bright Belanus, yes!"

Gratified by his reaction, she redoubled her efforts, stroking his thick sex with both hands and taking his head between her lips. She licked and swirled her tongue over him, drew fanciful patterns on his velvety flesh.

He only grew harder. Thicker. Seeping a salty sweetness that called to her, enticed her to take him deeper.

Now it was his turn to surrender to pleasure, and she found the prospect entirely agreeable. Bryce always treated sex like an itch to be scratched, a problem to be dealt with quickly with as little fuss as possible. Colin's voluptuary approach made his lovemaking a celebration of the senses, and he was a feast she intended to enjoy.

His cock jerked against her lips, warm and resilient. Living steel sheathed in silk and velvet. She pressed her mouth on him, nibbling his length with delicate care, laughing when he called to Belanus for strength.

"It's a ruthless woman, you are," he chided as she brushed her lips lightly over his plum-like head. He suffered her un-practiced attentions with gratifying zest, groaning with every stroke of her tongue.

His hungry growl when she took him deep into her mouth sent shivers up her spine, knowing she was teasing a predator and would soon reap the consequences. She creamed at the thought of his prodigious control snapping, anticipating the fury of his lovemaking.

Alana sucked hard on his cock, fondling his balls with one hand and his shaft with the other, trying to hasten his outburst. With all the time he'd spent pleasuring her, surely he couldn't last much longer.

It happened suddenly with only the abrupt tightening of Colin's butt cheeks to warn her. He sat up, jerking her into his arms and tumbling her onto her back in one fluid motion.

Before she could even gasp, he had her legs hooked over his shoulders. He buried himself inside her with a sharp thrust that stretched her swollen inner membranes with delightful force, his thick cock delving deep into her yielding flesh and settling snug against her core. He pounded her, his hips pistoning in a fast, relentless rhythm that didn't slack even when rapture burst through her in a precipitate outpouring of delight.

He swept her higher, driving her up the heights of pleasure, merciless in his passion, his gaze turned inward as he pumped her, focused on some unseen goal.

Moaning, Alana clawed the bed as savage need coiled once more in her belly, cream gushing as Colin slammed into her. Peak after glorious peak fell away beneath her in rapturous splendor, each more breathtaking than the previous one. Lights flashed before her eyes, scintillating and golden.

"Yes! Give me more!" He urged her onward, inciting her with hands and mouth and tongue, his cock's mind-blowing friction fueling a firestorm that rampaged through her senses. Each hard thrust fanned the flames engulfing her body, stoked her burning thirst for more.

She came with explosive force, one that overshadowed her previous orgasms and catapulted her screaming into the star-spangled heavens. She soared weightless, borne by a towering wave of rapture strengthened by renewed surges of ecstasy that buoyed her ever higher.

Colin jerked in her arms, roaring his release as he continued pumping her, drawing out the climax. The raw pleasure lasted for endless moments, overwhelming her nerves with sheer sensation, before tumbling her onto a gentle shore.

Replete, she lay panting beneath her virile blanket, boneless with carnal languor. Unbelievable. She'd never dreamed so much pleasure was possible. If she didn't have to move until Beltane, it would still be too soon.

"So, why's Alcott after your brooch?" The question floated through Alana's euphoria, idle and unthreatening. A simple query with an equally simple answer.

She responded without thinking, all caution held at bay by satiation. "He wants to use it to summon Papa Dare."

The male heat covering her slipped to one side, then snuggled her against a broad, firm chest. "Who?"

"My great-grandfather, Adair MacArdy. It was his brooch." Memories of Papa Dare flashed before her mind's eye. He'd raised her after her parents and grandparents had died in a plane crash, had taught her how to use her wood magic and to amplify it using the brooch. He'd led her through her grief and wrestled with the problems of female adolescence. He'd stayed until he was sure she would be all right. Then he'd given her his brooch, the secret of his long life, the reason behind the wild success of her business, and had passed on after one hundred and twelve years.

Alana blinked back tears at the reminder of her loss.

"Summon him for what?" Gentle hands stroked her belly, a rhythmic back-and-forth that soothed her distress.

"Bryce thinks it's part of some treasure Papa Dare had, so he stole my brooch. He'll use it to enslave Papa Dare, make a simulacrum of him and force him to reveal the location of his treasure." The discussion reminded her of what waited beyond the wards. She groped for her brooch, relaxing only when its magical warmth enfolded her.

"Is it? Part of the treasure, I mean." There was no change in the rhythm of Colin's strokes, nothing but absent interest in his voice.

She sighed. "I don't know. Maybe." Certainly, there were hints aplenty from Papa Dare's stories.

"How does Alcott know about the treasure?"

"He found a ring." Bryce had brandished it at her, so sure she could do nothing against him. "Somehow he connected it to Papa Dare. And from him to me," she finished in a whisper. The glee on the earthworm's face when he'd admitted he'd sought her out merely to steal her brooch was still stark in her memory.

How could she have been so blind? Bryce had never wanted her. No wonder he'd barely made an effort at pleasuring her during sex. To think she'd hoped things would improve. That this Samhain would add a spark to their lovemaking. She bit her lip, remembering her excitement that morning when she'd shaved her nether lips. What an idiot she'd been!

"Is there anything to eat?" Alana suddenly realized she was famished. She couldn't remember when she last ate.

"Just soul cakes." Colin used his chin to gesture toward the foot of the bed.

Of course. The traditional bannocks were spread out on the window seat beside a basket filled with brown bottles of ale. Alana left the bed to get one, strangely grateful for her skirt and blouse as she forced her shaky legs to carry her to the window. She ran her fingers though her hair to give them something to do, the brush of her unbound tresses along her back sending a thrill up her spine.

The oat bread was chewy and sweetened with honey for energy to help lovers last through the long night. She consumed it eagerly, conscious of her latest exertions. The delicious ache between her damp thighs wouldn't let her forget.

"Want some?"

Colin lounged on the bed, his arms folded behind his head, one leg bent at the knee with its foot flat on the mattress, his soft cock in its nest of curls exposed to her gaze—completely unabashed by his nudity. And why should he be? He was clearly an excellent example of the male of the species. "Please. An ale would be good, too, if you don't mind."

Holding her bannock between her lips, Alana twisted off the cap of one bottle, then handed him his brew and a soul cake. "Why upstairs?" she blurted out after taking a mouthful of oat bread, asking the question that had been nagging her.

He took his time quaffing ale, the strong column of his throat working steadily as he drank. "It was the nearest haven. Simulacra are fast, faster than most people. We wouldn't have made it out the door even with my distraction, so upstairs was the only option." He bit into his bannock before continuing. "It helps that it's above ground. In most cases, simulacra have to maintain contact with earth or stone. If the HardWood used brick in its construction, for example, we'd already be in trouble."

About to sip from her own bottle, Alana paused. "Most cases? There are exceptions?"

Colin gave her a tight smile from behind the soul cake. "Samhain—the time when spirits walk freely. If the necromancer is strong enough, he can force a simulacrum off the ground even if it doesn't have any contact with stone."

She stared at him in horror, the oat bread like sawdust in her mouth. "Then—"

He shook his head. "Not yet. Alcott's barely stressed the wards. But maybe. Eventually."

"So we're trapped here?"

"Not hardly!" Colin retorted immediately, his tone almost indignant. The quickness of his reply reassured her of his sincerity.

Alana searched the room for another exit, but only the window presented itself. "The window?" she asked incredulously. They were more than twenty feet up because this side of the building had three stories, counting the ground-level pub in the HardWood's basement.

"Uh-hmm." He raised his bottle in the affirmative.

She drank some ale and finished another bannock while she considered his answer and the confidence implicit in his casual delivery. "There's no ledge."

"No problem." Thumping the mattress, he brushed crumbs off the sheet, then patted the bed in invitation and set his empty bottle on the floor.

Nonplussed by his assertion, she walked across the room, fully conscious of his warm, admiring gaze sweeping her body, and sat down where he'd indicated, wondering how he intended to escape.

Colin wrapped an arm around her waist as he settled back on the pillows and urged her down beside him. "He didn't just give it back to you." He returned to his original topic as though there hadn't been a long break in their conversation.

Alana went still at his statement but couldn't pretend to misunderstand. Smiling grimly, she gave a careless shrug. "When I realized he was the one who took it, I stole it back."

He laughed softly, his arms closing around her as he spooned her against his chest. He held her that way for several heartbeats in restful silence.

"Would it work, do you think?"

She stiffened at his question, his reassuring embrace suddenly feeling constrictive. Why'd he ask that now?

"Maybe," Alana answered cautiously. "Papa Dare had it forever. There's bound to be a resonance."

"Then unless you break its link to your great-grandfather, there'll always be a chance Alcott will succeed." His voice was calm—logical and dispassionate—as though he didn't have any stake in the matter.

She twisted around in his arms, needing to see his expression. "What do you mean by 'break its link'?"

He met her gaze steadily, his face revealing nothing untoward. "Rework it so it can't be used to summon your great-grandfather."

Alana clutched the big brooch, its rounded metal edges biting into her palm. "Rework it?" Her voice broke at his suggestion. Lose her most cherished memento of Papa Dare, never mind the magic that allowed her to tend to the gardens in the Pleasure Quarter?

"I could do it," Colin was quick to offer.

She bit her lip. Was it all a ploy to get his hands on the brooch? Dared she trust him? He seemed to have her best interests at heart, seeing how he'd helped her elude Bryce's simulacrum. But she wouldn't have thought Bryce could turn to necromancy, so her judgment wasn't all that reliable.

"I can't risk it."

Leaning back into the pillows, Colin blinked at the non sequitur. Risk what? Him reworking the brooch? He wasn't as bad as all that! In fact, he prided himself in his craftsmanship.

He kicked himself at his ego. Alana's doubts didn't seem based on his skills—or lack thereof. He speared his fingers through his hair, at a loss for another answer.

"The simplest solution is to destroy it. It lacks elegance, but it'd be over quickly." It galled him to make the suggestion, the artist in him horrified by the prospect, although the trained soldier knew it was the most expedient solution. "It would cut the link between it and your great-grandfather."

Alana was shaking her head even before he finished speaking, her lips set in absolute rejection. But, then, he hadn't thought she'd actually consider it.

Colin frowned inwardly. If he couldn't convince her to let him rework the brooch, he'd need every erg of power he could get to protect her from Alcott and his simulacrum.

Just then, the walls flashed, another sudden ripple of yellow light that was there and then gone. He'd noticed it happening earlier, while he'd been making love to Alana, but now it was happening more frequently.

"What was that?" She grabbed his arm, staring at the wood panels as though expecting a simulacrum to emerge from the blank walls or break through the door.

"The wards," Colin bit out tersely, rubbing the back of her hand. "Alcott's attacking them." There was no danger of them failing any time soon, but one thing the necromancer had was time. With midnight still approaching, every minute that passed increased Alcott's access to power.

Her grip tightened, her knuckles turning white as her short nails bit into his skin. "What do we do?"

"For the moment? Just stay here. It's still some hours to midnight. He's going to get stronger." While Colin got weaker, save for the energy he was drawing from the festivities. "Facing him down now would be a losing proposition."

Of course, if the confrontation went down here in the Pleasure Quarter, Colin could tap the emotion in the air to boost his fire magic, but that would put civilians at risk. He didn't even want to consider what would happen if someone was killed: the boost to Alcott's power would be enough to give the fool an addiction to death magic. From what he'd heard, it was that potent.

Best to distract Alana and gather what power he could. Fretting wouldn't change their situation.

She moaned when he licked behind her ear, his restless hands gliding all over the smooth expanse of her welcoming body. "So we're just going to lie here while Bryce gets stronger?" The desire and delight coming from her told him she wasn't adverse to his attentions.

Colin caught her soft lips, his stubble rasping against her jaw. "We're not just lying around," he informed her between deep, torrid kisses. "We're charging up . . . or, at least, I am."

4

Another wave of light flickered over the walls—still mostly yellow flashes, not that Colin expected that to last. They'd been coming more often in the past hour, sometimes with barely a pause between attacks. Alcott had to be nearby to sustain such an effort, even with midnight approaching.

Colin gritted his teeth, pulling Alana closer, his protective, possessive instincts demanding he keep her safe. But even as flush with power as he was from all the life energy tonight, he couldn't deny the season: Samhain would boost Alcott's power. With summer over, Colin's fire element was on the wane—and thus the power he drew from it. In a face-off with the earth mage, Colin would be at a disadvantage. Add the simulacrum downstairs, and his chances of winning declined to suboptimal levels.

They had to even out the odds.

Alana stirred, twisting in his arms to face him. "What are you thinking?"

He had to drag his thoughts from the pretty sight her new

position afforded him. "Alcott will get through within an hour or two. How were you planning on handling him?"

"I—" She shrugged, a careless movement that drew his gaze to her pale shoulder and skin so fine he could see the blue lines of her veins. "Just stay ahead. Keep Papa Dare's brooch out of his hands."

"And then?"

"After dawn, report him to the garda." After the lawless period of Samhain ended, she meant. Evidently she hadn't thought beyond filing a report.

"And tell them what?"

Sitting up, Alana stared at him as if the answer was obvious. Her hand closed around her brooch as that damned knot of suspicion in her flared. "That he's using necromancy!"

Colin pushed on, needing to make her recognize the difficulties ahead. "With what proof?"

"I—" She closed her mouth, sucking on her bottom lip as she took in what he was saying. Her thumb rubbed the malachite stone of her brooch, a habit of hers when lost in thought. He'd seen her do it often enough in the months he'd been her neighbor.

"Who else has seen him using necromancy? I haven't," Colin pointed out, pushing himself upright so he wouldn't be at a disadvantage. "It will be your word against his."

"But the simulacrum downstairs! People saw it."

He held her gaze, trying to communicate his seriousness. "There are hundreds of earth mages in the city. Any of them could have done it. Even if the garda found a simulacrum, there's no way to tie it to Alcott."

Her breath hitched. "You're right. They can't arrest him on my say-so." Despair and frustration spilled out from Alana as her eyes watered. "That's it? Bryce wins?"

Colin pulled her into his arms, cursing his bluntness. "No.

But so long as the brooch exists, Alcott can get his hands on it. If not tonight, there's always next Samhain."

Blinking away her tears, she pressed her clenched fists to his chest, keeping some distance between herself and Colin. "You think destroying Papa Dare's brooch is the solution." She stared at him in demand, her jade-green eyes unflinching. "Don't you?"

He met her gaze steadily. "Breaking the link is a permanent fix. Going to the garda, evading the simulacrum—"

"Simulacra," Alana interrupted. "There are five of them."

Damn. He couldn't handle more than one by himself. They'd have to get to his shop if they were to have any chance at all of defeating Alcott. But going up against five of those abominations made things much more difficult.

Frowning at their blighted prospects, Colin continued with a nod of acknowledgement: "—evading the simulacra, safeguarding your brooch, those are all temporary measures. To eliminate the risk of a necromancer summoning your great-grandfather, we have to cut his ties to the brooch."

He paused for effect, studying her unhappy expression. "Either that, or kill Alcott."

Perched on the window seat, Alana stared unseeing into the darkness as she grappled with Colin's statement. He was right; the options he presented were the only permanent solutions. She wouldn't accept Bryce's word even if he swore on his mother's grave not to pursue the brooch. Even the law agreed that such a necromancer couldn't be trusted: creating even one simulacrum was a capital offense. But Colin's calm, straightforward delivery still shocked her.

She nibbled absently on a bannock, torn between the alternatives. She couldn't imagine planning to kill Bryce in cold blood. But at the cost of losing her only keepsake of Papa Dare and the damage to her business—the source of the funds she'd need to rebuild her cottage? She bit her lip at the selfishness of her thoughts. Protecting Papa Dare was her highest priority, of course. But what if reworking the brooch still didn't deter Bryce? If the brooch's spell was lost, her wood magic wouldn't be enough to fight off his simulacra.

And that still begged the question of whether she could trust Colin. Did he have his own reasons for wanting the brooch? He seemed to have her best interests at heart, but how could she be sure? She'd thought Bryce was genuinely interested in her, and look where that had gotten her.

"Eat more. You have to keep up your strength."

Alana startled at the soft words. Colin had been good about leaving her to her thoughts that his murmured instruction came as a surprise.

A brown-sleeved arm appeared at the edge of her vision, reaching for a soul cake.

Turning to him, she registered his garb. He was completely clothed once more, decked out in black turtleneck, chestnut-brown suede leather jacket, khaki denims, and black boots. Once more the dangerous rogue, no longer her smiling lover.

"Already? It's still some time to midnight." If he was dressed, that meant he believed Bryce would break through soon. She put on her bra and did up the snaps of her blouse. Unfortunately, her G-string was a lost cause, but she left its strap around her hips anyway, not wanting to leave anything that might help Bryce track her.

"Soon," he told her, watching the walls. The flashes of light flickering over them were now a bright orangey red, like a field of corn poppies bowing before the wind. And just as frail?

Gathering up her hair in a high ponytail, Alana watched Colin in turn as she secured the heavy mass with her twist. Despite her doubts, she took comfort from the mantle of seasoned competence he wore like a favorite sweater. "Shouldn't we prepare to get out of here?"

Colin gave her a sidelong glance and a brief shake of his head. "Best not to telegraph our plans, given the simulacra's speed. It'll give us more of a head start."

"You do this often?" she asked, just to make conversation. With the breakthrough imminent, she didn't think she could force herself to eat and wanted something to occupy her mind. Finding out more about her neighbor suited her well enough.

He grinned suddenly, a fierce light in his golden eyes. "Normally, not with such beautiful company."

"Oh, you."

She was about to smile when a chill tightened her belly and raised the hairs on her arms. She fisted her hands against the sensation. "They're out there." She nodded at the door where dry wood complained of cold, unliving earth.

"The simulacra?" Another wave of red light washed over the walls as he spoke, flashing and glittering until they looked like the sea at sunset.

"Right outside." She could feel them.

"Better get ready then." Colin closed his eyes briefly, taking a deep breath that swelled his chest and flexed his shoulders, evidently centering himself to oppose Bryce's attack when it came. All signs of the urbane jeweler and her generous lover were gone, replaced by a resolute soldier.

"I could harden the wood," she offered, unwilling to stand around doing nothing.

His hand slashed the air in negation. "You can't hold them back once the wards fail. I'll handle the rearguard; you see to our escape route." The hardness in his voice brooked no argument. The square set of his jaw only reinforced his air of implacability.

Alana cleared the window seat and pushed open the casement to eye the flat side of the building and the long drop to the deserted tables outside the pub. "How? Make a rope from the beddings?" That was doable, if precarious. What if the sheet tore under their weight?

"Call a tree. We'll have to stay off the ground. It'll make it harder for Alcott to track us." Colin moved a few steps forward, placing himself between her and the door.

Swallowing at his maneuver, she called to the nearest oak, willing it to aid her. Its massive trunk bent ponderously, its thick branches extending oh-so-slowly toward the window. *Hurry!*

The wall around the window turned a brilliant, solid red. Once. Twice.

"He's breaking through."

Her nails bit into her palms as Alana forced herself not to use her brooch. She couldn't urge the oak to move faster lest the branches broke—and fresh growth wouldn't help them since it wouldn't bear their weight.

The oak's branches were only halfway to the window when the color on the wall vanished—and with it the wards' protection. A split second later, wood panels groaned behind her, creaking as they fought to resist the unliving earth pressing on them.

Dread had her stealing a glance over her shoulder to see the door and jamb cracking under the strain, and her lover limned with fire. As she watched, the wood shattered, sending splinters flying at them and revealing two simulacra.

Colin burned the slivers in midair, reducing them to gray ash that crumbled to dust. With another wave of his arm, he covered the simulacra with pale blue flames.

Uncanny screams came from malformed mouths, spine-chilling in their torment. They clung to the jamb despite it all, the blaze spreading to the shattered wood. The bigger one forced itself into the room, staggering as luminous fire engulfed its body. It brought with it the stench of swamps and scorched wood, each step charring the floor.

Hard thumps drew Alana's attention to the window where several thick branches rested against the side of the building. Relief surged through her, making her knees weak. "Colin!" She grabbed his shoulder to urge him away.

He shrugged off her hand. "Go!" he ordered, throwing a scarlet fireball at the closest simulacrum. He planted his feet as though preparing to wrestle. Obviously, he wasn't going to leave before she did.

Alana leaped for a branch, hoping Colin wouldn't put off his escape until it was too late. Scrambling for a handhold, she turned back to check on him. "Hurry!"

Retreating a step, Colin raised a wall of flames, then spun for the window. He launched himself off the seat an instant before a howling simulacrum grabbed at him.

Navigating the trees hadn't been too onerous. Bright moonlight aided them in picking their way through the massive branches, though it was still difficult to judge distances with any accuracy. Luckily, the spirits of the night were haunting at ground level, allowing Colin and Alana to travel unimpeded.

The trees eventually ran out at the edge of the gardens, forcing them to climb down to the ground. From there, they'd have to cross several city blocks to get to his shop.

Colin ignored the urge to creep from shadow to shadow. He could see precious little cover in the yellow light of the sodium streetlamps—not even a single car was parked on the road—and going slow carried just as much risk as running. Besides, those abominations might be lurking in the same available darkness.

"Where do we go?" Alana's question was calm, almost dispassionate. She wasn't even huffing for breath after their scramble through the trees; of course, it probably helped that the trees wouldn't have let her fall if she'd slipped. If Colin hadn't sensed the wariness she radiated, he'd have thought she trusted him.

Shrugging off his annoyance at her suspicions, he probed the shadows lining the desolate street for ambush or wandering spirits that might report their location to Alcott. Finding none, he stepped out of the bushes, keeping a firm grasp on Alana's hand.

"My place. I've a commercial gas tank in the shop." With that much fuel behind his fire magic, he might be able to stop a few of the simulacra. "I also have a Breo-saighead there." Stashed in his arms locker where it wasn't doing him any good, damnit.

"*What?*" Alana dug in her heels, throwing him off his stride. She stared at him, her eyes almost cat-green in the yellow streetlight, as he turned back to her. "Isn't that a military weapon?"

Colin urged her onward with a gentle push. "Personal arms for reservists. It's standard issue for fire mages." Right now, he bitterly wished he had it on him. The wand would let him transform a simulacrum to so much magma, then turn it to solid rock. Even if Alcott could undo the process—reduce stone to sand, not just rocks and pebbles—it would cost Alcott power.

Also, if Alana changed her mind about letting him rework the brooch, he'd have his tools close to hand and could conserve most of his own power for fighting Alcott's simulacra. Blocking their attack at the HardWood had required a significant portion of his reserves, even with all the sexual energies around him then. Now that they were outside the Pleasure Quarter, he'd have more difficulty recharging.

They had to get to his shop. It was their only chance.

Alana picked up her heels at his explanation, radiating bright optimism. Perhaps the chance of fighting back had given her hope.

They crossed several blocks without any mishap and—thankfully—without seeing another living person. Only autumn flowers in planters and low maples lined the streets, empty but for the occasional trash and dry leaves rustling in the breeze. Even the animals were in hiding for Samhain.

The next corner revealed his building and Alana's flower shop across the street. Both appeared untouched, the security grilles covering the dark windows unmoved. Colin allowed himself a cautious breath of relief. It was beginning to look like they'd actually make it.

A low moan joined the whistle of the cold wind, rising ominously into a wordless howl.

Three simulacra stepped into view, cutting them off from Colin's shop and his weapons. Behind them, two more simulacra blocked the path back to the gardens and any chance for retreat.

Damnit. They had no chance of breaking through. And at five to one, he didn't have a hope of keeping Alana safe.

"What do we do?"

He gritted his teeth, knowing he had only one option left. It left a bitter taste in his mouth. As a soldier, he'd been taught that the objective was to make dead heroes of the enemy, not be one himself. "Give me your panty."

Without asking questions, Alana slipped off her ruined underwear, her long legs flashing in the streetlights. She handed it to him with a puzzled expression, but he didn't have time for explanations.

Studying the two simulacra between Alana and relative safety, he planned his attack, making sure he had a firm grip on her wet panty and the life energy it represented. He'd have to act quickly to give her the best chance at escaping.

"While I keep them busy, run. Find a strong tree somewhere, and hide until dawn. Then go to the garda." His corpse would bolster her credibility. He just hoped Alcott wasn't close enough to gain power from his death.

* * *

Alana stared in horror as Colin threw himself at the wailing simulacra, fire outlining his body, brandishing her torn G-string like a whip. He was going to get himself killed!

A simulacrum screamed as Colin lashed out at it, flailing at him as he pressed his advantage. His attack opened a gap big enough for her to slip through, back to the gardens and the trees that might protect her.

"Run, Alana!" he shouted, his voice hoarse with pain. Then another rushed him in a blur of motion. It slammed into him—and the flames that surrounded him flickered out.

"*NO!*" She summoned all the power she could—more magic than she'd ever wielded before—and forced it through her brooch. Called all the plants around them to Colin's aid.

Green shoots sprouted from between the cobblestones of the street, grew out of the gutters. Vines crawled from the planters by the lampposts, thickening and turning woody as they swept across the pavement. The trees along the sidewalk stretched out their branches, trying to reach over.

Hard canes smashed into loamy bodies, felling unliving earth, breaking the simulacrum to clumps of soil around her lover's slumped form. Grasses wove themselves into a thicket in the middle of the street, barricading the other simulacra, and screeching silently at the effort.

Darting forward, Alana shook Colin, trying to rouse him. The soil covering him burned like dry ice, leaching warmth and life from her hands. She brushed it off him desperately, her skin prickling with horror at the contact. She had to be quick; the plants wouldn't hold the simulacra for long. Already the clumps were reforming despite the canes that continued to beat at them and the vines that swept them apart.

"Colin?"

He was cold and unresponsive, his face pale even in the glare of the yellow streetlights. If he was breathing, she couldn't tell.

Drawing on her wood magic to strengthen her limbs, she dragged him out of the freezing mound of life-draining earth. "Colin, wake up! I'm not leaving you here."

He seemed to register the threat at some level. His lashes fluttered weakly. Then he broke out in a coughing fit, the pain-wracked hacking like morning birdsong to her ears.

Relief brought tears to her eyes—tears she couldn't let fall, not when danger had them nearly at arm's reach. "We have to get out of here."

Gasping, Colin shook himself, throwing off sand and soil with a sudden flare of light. He staggered to his feet, unsteady yet somehow managing to place himself between her and the simulacra from which she'd saved him.

"This way!" She grabbed his hand and ran headlong down the street toward the Pleasure Quarter and the protection of its trees. Hopefully, the plants she'd summoned could contain the simulacra just a little longer.

A few feet into the gardens and she heard gurgling water, just as she remembered. She led him down the slope into a creek and turned to follow its course, splashing through water cold with the onset of winter. It numbed her toes and chilled her legs, her hurried pace splattering her buttocks. If Bryce was tracking them through the ground, surely wading through water would mask their presence.

"I told you to run," Colin growled, barely audible, though she detected an undertone of pain. He followed her, his movement still rather tentative, though he hardly made any noise, not even when they'd entered the water.

Alana chanced a quick glance over her shoulder to make sure he was really behind her and was relieved to find their trail empty. "I couldn't leave you like that," she hissed back. "What were you thinking!" She took the time to glare at him, since they'd apparently evaded the simulacra temporarily.

"I had to keep you safe." Evidently somewhat recovered, he glared back at her, his chest flexing in outrage at her temerity in questioning his motives.

That moment when his fire had vanished as he'd disappeared under the simulacrum flashed before her mind's eye. Right then she'd thought he'd died.

Alana swallowed with difficulty, her heart once more lodged in her throat. She grabbed his lapels to pull him down so she could search his face, the moonlight filtering through the canopy of little help. "Are you all right?"

Colin stilled, a faint crease appearing between his brows. She could tell he was debating whether he could fob it off as a minor inconvenience.

"It wasn't fun while it lasted, but there's no physical damage." He shrugged both shoulders, as if settling a heavy weight. "It's over and done with. I'd rather not dwell on it." He touched her cheek, a featherlight caress that warmed her whole body. "Thanks for pulling me out. Now, let's concentrate on winning."

She suspected that was all he'd say about it. But he was right: they had other things to worry about. Respecting his wishes, she turned back downstream, trying to find the path that led to the grove she wanted and hoping nothing in the creek took offense at their presence while she did so.

"I've never seen plants grow that quickly, even with wood magic. How'd you do it?"

"My brooch is a charm," Alana answered absently, keeping a lookout for water sprites. "It amplifies my magic."

It was another nightmare flight, but this time she wasn't alone. This time she had someone at her back, sharing her danger. Someone willing to die for her, if necessary. That seemed to make all the difference in the world.

A shrubby willow to one side caught her eye, arresting her cautious advance. Bent over the creek, it looked like a woman washing her hair.

They'd gotten far enough. If she remembered correctly, the break in the bank beside the willow joined a trail that led to the central grove she was heading for. Alana turned to leave the creek and its cold waters.

"Wait." Colin stopped her with a warm hand on her shoulder. "Alcott's tracking you. It has to be you. He probably isn't that familiar with the malachite's resonance."

She frowned at him. "So?"

He dipped down and lifted her in his arms in one smooth motion, displaying miraculous powers of recuperation.

"Colin!" Alana squealed in surprise, wrapping her arms around his neck instinctively to anchor herself against his chest. "You can't carry me!"

He raised his brows at her. "That's exactly what I'm doing. This way, you won't touch the ground." He hefted her higher in a heart-stopping bounce. "This where we're going?" he asked with a nod at the break.

Still taken aback by his actions, Alana nodded back silently. No matter how much she wanted to stand on her own feet, arguing when he had a good reason for his actions would be stupid. They couldn't make it easy for Bryce; thus far, the earthworm seemed to hold all the aces.

Colin scaled the steep bank, carrying her with an ease she found remarkable. She wasn't as heavy as some women, but she was taller than average, which surely made her an awkward burden. Yet he bore her weight without any obvious strain, striding along the faint path without stumbling or banging her against anything, sidestepping obstacles without her assistance.

Suspended in his arms, she felt . . . delicate. Protected. Intensely feminine. A sentiment she never thought she'd ever experience—or crave.

Alana guided him through the woods, puzzled by her reaction. Bryce, who was much bigger, taller, and stockier than

Colin, had never engendered such a feeling in her. Why now, and why with Colin? Was it simply because of circumstances?

She hadn't found any satisfactory answers to her questions by the time they reached the end of the trail.

Still carrying her in his arms and breathing easily, Colin stepped into the clearing and out into the moonlight. To their right was a large stand of oaks right where she expected, the broad, leafy canopy stark under the full moon.

"Over there."

The grove didn't have any paths wending through it, but once past the shrubs ringing the clearing, the going was easier since the heavy shade deterred most bushes. To Alana's relief, the trees were devoid of unearthly presence. They'd been lucky so far not to encounter any spirits; she hoped their good fortune would hold.

She pointed Colin to the central oak, which had battens affixed to it, climbing the massive trunk.

Supporting her body with his own, he set her feet on the wooden slats, obviously making sure she didn't touch the ground. "Go on."

She heard him scrape his heels clean before he climbed after her, staying close to her heels. He probably had a good view of her naked sex from his position.

The thought was perversely thrilling. It sent wild darts of excitement stinging her core and nipples, drawing a throb of restless hunger from the suddenly tight buds and cream dewing her nether lips. What an inconvenient time for desire to raise its head!

Alana slowed her ascent, worried that her distraction might cause her to slip and endanger both of them. After the way Colin had nearly sacrificed his life for her, she couldn't chance that.

"Something wrong?" The soft question came with a gust of

breath that warmed her lower calf. He definitely had a good angle on her.

"Oh! Ah, no." She tried to climb faster, to get the awkward moment over with, but the clenching of her core was maddening.

"Something smells good."

Alana's cheeks heated at the lighthearted words. Colin had to be teasing her. After all the hours they'd spent in bed, he had to know the scent of her musk, considering he'd practically devoured her.

They finally made it to the top without any mishap. The tree house was exactly as she remembered it: a solid platform of wood nestled among the gnarled spreading branches of one of the largest oaks in the park. Plain balusters formed a low rail around the edge, more as a reminder of boundaries than for protection. Screened by the oaks' branches, the tree house had a commanding view of the clearing they'd crossed.

An empty clearing, so far. Except for some pale lights bobbing in the shadows across the field, nothing moved beneath them.

And still no sign of pursuit. She allowed herself a sigh of relief. It was now past midnight: every minute they remained undiscovered was one that weakened Bryce and one more closer to dawn and the end of Samhain Night.

But there was only one way to ensure that Bryce wouldn't win and that Colin wouldn't sacrifice himself for her again.

Alana fumbled with the pin but eventually managed to release it. Turning around, she thrust her brooch at Colin with a trembling hand. "Do it. Rework it so Bryce can't use it." Even if its magic was lost, she would count herself well ahead if it meant Papa Dare wouldn't be reft from Tir nan Óg. Her business might suffer without the brooch's power to help her, but she would face that when it happened.

* * *

Colin stared at the ornate brooch, knowing what it cost Alana to make this choice. He wanted to tell her she didn't have to do this, but he couldn't pretend Alcott wasn't going to find them eventually. His reasoning earlier still held true: breaking Adair MacArdry's link to the brooch was the only sure way of guaranteeing Alcott wouldn't be able to use it to summon Alana's great-grandfather from the grave.

But Colin's fight with the simulacra had drained his reserves. And without access to the tools in his workshop, he'd have to use pure magic to rework the brooch. "If I do that now, I won't have anything left for fighting Alcott. I can't protect you." It would be easier if he merely destroyed it.

"You don't have to fight them alone. I can help," Alana countered, her pale eyes sparking in her ferocity. "Even if the power of the brooch is lost, I'm not helpless."

She caught his lapel with her free hand. "At least we can deny him this. Without it, maybe he'll leave. He'd have nothing to gain in attacking us."

Except their silence. The creation of simulacra was illegal necromancy, even for the military.

He took the brooch. "All right."

Colin knelt on the platform, studying the malachite center stone and the baroque curves and twists around it, wondering what to make of it. The brooch really was a gaudy piece, heavy with gold and warm with magic. The change would have to be drastic to break its tie to Adair MacArdry.

How much easier to just destroy it: that would require less energy, leaving him more to fight with. But he couldn't betray Alana's trust, not when she'd finally given it to him.

It would be a challenge to rework it without ruining the spell. And make it a graceful example of his skill? He grinned inwardly, having to admit to a certain amount of conceit. Merely cutting the link wouldn't be enough to satisfy his artistic ego.

Now, what to change it to that would complement Alana? He closed his eyes, praying to Brigit for inspiration.

He was answered with a vision of a necklace with fine golden links that matched Alana's delicate features. *Yes!*

His power spilled into his hands with a billowing surge of heat, as though the door of a roaring furnace had opened.

The brooch glowed on his palms, the gold turning molten. It flowed in thin strands, a cobweb of light and metal obedient to his will. Moonlight made it glow silver, as if Arianrhod were lending him her grace.

He wielded the last of his magical reserves in a heady rush of power, completing the brooch's transformation with a flash of sparkling light. Drained but exultant, he spread his tremulous hands, allowing the delicate necklace he'd crafted to hang between them, its fine chains describing a web that supported a malachite pendant.

A quick probe told him something still resided in the dark-green stone, but that could be merely an echo of the original spell. Only a wood mage would be able to tell for sure.

Colin presented it to Alana with a flourish, masking the weakness he felt with insouciance. The trepidation and sorrow on her face roused an inkling of tenderness inside him. No matter how well he'd plied his magic, she'd just lost her last link to her great-grandfather. Levity had no place here.

5

Alana placed trembling hands on the fine gold chains around her neck, conscious of the warm pendant nestling between her breasts. Gone were the baroque twists that hinted at hidden things; she'd loved to stare at them as a child, seeing flowers and sprites in their curlicues. Was its magic also lost?

"It'll look better on bare skin." The snaps of her blouse parted with a quick yank of Colin's hands, the rapid clicks like fireworks in the silent woods, allowing the chill night air to waft across her bosom.

Startled, she jerked her head up to see him smile in approval, his golden eyes glowing with hunger. Dampness trickled down her thighs at the predatory smile that marked her as his rightful prey.

His hands closed over her breasts, hotter than before, so large to be capable of such delicate work. "That's better." In the moonlight, they were dark over her milk-white skin.

She caught his wrists, gasping when his thumbs played with her furled nipples. "What are you doing?" The fire in her blood made her knees weak, had her core throbbing with emptiness. How could she want him again when they'd already spent much of the night making love?

"What does it look like?" The intent look he gave her made no subterfuge as to his meaning.

A perverse thrill ran through her, seizing her lungs and scrambling her thoughts. "But— Now?" She searched the dark woods. "Bryce could be here at any time."

"Exactly." Colin frowned down at her. "I need to recharge." Through sex. He needed her pleasure to replenish some of the power he'd expended reworking Papa Dare's brooch.

"Oh!" She'd forgotten about that in the dread of the moment, faced with the loss of her memento. Of course, Colin wouldn't let her face Bryce alone, wouldn't want to be next to powerless when he could do something about it. "All right."

Pushing her ponytail to a more comfortable position, Alana lay back on the platform—like a virgin sacrifice of old, back when life was slower, and cities were the exception. Probably a silly reaction, but she couldn't shake the excitement coursing through her, raising gooseflesh on her arms, making her wet and hungry and aching for his possession.

Her senses sharpened, anticipating Colin's passionate lovemaking. She could feel the grain of the worn planks beneath her fingers, the long strands of hair against her back, her pendant heavy between her breasts. She could smell her desire in the air, mixed with the scent of dry, dusty wood and green moss. The trees rustled approval and encouragement.

She lifted her skirt in invitation, baring her swollen nether lips to his gaze and the caress of the night wind. She played with herself, gliding her fingers through her cream and circling her erect clit. Pleasure sparkled through her, calling her to move, to rejoice in the carnal dance. To reward him with ready power.

"That's it. That's right," he crooned, almost singing to her.

His eyes seemed to glow in his face, his nostrils flaring, a distinct flush spreading across his cheeks as he watched with predatory intentness.

Alana immersed herself in her craving, letting her need consume her, moving her hips as her fingers dipped into her sheath. Her inner flesh quivered, sensitized to the slightest touch from so many hours of lovemaking, and responded with a gush of cream.

"I want you here," she whispered huskily, desire stealing her voice.

"You'll have me there." Silhouetted against the full moon, Colin lowered himself between her thighs, dark fire gleaming in his short hair. He covered her legs with his body, blanketing her with his male heat.

He kissed her creamy fingers, his tongue darting out to lick their slick lengths and dipping down to join them in exploring her depths, impressing shimmering delight on her avid senses. He parted her lips, nibbling on her tender flesh and pricking her with his stubble.

Alana moaned as her labia caught fire at a thousand needle points of pleasure. Her nipples throbbed, echoing the exquisite sensation. She stroked them with her free hand, trying to soothe the aching buds, though her meager efforts were like nothing compared to his firm touch.

Colin devoured her with relentless greed, mingling his fingers with hers in her channel and caressing her delicate inner membranes. Lapping her cream, he drove her up the path of ecstasy with breathtaking haste, sending molten desire surging through her body.

She eagerly embraced the pleasure coursing through her, scaling the now-familiar heights with willing fervor, knowing that doing so would bring him more power. The knowing touch of his mouth and tongue on her sex as she played with herself served as piquant spice, fueling her excitement.

The first tremors of her imminent rapture rumbled through her, a precursor of glorious release. She pursued it avidly, unfettered by lingering worries about selfishness.

As though he also sensed it, Colin slipped his tongue behind her fingers, teasing her clit with artful swirls, unleashing a wild torrent of burning bliss through her body.

Her back arched at the violence of her release, the waves of blistering delight curling her toes in their ferocity. She cried his name in the throes of her ecstasy, wanting him to share the wonder of her climax.

He rose over her, aiming his cock at her nether lips with dispatch. He took her with equal haste, his thick length scraping along her swollen, hypersensitive inner membranes in wonderful friction.

Alana groaned as his possession magnified her pleasure, ramping it up several levels. She'd thought she'd learned all her body was capable of during the long hours of lovemaking at the HardWood; now she discovered she knew precious little.

He pumped her with that relentless cadence, his slim hips pistoning above her, grinding his pelvis against her mound.

A fresh surge of delicious sweetness burst over her, foaming through her veins. "Oh, Colin!"

He grinned down at her, a roguish slash of bright teeth in a shadowy face haloed by dark fire. "There's more," he promised in a throaty growl. "Much, much more."

He hooked his arms under her knees, trapping her thighs between them, propped her ankles on his shoulders, and raised her. He plunged into her again, deeper this time, the head of his cock finding and chafing her joy spot with assiduous attention.

Rapture exploded through her like a fireball of pure, undiluted ecstasy, drowning her in utmost sensation. Alana screamed, needing to voice her release. A cry of triumph she couldn't stifle. It went on and on—heat and pleasure and delight—rolling inexorably, catapulting her to the heavens.

Colin continued thrusting into her, his cock still hard, a blunt instrument of erotic compulsion. Cupping her breasts, he caught her furled nipples, tweaking them with a knowledgeable touch that lanced her core with darts of sensual lightning.

Swift Flidais! His stamina was remarkable! How could he still be erect? She didn't realize she'd actually spoken aloud until he answered her.

"I could keep this up for hours."

She gasped at his confident statement, too breathless to say anything more. It made sense that he was such a superb lover since he drew power from her pleasure. As her focus narrowed down to the tumultuous delight rampaging through her body, she was profoundly grateful that her magic allowed her to tap the strength of the trees; otherwise, she wouldn't be able to walk straight for some time.

"Alana!" The gravelly bellow that shattered the early morning silence was unmistakable. An insistent bass she never wanted to hear ever again. "I know you're here."

A strong wind whistled through the grove, seeming to underscore his demand.

Poised at yet another cusp of ecstasy, Alana shuddered, straining for the completion hovering just beyond her grasp. But Colin pulled out, leaving her bereft.

Easing his cock back into his pants, he rolled to his knees to peer through the leaves at the clearing below, a snarl twisting his lips.

Equal frustration boiled through Alana, leaving her breasts and sex swollen and aching. Need pooled heavy in her hungry core—so much need she wanted to scream. Or kill someone. One man in particular.

How dare Bryce interrupt them!

Rising to her rubbery knees, she wrapped her arms around Colin, pressing herself against his warm back. "Can we ignore him?"

"For a while perhaps." Colin placed his hands on hers, chafing them gently. "The longer we can put off fighting him, the better for us. Problem is: he probably knows that, too. He'll do something to force the issue."

Below them, the earthworm stood dappled by bright moonlight gesturing at something out of sight. Something glinted on his left fist as he clenched it.

The earth shook, then twisted with a dull roar.

Alana gasped as the tree house tilted. She grabbed a branch with one hand and clung to Colin with the other. Using her wood magic, she willed the branch to support them, tapping the oak's strength to augment her own. Leaves shook around them, slapping against bark and breeze, spiraling away when the tumult proved too much for their dry stems.

Colin reached up and found his own handholds, his feet braced on the balusters, taking his weight off her arm.

A tree screamed in silence—a phantom sound chill with evil portent. Then a loud creak filled the air.

Alana moaned at the sudden crash, the loud cracks of branches breaking like so much deadwood. Her heart shriveled as she realized what was happening.

"What is it?" Colin asked in a low tone, careful not to whisper so his voice wouldn't carry far. The stark expression on Alana's face made the hair on his nape stand on end, twisted his gut into snarls.

She looked so lost as she met his gaze, her cheeks ashen. "His simulacra. They're killing the trees."

His stomach dropped to his toes straining for purchase. He knew there was no way he'd be able to talk her out of revealing herself to save the trees.

And she'd be right. As soon as she showed herself, Alcott would stop attacking the trees—in favor of attacking her.

When another creak rented the leaves' crisp rustle, she voiced the inevitable words: "I have to go down."

Releasing his grip on one of the branches, he skimmed her tight jaw with his finger. "Not without me." He glared at her to forestall any silliness on her part, such as assurances that he needn't do anything more.

She gave him a searching look, radiating concern and worry, then nodded at him, her lips quivering with a wan smile. Her pretty breasts rose and fell as she inhaled deeply, the pearly slopes catching the moonlight.

Then the limb they clung to moved, twisting slowly until it could also support their feet. Once they were stable, they climbed down to the tree's trunk—still high above the grove but a more secure position.

While they perched on the forking branches and Alana put her clothes to right, Colin assessed their opponent carefully, noting how the necromancer hung back, using his simulacra as a defensive screen yet never giving them his back. Though the full moon was low over the western horizon, screened by tree-tops, he could see enough.

Alcott was taller and thicker-set than he, outweighing him by several pounds. Despite his size, he looked ordinary, dressed in black jeans and a white dress shirt—nothing at all like the stereotypical necromancer beloved by dramas. Only his pallor hinted otherwise.

Despite appearances, Colin didn't underestimate the other

man's capabilities. To have created and hidden his simulacra for at least five years—necromancers could make only one simulacrum in any Samhain—implied a great deal of cunning and guile, not merely native power.

In a magical battle, the other man also held most of the advantages: his simulacra and the time. Not only was it nighttime but Samhain Night. As an earth mage, Alcott might have enough power to command wandering spirits.

It didn't help that Colin's reserves were still fairly low, despite the charge he'd gotten from Alana's orgasms.

There were only two points working for Colin. First was Alana, who'd proven she wouldn't run from a fight. If they'd had more time, he might have taught her how to combine her wood magic with his fire magic. Unfortunately, recharging his reserves had had to come first. But if he hadn't bungled the transformation of the brooch, its spell could offset that oversight.

Second was the hour: it was past midnight and less than a couple of hours until dawn. Alcott's power was on the wane and would continue dropping. Assuming Colin could stretch out the fight, the balance of power would tip in his favor when the sun rose.

Alana tapped his shoulder, nodding her readiness, a grim set to her delicate features. She led the way down, touching the rough bark every so often, evidently using her magic to safeguard their descent.

At the edge of the clearing, Colin signaled her to wait, to give him time to locate all five simulacra. He wouldn't put it past Alcott to try to set up an ambush.

At the far end, one of the garden's giants lay on the ground, a dried-up trunk bereft of bark and leaves, its thick branches reduced to kindling, its roots torn from its moorings. The sight made him wince. It had to be much worse for Alana, who'd tended to many of the Pleasure Quarter's gardens.

He quickly spotted the five abominations clustered around another tree, thankfully not one near him or Alana.

However, dozens of curious sprites ringed the clearing, their pale bodies lightening the shadows between the trees, their high-pitched chitter far too shrill for human ears, night-black eyes wide with excitement. Even they gave the simulacra wide berth.

Hopefully, they wouldn't help Alcott.

But if he and Alana showed any weakness, the sprites might swarm them. For good or for ill.

Colin took a deep breath, mustering the slight reserves of extra energy his lover had supplied him. He could feel the power available through his fire element strengthening as sunrise approached, but the reinvigoration would take time they didn't have. Once centered, he stepped into the moonlight, keeping a close watch on the simulacra.

"Stop it," Alana ordered Alcott as soon as they entered the clearing. She fingered her necklace, her thumb rubbing the malachite pendant suspended between her breasts. "There's nothing for you here. The brooch is gone."

The necromancer bristled visibly, his lips curling in a sneer. "Do you expect me to believe that?"

That was one answer Colin hadn't expected. He caught Alana by the elbow and drew her behind him.

"I know Sheridan's a jeweler. Well, a decoy won't work."

Colin injected derision into his voice. "Use your magic. It's the same stone."

If he pricked Alcott's vanity, the necromancer might lose his temper and, perhaps, some control. At the very least, it might make the other man less cautious . . . and maybe force a mistake? He could only hope.

In the middle of the clearing, Alcott waved an arm at his simulacra, which abandoned the tree they were killing. They closed around the necromancer like a retinue of bodyguards, albeit one that stank of swamp gas.

The bastard's expression shut down with the familiar blankness of someone conducting a mental probe.

After a few heartbeats, a furious scowl spread across the necromancer's face, contorting his broad, pallid features, his black eyes disappearing in narrow slits. "You whore!" he thundered in tones of outrage. He raised his large fists, obviously preparing to use his magic.

A holly, its spiny leaves unmistakable, sprang up from under Alcott, throwing him off his feet and slashing at the necromancer with its formidable defenses.

A whoop from Alana told Colin what had happened: she'd used her wood magic and discovered that Colin had succeeded in preserving the spell on her charm. He grinned at that victory, renewed optimism filling him with savage delight.

The necromancer had made a mistake in confronting them personally. By doing so, the other man had opened himself to direct assault. If he had remained hidden, he might have worn them down without risk to himself. His frustration at Alana's escape must have driven him to handling matters personally. Did that mean his control over the simulacra was less than complete?

"Kill them!" Alcott shouted from where he sprawled on the ground, his arms flailing around his head in defense against the holly's assault.

His creations obeyed with inhuman speed, their dark forms blurring in the moonlight, their passage raising a whistle of wind as they crossed the field.

Colin sent the merest flame at the closest simulacrum, trying to conserve his power. The extra energy he'd drawn from Alana's pleasure wouldn't last forever. He had to make every bit count.

Blue flames engulfed his target, the high heat wresting uncanny howls from the abomination, the soul inside it flinching from the life fire symbolized.

Innocent though that soul was, Colin refused to handicap his defense of Alana. If they failed here, the necromancer would do much worse.

The other simulacra froze in their tracks, evidently horrified by the flames. More plants shot up around them, vines and whatnot, slamming through animated earth.

The ground erupted around Alcott, clumps of soil flying through the air like shrapnel from an explosion. The blowout buried the holly under a pile of rocks.

Climbing to his feet, the necromancer gestured sharply at the simulacra in front of him, a familiar-looking black onyx ring gleaming on his left hand.

Colin stared, doubting his eyes. It wasn't that he had seen the ring before; in fact, he didn't think he'd ever had. But as an artisan, he recognized another craftsman's style, and the ostentatious lines of Alcott's piece were uncannily similar to Alana's former brooch.

Could it be?

When Alana had said Alcott's ring was from Adair Mac-Ardry's hoard, he hadn't realized that it was by the same craftsman. Which meant the ring might be a charm, one that amplified earth magic like the brooch worked with wood magic.

It made sense now. Alcott wasn't after money—he wanted power. If the hoard contained more such charms, its magical potential was incalculable.

"Keep the simulacra off my back." Colin could only hope

Alana could handle them, could hold them off long enough for his gamble to work.

If Alana couldn't, they were lost.

Channeling her magic through her pendant, Alana called on more holly to block the simulacra, steeling herself against the deaths that would ensue. If they didn't stop Bryce, there would be even worse.

But what was Colin doing?

The prickly bushes grew quickly, reaching out to snag at un-living arms and bodies, screaming silently as life was drained from their branches, yet still coming on.

Colin extended his arms, his hands curved as if they bore an invisible bowl between them. Nothing seemed to happen for the longest time, except for a roiling of the air around his hands, like moonlight on water, barely visible to the eye.

Then Bryce swore, cupping a protective hand over a sud-denly glowing band on his left ring finger. "Kill them!" he shouted at his creations.

She finally understood: Colin was attacking Bryce's ring. But why? As soon as the question came to mind, the answer occurred to her: it had to be the source of the earthworm's con-trol of the simulacra.

But Colin was weakened, his reserves drained by reworking her brooch and the earlier fight. He couldn't keep up his attack and fight off the simulacra at the same time. He might not even have enough energy to succeed in his assault.

Another wave of power sent more plants sprouting from the ground to block the simulacra, buying Alana time to think. She couldn't help Colin directly, but she could boost his power.

Thrusting a hand under her skirt, she teased her clit to throb-bing awareness, welcoming the heat pooling in her belly. With her other hand, she tore open her blouse to fondle her breasts, plucking and rolling her nipples the way Colin had during her lap dance earlier that night. Need seared her at the memory of his skill, the way he'd teased and tormented her with pleasure.

"Whatever you're doing, keep it up," Colin ordered her.

Baring her breasts to the night air, Alana pressed herself against him, stropping the tightly furled buds of her nipples against his suede-covered back, raising sparks of delight in the hard nubs.

"Bright Belanus," Colin murmured prayerfully, his muscles flexing at their point of contact.

"Damn you both." Shoulders bunching, Bryce glowered at them, his bushy brows knitting across his forehead, a muscle twitching by his square jaw. "You'll die for this."

Alana plunged her fingers into her sheath, panting as hunger spiraled through her core. Cream dripped down her thighs, hot and thick, perfuming the air with her desire.

On tiptoe, she whispered into Colin's ear: "Defeat him, and you can have this."

He chuckled. "What an incentive." He raised clenched fists in front of him, his shoulders squaring, muscles bunching against her cheek. Light wreathed his hands, a pale glow barely visible in the moonlight.

His efforts seemed to have some effect—the simulacra had come to a halt, rocking in place as though caught between opposing forces.

Gesturing stiffly, the earthworm growled something Alana couldn't make out, the ground around him breaking and shifting, clumping together in uneven, knee-high mounds. The drifts surged toward her and Colin in rising waves, threatening to knock their legs out from under them.

Colin slashed a hand toward Bryce, a line of fire leaping from his outthrust fingers.

Swearing, Bryce leaped away from the flare. His distraction allowed the ground to settle back.

But Colin's riposte must have taken its toll in energy; the simulacra resumed their advance, gaining a few feet before once more coming to a standstill.

Colin needed more power!

Alana set on her flesh with a will, closing her eyes to block out all distraction. She rode her fingers, working her clit to nearly painful erection. Pleasure flashed through her, fleeting in sweetness, whetting her need for more.

She wanted Colin inside her, filling her with his virile length and plumbing her depths. She wanted his lips on her, exploring her willing body, marking her with prickling delight.

She gasped as an exquisite tingle of sensation played over her hypersensitive nerves, replete with excitement. Cream flowed over her fingers, trickled down her calves, fed the grass beneath her.

"Yes, that's it," Colin crooned. "Just a little more."

Alana redoubled her efforts, coaxing her engorged clit to greater pleasure. She pumped her sheath, reaching for that one spot guaranteed to bring fruition to her handiwork.

"Yes!"

Wondering at Colin's exclamation, she opened her eyes to look over his shoulder.

An orange glow surrounded Bryce's left fist, centered on the gold ring. It pulsed rapidly—turning yellow, then white, then yellow, then back to orange—over and again in a hypnotic coruscation.

The earthworm shouted something, pain and fury mingling in his harsh bass.

The malevolence in his voice made Alana jump, her palm grinding on her mound, her fingers rasping over a nub of hard flesh. The tension in her core ratcheted upward, a sudden wave of need that had her nerves quivering with expectation, poised once more on the verge of ecstasy.

"Now," Colin ground out, forceful determination informing that one word.

The glow around Bryce's fist vanished, reappearing around Colin's outstretched hands. Silence fell over the clearing, as if everyone—even the sprites and the night wind—was stunned by the shift in light.

The contrast made one sound seem louder than it was: the black onyx on Bryce's ring shattered, the high crystalline ringing reverberating in the night.

Bryce shrieked.

The simulacra remained still for a few heartbeats. Then, slowly, as though bewildered or resisting habit, they turned to Bryce. They converged on him, ignoring his screamed commands, ponderous in their approach.

"No! I order you to obey me!" Clutching his left hand to his wide chest, Bryce flailed his other hand at the simulacra, gouging chunks of soil from his creations.

Growling with an undertone of fury, they continued their advance, moving faster and faster despite the necromancer's attempts to hold them back. Too many for him to repel, they came at him from all sides.

In a final burst of speed, the simulacra overwhelmed Bryce, burying him beneath unliving earth. He disappeared from sight, his screamed imprecations abruptly silenced.

The ungainly mass heaved once, twice, as the deadly battle continued. Finally, it settled into quiescence.

A cool gust of night air dispelled the lingering swamp stench, leaving behind the familiar tang of verdant forest.

Alana turned away, reminded of how she had nearly lost Colin to a similar attack. Scenes flashed before her mind's eye. The jeweler's polite, businesslike demeanor in the previous months. The guilty fantasies she'd entertained about him. His newly discovered roguish playfulness. His fiery lovemaking.

His willingness to sacrifice himself for her escape. A man who had no ulterior motive in sharing her bed.

Her lips quirked involuntarily. Well, none except for the power her pleasure brought him. No one would fault him for that.

And she had almost lost him. Might still lose him when Samhain Night ended.

Alana took a deep breath to settle her roiling stomach, and a spicy summer scent filled her lungs, mixed with the smell of leather and male sweat. A masculine essence that reminded her of more basic things.

Her core clenched with hunger, its emptiness bordering on pain. Her sheath fluttered around her hand, forgotten in their sudden change in fortune. Hot cream trickled onto her palm as her swollen clit pulsed, her body demanding relief.

The need to confirm Colin's safety in the most basic way possible stirred, fanned by her awareness of their limited time together and the approach of dawn.

She rested her forehead on his back, trying to rein in her desire, but couldn't. "Colin?" she said huskily, wrapping her arms around him, pressing her body to his, rubbing her tight nipples against his back, unable to say more.

Colin's chest expanded—once, twice—as though he labored under some strong emotion. He spun around to face her, his face stark with carnal hunger. "That was inspired, Alana! You were wonderful!" He rained kisses on her cheeks, peppering them between words. "Absolutely wonderful."

She caught his stubbled jaw between her hands, craving a fuller kiss, a deeper possession. "If I'm so wonderful, shut up and take me!"

With a wild whoop of exultation, Colin bore Alana to the grass, more than willing to obey her command. How he wanted this spirited, delicious woman!

This time she allowed him to strip her completely, leaving her pale body glowing in the moonlight like some faerie queen awaiting her mortal lover, her sable hair spread under her shoulders like a cape. Her nipples pebbled in the chill air, pouting at his delay.

He flung off his own clothes with reckless haste, eager to feel her naked against him. He knelt between her thighs, his swollen cock aching with anticipation. He plunged into her, growling as she clasped him in a snug, creamy grip. A surge of life energy slammed into him at her gasp of pleasure.

Colin crowed in laughter, pressing fervid kisses on Alana's smooth throat and shoulders and breasts. Exhilaration coursed through him, powering his frenzy with the heady knowledge of their survival.

They'd vanquished the necromancer, and all because of her quick thinking.

Alana welcomed him with matching ardor, meeting his thrusts with breathless abandon. Her nails bit into his shoulders as she clung to him, her slender legs locking around his hips.

The sounds of their mutual pleasure filled the darkness. The steady slap of wet flesh. The sighs and moans of delight. The grunts and groans of desire.

Wave upon wave of her excitement flooded his senses, recharging his spent reserves. And still she gave of her enjoyment, purring her gratification as her body clenched and fluttered around him, milking his cock with the beginnings of her release.

He adjusted his angle to better tease her clit, rolling his hips to vary his pounding motion. It wound the hunger mounting in his balls to singing tension. He forced it back, wanting to savor her lust.

With a husky prayer to Flidais, Alana spasmed around him, her climax triggering his own release.

Raw pleasure exploded from his balls, searing his nerves with carnal fury. It shot out his cock in a blaze of delight that should have sent them up in flames.

He threw back his head, howling his ecstasy into the night. Challenging any who dared take his woman from his arms.

Boneless and euphoric from Colin's lovemaking, Alana snuggled deeper into his embrace, wrapping her legs tighter around his hips and soaking up his male heat. Despite the chill in the morning air, she couldn't bestir herself to dress, not when Samhain Night would soon be over. She wanted to savor every perfect minute with Colin that she could. Who knew what would happen after the sun rose?

The eastern sky lightened slowly, bringing an end to Samhain and a return of society's rules. The first tentative bird calls soon melded into a chorus of territorial twitters.

The pungent odor of bruised leaves joined the musky scent of sex and sweat, an unusual blend Alana would always associate with the memory of this night.

In the gray light, she saw that they lay in a large circle of fresh growth: flowering white clover surrounded by red-berried hollies. In the middle of the clearing, just a few feet away, was a tall grassy mound—all that remained of Bryce and his simulacra. The spaces between the trees were empty, the sprites gone until next Samhain.

A warm, bristly kiss on her shoulder, right on the sensitive spot where it met her neck, told her Colin was awake. A blunt nudge at the juncture of her thighs told her he was more than ready to greet the day.

She welcomed him into her body, relishing the slow glide of skin on skin and the lack of all demand, content with the sweet give and take. They flowed together, rocking gently, savoring the gradual approach of pleasure.

This time when they kissed, Colin lingered, taking his time as he explored her mouth, his tongue capturing hers in a lazy tangle, his stubble a sensual rasp on her face.

Alana caressed his shoulders and broad back, reveling in their lean strength. She fluttered her inner muscles, milking his thick length inside her as he pumped her with leisurely strokes.

Her climax broke through her with the sweetness of an afternoon shower in summer, soothing in its restraint. A dreamy outpouring of delight. Welcome contrast to the violence of Samhain Night.

Colin signaled his release with a soft gasp. The rhythmic jerks of his cock inside her strung out her pleasure like silken pearls on a gold wire, delicate and precious. A fragile bliss neither of them wanted to risk with speech.

The first streaks of dawn were painting the sky in pinks and golds by the time Alana untangled herself from Colin and dressed, plaiting her hair in a simple French braid. The yellow streams of light gilded the grass-covered mound, lush with unseasonal greenery.

Bird calls filled the clearing, a sound of such reassuring normalcy that she sighed, finally truly convinced that the nightmare had ended.

"It's over." Papa Dare was safe. Her little cottage was destroyed, but it could be rebuilt. Even better, she would have time to rebuild it, now that Bryce was gone.

"Is it?" Colin's hand touched her cheek, tilted her chin up to look into her eyes. His golden gaze held an invitation, warm with unspoken meaning.

"What do you mean?" Alana's heart picked up speed, its loud beat ringing in her ears.

"It's only over if you want it to be." His light tenor was vibrant with promise as his thumb glided over her bottom lip. "I've got a big bed. You're welcome to share it." By the meaningful quirk to Colin's lips, he wasn't offering merely a place to sleep.

As the morning breeze caressed her damp sex, Alana decided his offer had merit. Everything else could wait. Stepping into the circle of his arms, she pulled his head down for a kiss. "That's an excellent idea."

Here's a sneak peak at *Sin*,
by Sharon Page, on sale this month!

Chapter One

What would her jaded lord do with his hands while the lovely courtesan knelt between his legs and kissed him intimately?

Venetia Hamilton tapped the end of her brush against her lips as she studied her watercolor painting. Even though her earl—yes, she'd decided he was an earl—was a most experienced man, this time he'd met his match in the delightful auburn-haired woman pleasuring him.

She couldn't resist smiling at her imaginary earl's downfall in the arena he believed he reigned supreme. Since his lordship was so steeped in vice, so bored by customary sensual acts, he'd begin with definite ennui, merely an onlooker to his own seduction.

In his right hand, Venetia sketched a glass of fine champagne. In his left, since he was in the theater box of the pretty woman, she gave him a peeled orange the size of an ample breast, large enough to fill his strong hand. No, he would not touch the woman, she decided. But in his expression . . . there she could show not only the desire, but the growing wonderment as his heart began to open, to unfurl, to delight in the pleasures bestowed upon him.

She turned her attention to the audience, for her earl was receiving these daring caresses to his intimate parts in full view of the Drury Lane theater. Ah, the expressions told the tale—the matrons pretending to be scandalized, but really enraptured by his magnificent proportions, his exquisite form, his handsome face. Envy on their husbands' faces. And the leering looks of the mob in the orchestra.

Now she must tackle the earl's expression. Capture perfectly the growing astonishment on his face as this act that he must have experienced a thousand times—at least—became new and special and wonderful once more . . .

She took short, unsteady breaths as she stepped back from naughty fantasy to the reality of her tiny studio. When she drew, she became one with the scene—not a participant, but a figure in the shadows, holding a brush, telling a life's history in one erotic moment.

Her body hummed with desire, ached with it. She should be ashamed to admit it, but she wasn't at all as proper as her mother had raised her to be. She was, after all, her father's daughter.

With a sigh, Venetia plopped her brush in the jar and swirled it until the water blushed pink, lit by the fragile spring sunlight that spilled through the paned window. The only raven-haired scoundrels in her life lived on the canvases stacked on the narrow shelves of her studio, all safely hidden beneath muslin covers.

She knew perfectly well that love was a woman's folly. That rakes never truly reformed—

A sharp rap on the door had her almost knocking over the water glass. The rap came again. Followed by a breathless, "My heavens, Miss Hamilton!"

She had to take the time to turn the easel so her painting faced the wall and Mrs. Cobb burst through the door just as she hid the scandalous picture.

Mrs. Cobb puffed from the jaunt up the stairs. Her cheeks blazed red, her cap was askew. She held out a card. "There is a *gentleman* to see you, mum. A gentleman calling upon you alone!"

"Which gentleman?" Her father? Rodesson outwardly appeared to be a 'gentleman.' But he wouldn't dare visit.

Her housekeeper pushed her cap upright. "The Earl of Trent, mum! I put him in the drawing room. Tea? Should I put the kettle on?"

Venetia's heart tapped a frenzied dance in her chest. She pushed her chair back, snatched up the studio key, and crossed the floor in a heartbeat to take the card. Her thumb slid over thick, textured vellum embossed with a crest. Her gaze fell to the title, in bold text. It did indeed read THE EARL OF TRENT.

She slumped against the doorframe in disbelief. How *could* the earl know who she was?

Mrs. Cobb lurked over her shoulder, demanding a decision on tea as Venetia locked the door to her studio with shaking hands.

"N-no tea," Venetia stuttered. Lifting her skirts, she hurried down the hallway in the most unladylike way. But if she was running into disaster, she wanted to get it done with.

Plodding footfalls told her Mrs. Cobb was following but couldn't keep up.

The most preposterous notion dawned as Venetia sped down the stairs. What if her father had gambled again, hoping to win his vowels back from the earl? What if this time Trent had won *her* at cards?

Reaching the open drawing room door, she stopped, smoothed her skirts, and gulped down steadying breaths. She must be careful. If she ruined her reputation, she ruined her sisters' reputations. Maryanne, Grace . . . they at least deserved a chance at the lives Mother hoped they would lead—marriage, children, happiness . . .

The earl, she noted, had found the only warm spot in her chilly drawing room. As soon as she stepped inside, the cold seeped through her dress and wrapped its icy fingers around her bare neck. Since she never received guests, she never heated the room. At least a fire now crackled in the hearth.

His lordship stood so close to the licking flames, she feared a spark might set his trousers alight. His left elbow was propped on the mantel, between the unfortunate bric-a-brac left by the previous tenant—two candlesticks shaped like nude women and a bronze of his favorite mount.

Venetia closed the door gently behind her, then stopped short, still clutching the doorknob.

The earl balanced an open book in his large gloved hand and he lazily flipped the pages. The faint sunlight cast a bluish gleam on his coal-black hair and slanted across his straight shoulders. Even in a casual stance, he easily topped six feet and she couldn't help but admire how his midnight-blue superfine emphasized the taper from wide back to narrow waist and lean hips. Skintight trousers displayed magnificent legs and disappeared into Hessians with a mirror finish.

She arched on tiptoe to spy around his broad frame. Pictures. The book did indeed contain pictures but she couldn't see the detail—he stood too far away. But *Tales of a London Gentleman* was bound in burgundy leather, in exactly the same shade as the book lying across that massive hand.

The earl paused at a plate, then turned the book in his hand to study some detail that had caught his fancy. A flush prickled along the back of Venetia's neck.

He moved to capture the light more fully on the page, and

she saw his profile. Raven hair, darkly lashed eyes, patrician features, and wide, firm lips.

Her stomach pitched to her toes. *Trent* was the dark-haired gentleman who had appeared in her father's pictures. The man she'd copied for *her* book. She'd thought him an invention of her father's brush. But since he stood before her in the flesh, obviously her assumption had been wrong.

It made sense. Rodesson attended brothels and orgies and hells. Why wouldn't he base his pictures on actual patrons? On the actual scenes he had witnessed?

The titles flew through her whirling mind. *The Fair Lady Bound. The Jermyn Street Harem. The French Kiss.*

Even *The Trapeze* in which the nude lady had been seated on a suspended bar over the gentleman's upright—

Venetia pressed her hand to her churning stomach. Her father had changed Lord Trent's appearance, she saw that now. She, in utter innocence, had decided to make *her* gentleman more handsome. By horrific accident, she had succeeded in making him look more like the actual man.

A soft groan spilled from her lips.

The earl looked up sharply and she stared into vivid turquoise eyes, the color startling and beautiful in contrast to his long sooty lashes and straight black brows.

That extraordinary shade had not appeared in her father's pictures. Could *she* capture it? If she blended cobalt blue with a touch of—

"This is my personal favorite, Miss Hamilton. I think you have caught my likeness perfectly in this one." Dangerous amusement rippled through Lord Trent's seductive baritone and his deep masculine voice held her transfixed. "You have a remarkable talent."

A remarkable talent. She felt a warm flush of pride, even as her knees almost buckled.

"My-my lord." She managed a curtsy, a wobbly one, her plain gray skirts crumpling as she dipped. "I am afraid I don't understand to what you are referring."

He closed the book. His brows arched over those turquoise eyes—*cerulean* blue would do it, blended with a dab of yellow oxide—

"Your book of erotica in which I play the starring role."

GREAT BOOKS, GREAT SAVINGS!

When You Visit Our Website:
www.kensingtonbooks.com
You Can Save Money Off The Retail Price
Of Any Book You Purchase!

- **All Your Favorite Kensington Authors**
- **New Releases & Timeless Classics**
- **Overnight Shipping Available**
- **eBooks Available For Many Titles**
- **All Major Credit Cards Accepted**

Visit Us Today To Start Saving!
www.kensingtonbooks.com

All Orders Are Subject To Availability.
Shipping and Handling Charges Apply.
Offers and Prices Subject To Change Without Notice

Is It Hot Enough For You?

DO YOU LIKE YOUR ROMANCE NOVELS EXTRA HOT?
Then Kensington has an offer you can't refuse.
We'll deliver our best-selling erotic romance novels right to your doorstep, and the first set of books you receive are **FREE**, you only pay $2.99 for shipping and handling!

APHRODISIA—

redefining the word HOT! Not for the faint of heart, these trade paperback novels don't just open the bedroom door, they blow the hinges off.

Once you've enjoyed your **FREE** novels, we're sure you'll want to continue receiving the newest Aphrodisia erotic romances as soon as they're published each month. If you decide to keep the books, you'll pay the preferred book club member price (a savings of up to 40% off the cover price!), plus $2.99 for shipping and handling charges.

- You'll receive our **FREE** monthly newsletter featuring author chats, book excerpts and special members-only promotions.
- You'll always save up to 40% off the cover price.
- There's no obligation—you can cancel at anytime and there's no minimum number of books to buy.

SEND FOR YOUR FREE BOOKS TODAY!
Call toll free 1-800-770-1963 or use this coupon to order by mail.

YES! Please send me my FREE novels from the club selected below:

Aphrodisia – code BABA06

Name

Address

CityStateZipTelephone

Signature
(If under 18, parent or guardian must sign)

Send orders to: Romance Book Clubs, P.O. Box 5214, Clifton, NJ 07015.
Offer limited to one per household and not valid to current subscribers. All orders subject to approval. Terms, offer and price subject to change without notice. Offer valid in the US only.

Visit our website at www.kensingtonbooks.com.